THE RUTHLESS GENTLEMAN

LOUISE BAY

Published by Louise Bay 2018

Copyright © 2018 Louise Bay. All rights reserved

This is a work of fiction. Names, characters, businesses, places, events and incidents are either the products of the author's imagination or used in a fictitious manner. Any resemblance to actual persons, living or dead, or actual events is purely coincidental. The author acknowledges the trademarked status and trademark owners referenced in this work of fiction, which have been used without permission. The publication/use of these trademarks is not authorized, associated with or sponsored by the trademark owners.

ISBN – 978-1-910747-53-7

BOOKS BY LOUISE BAY

The British Knight

Hollywood Scandal

Duke of Manhattan

Park Avenue Prince

King of Wall Street

Love Unexpected

Indigo Nights

Promised Nights

Parisian Nights

The Empire State Series

Hopeful

Faithful

Sign up to the Louise Bay mailing list

www.louisebay.com/newsletter

Read more at www.louisebay.com

ONE

Hayden

When faced with an impending crisis, there were two sorts of people in business—those who said they weren't going down without a fight, and those who didn't bother to entertain the possibility of failure in the first place. I was firmly in the second category.

I'd built my reputation differently to a lot of businessmen in the City of London. Instead of relying on family connections, drinks with old boarding school mates, and trying to impress, I concentrated on the numbers, obsessed over details and made smart decisions. I liked to make money. A lot of money. I didn't care to shout about it.

Over the last ten years, I'd taken Wolf Enterprises from spare-room startup on the outskirts of London to one of the biggest companies in Europe. I was responsible for tens of thousands of jobs and a balance sheet of billions. For a decade, I'd known nothing but success after success. But, in the last twelve months, something had shifted. I'd been missing out on important sales, undercut on contracts, and locked out of bids. My empire was wobbling.

I wasn't about to let it collapse.

I just had to convince my investors over lunch that I could turn things around.

As I arrived at the entrance, I spotted Steven and Gordon across the room. I checked my watch. I'd arrived at the restaurant exactly on time, which meant they were early. A bad sign, as they ordinarily made a habit of keeping people waiting. They meant business.

But so did I.

The hostess showed me to a seat opposite them at a table near the back. These guys did nothing by accident. A public lunch rather than a private meeting. Arriving early. Seating themselves so the dynamic would be two against one—it was all carefully orchestrated, designed to send a message before they'd even spoken a word.

"Gordon, Steven, good to see you," I said, acknowledging Gordon, the more senior of the two, first. I understood the pecking order. It was the small things that mattered most in business.

"I love this view," Gordon said, opening with something casual, yet subtly dismissive. He hadn't even bothered to greet me.

I glanced out the window. The square mile in the East of London, known as "The City," was one of the oldest parts of the capital and crammed full of the biggest banks, insurers and investment houses in the country. It was the financial hub of Europe, where the suits were sharp, and the minds sharper.

Money ruled these streets, and I'd not been making these men enough.

They wanted me to know it.

As if I could forget.

"You can keep an eye on all your investments up here," I said, lifting my chin at the view.

Gordon smiled but fixed his gaze on mine. "Quite."

They thought they'd ambushed me, but I was more than well prepared. "I need to bring you up to speed on a few things."

"We hear you lost the Lombard deal," Steven said.

And there it was. No more niceties. Swords had been drawn.

There was no point in asking him how they knew. Part of the reason I'd wanted them as investors was because they were among the most well-connected people in the City.

I sat back in my chair. "I found out late last night that we'd been outbid and they'd signed with another buyer."

Steven and Gordon stayed silent, waiting for me to fill in the gaps.

"You know who beat you?" Steven asked.

"Cannon Group." I kept my expression fixed, though my hands twitched in frustration. I wanted to pull them into fists and punch something. Hard. Over and over. Fucking Cannon. The last four companies I'd tried to acquire, I'd lost to them.

"This is the fourth acquisition in a row that you've lost," Steven said. "We think you're losing your touch."

It was a justifiable accusation. I'd made my career as a deal maker—spotting small, undervalued companies and buying them, only to triple their value within three to five years and sell. It was what I did. Except that Cannon was beating me to every company I targeted.

"Have you made an enemy over there?" Steven asked. "It seems personal."

"I don't believe in conspiracy theories," I replied.

"When you're on top, you're a target." I shrugged even though I knew that where Cannon was concerned, it was indeed personal.

"Be that as it may, you need to figure out what's going on. We invested in you not just because you could spot a good deal, but because you could close on it. If that's changed, we need to reconsider our relationship," Steven said.

"This is as frustrating for me as it is for you—" I started, stepping neatly around Gordon's attack dog.

"Frustrating? This isn't just frustrating. It's plain bad business," Steven continued. "We're not in the business of backing losers."

"And I'm not in the business of losing, which is why I've moved on to bigger and better things."

Gordon cleared his throat. He was as old school as it got, from the monogrammed cuffs on his shirt to the fifth-generation family home in the country. He never raised his voice and certainly didn't engage in public confrontations. Of the two, he was the one I had to watch.

"We want to know how we can help," Gordon said. "We think you're excellent at what you do. We just want to see you back on top."

Although Gordon sounded caring and charming, he was delivering the same message as Steven had been, just in a very different way. Our relationship was teetering on the brink.

If Steven and Gordon walked away now, it would send a clear message to the City—Hayden Wolf was a dead man walking. My deal-doing days would be over, and the business I'd built to honor my father would crumble.

I tried to appear calm, as if adrenaline wasn't threatening to overwhelm me. "I am a deal maker, but I won't just buy for the sake of it. Cannon are making the headlines at the moment, but they're overpaying for assets." If their strategy was to take me down, it was working, but at the cost of their business. They were paying far too much for companies worth far less just to screw me.

Gordon nodded. "I'm not concerned with Cannon's business practices or bottom line. I'm concerned with yours."

"Wolf Enterprises is on course," I said, giving no ground. "And my next acquisition is going to make you forget about the last twelve months."

The table fell silent as our waitress arrived with drinks for Gordon and Steven, then disappeared again.

"Wiping away the last twelve months would take a deal far larger than anything you've ever closed in the past," Steven pointed out.

"Yes, it would," I agreed.

"You expect us to believe that after a year that has marked your biggest failures, you're going to turn it around with a single deal to not only rival, but surpass any you've done before?"

"Not just to surpass any *one* previous success," I corrected Steven, but made eye contact with Gordon. "But to outdo them all, combined."

Steven laughed outright, but Gordon went still and silent, considering me with the same stare he'd used the day he'd decided to invest in an unknown kid with no references and nothing to lose.

"Looking to rise from the ashes?" he asked, narrowing his eyes.

I held his stare. "Exactly." Game, set and match to me. With decades of success behind it, Phoenix was the jewel in the City's financial crown. I'd promised Gordon ten years ago, at that very first meeting, that I'd own it someday. He'd laughed, but I'd meant it and now I was going to fulfil on that promise and buy Phoenix.

"This can't get out," Gordon said, his voice just above a whisper. "The minute news goes public that they're considering a sale it'll be pandemonium, a bidding war the likes of which we've never seen."

"I agree," I said, watching as Steven tried to puzzle together just what we were talking about.

"Cannon is targeting Wolf Enterprises, letting you set up the deal, then swooping in at the last minute to outbid you. They're getting their information from someone," Gordon said.

I'd been thinking of nothing else since I'd lost the Lombard deal. How had that been stolen out from under me? I'd kept it to such a close-knit group of people. All advisors signed ironclad nondisclosure agreements. I'd been so sure I'd had it in the bag.

"Corporate espionage?" Steven asked.

Probably, though I'd been reluctant to admit it. When I'd lost the first deal, I'd shrugged it off as one of those things. The second one, I changed my financial advisors. The third one and now Lombard? After the third deal had been stolen from under me, I'd ensured that only a trusted team of four, including my assistant, knew about Lombard. Which meant the leak had come from my own office.

The thought made me sick.

I'd handpicked the team. They'd earned my trust, something I didn't give easily.

If I was going to ensure secrecy, I was going to have to isolate myself further. To make this work, I'd have to trust no one, suspect everyone. My business, my reputation, everything I'd worked so hard to build over the last decade was at stake.

"If I want to get this deal done quickly and quietly, I need to disappear. No one can know I'm working on anything. The next time you hear from me, it'll be with a request to fund the deal."

"Disappear?" Gordon asked.

"An extended, working holiday. Preferably abroad. Let the vultures assume I went off to lick my wounds after the last deal fell through." Cannon needed to think I was down for the count.

"I know how much this deal means to you," Gordon said as Steven leaned forward. "I want to see you succeed. Do what it takes to make it happen."

I nodded. "I'm ready."

"Make this work, Hayden," Gordon said, rising from the table. "Because if you don't, it'll be the end of Wolf Enterprises."

TWO

Avery

I had a hangover the size of a whale. Being chief stewardess on a superyacht meant I was used to dealing with adversity with a smile on my face, so to anyone who was watching, I seemed just fine—my makeup perfect and my long, brown hair up in a glossy ponytail. My churning stomach and throbbing head told a different story.

"I don't know how you stopped us from trashing this place," Leslie, one of the crew members, said, coming up behind me as we looked over the main salon of the yacht I'd called home for the last five months. The dark circles under Leslie's eyes, her rumpled clothes and the way she kept clutching her forehead gave away the extent of her alcohol consumption last night. Yesterday we'd seen the last guest off and started drinking as we'd cleaned the place from top to bottom. Although the bottom was bound to be a little sloppy, given all the wine.

"I didn't want to ruin all our hard work," I replied. When we'd come back to the boat after taking our drinking ashore, I'd encouraged the crew to stay in the mess. I knew what it was like to arrive on a new yacht with the whole place in carnage, and I didn't want that for the next charter crew. I wanted to go home to California with a clear conscience.

I couldn't wait, or remember the last time I'd had a whole month off. Thirty days to hang out with my brother and dad, see my old friends. How I'd gotten through the last five months of the Caribbean season, I had no idea. It had been a brutal winter, and no doubt I'd spend the first week in Sacramento sleeping.

"Avery, Avery, this is the captain," my radio echoed out.

I rolled my eyes. "What does he want me for?" I checked my watch. "I'm off the clock."

The Caribbean season was officially over, and I had a plane to catch. But off duty or not, I never ignored the captain radioing me. Some captains were born assholes. Captain Moss wasn't one of them. He was a stern but fair captain who I imagined would have been very handsome thirty years ago before the weather and the job had taken their toll.

I unclipped my radio from my waist and depressed the button. "Captain, this is Avery."

"Wheelhouse, please."

My shoulders slumped. My whole body itched with the need to get off this boat. Five months on this thing and I was so done I was charcoal.

"Roger that, sir."

I turned to Leslie and we hugged. "I'll catch you in France."

"Or Italy."

Italy had some of my favorite ports—they were quieter than the south of France and the people more relaxed. And of course, pasta. "I hope so." Unless I'd renewed my contract with the same vessel, I never had my next season planned out much in advance, but I could hope for a season that involved *a lot* of Italy. Even if it was from the water.

I released Leslie and headed up to the wheelhouse, where the captain navigated the boat, barked orders, and generally made sure none of us died while we were on board.

"Avery, come in," he said as I knocked on the door. "Have a seat."

I slid into one of the two chairs bolted to the floor. "You've had a good season," he said, sitting opposite me.

"Thank you, sir."

"I'm putting a crew together for the Med season, and I'd like you to be chief stew."

"That's very flattering. Which yacht?"

"The *Athena*—refurbished in dry dock two years ago. She's a 154-footer. I've done a season on her and she's a nice vessel." As if he sensed he'd need to sweeten the deal, he added, "You'd get your own room."

I frowned. "Really?" Private space for the crew in yachting was as rare as hens' teeth.

He smiled. "Heaven, right? And the base salary's good —a forty percent uplift on what you had this season."

"Are you serious?" Salaries for chief stewardesses were well established and based largely on the size of the yacht. "How come?"

He shrugged. "The request came in from the yacht owner, actually. He's personally requesting every single member of the crew and willing to pay to get his way."

I wasn't sure how the yacht owner would even have heard of me. Usually, they simply hired a captain and left them to source the rest of the crew. "Forty percent more?

What's the catch?" There must be a reason the yacht owner was paying so much.

"Well, the first charter of the season's a long one. Eight weeks. So there'll be little time off during those first two months. I think he's trying to soften the blow."

Usually between charters of the five-month season, crew had a day or so to kick back and regroup. I slept like the dead on those days off. Eight weeks was a long period with no guest-free time. But a forty percent uplift was worth considering. My savings had trickled away into nonexistence, and I couldn't remember the last time I'd bought a new pair of sandals or a new outfit. I sent all my money home and even then it was only just enough. More money meant building an emergency fund and maybe a trip to Zara to add a couple of pieces to my wardrobe.

"But the upside is there's only one guest."

"Really?" That sounded too good to be true. "For a 154-foot yacht? There must be six bedrooms."

"Yup. The boat's got capacity for twelve."

I frowned. "That doesn't make sense."

"The guest is very private, apparently. Wants a working vacation." He shrugged. "Maybe he'll have guests once he gets settled."

"And how many interior crew will I have?" Maybe this was the big catch. "Would it just be me?"

"You'll get two. So the crew won't be different just because there's one guest. But, if we lose a member—for illness or incompetence—there won't be any replacements. We've been background checked."

It was unusual but not unheard of to be background checked. "Is it some celebrity doing a detox or something?"

"I have no idea. I've also been advised that we won't be

given details of who it is or their preferences for food or drink."

The whole reason guests went on these charters was to have every whim catered for, but if we didn't even know what this guy liked to eat and drink, then how would we make sure he had the best possible experience?

"Is he Russian?" Sounded like this guy was super paranoid. Rich Russians were all paranoid and not without cause. I had a girlfriend who worked on Boris Kasanov's *Sunset* for a few months. She'd thought working on the third biggest yacht in the world would be glamorous, but apparently the place had been full of scowling ex-FSB agents looking to take someone down. She'd left after a crew member had been accidentally shot in the leg and she'd been told to turn a blind eye or quit. She'd quit.

"No, British. From what I understand, the guest's privacy trumps any concerns over what we're serving them for dinner. I've only been made aware of preferences for privacy, and it's clear that if there are any slipups in relation to his requests, he'll leave and sure as hell we won't be getting a tip."

The last thing anyone wanted was an eight-week charter guest to leave—last minute bookings were rare. Even a forty percent uplift was not going to cover the lack of tip. It was a gamble, but one where I could tip the odds in our favor with great service.

"You know what these guests are like. I'm sure he'll have other requests when he's on board, and I think it's safe to assume this guy is going to be picky," Captain Moss said. "It will be tough but the money's good. We'll just get to know what he likes quickly and then adjust accordingly. You've managed a lot worse, I'm sure."

These details seemed odd but not so difficult. There

had to be something else. I'd never had a free lunch. Never even been offered a menu.

"There's one final thing."

I knew there had to be something. There always was.

"We have to be in Saint Tropez in three days."

I groaned. Freaking typical. There was no way I could do that. I shook my head. "I'm booked on a flight to Sacramento tonight."

"You're going to turn down a season with your own room at a forty percent pay bump just for a bit of downtime?"

It wasn't just that I was tired. I wanted to see my family, spend some quality time with my brother and my dad. I hated that I spent most of the year away from them as it was. If I could earn what I did on yachts back in California, there was no way I'd be anywhere but home. However glamorous it sounded, yachting was hard work, and for me, all about the money.

Which was what made this offer so tempting.

"The European sun will revive you. And remember you've got a tip on top of your salary. And you know if a guest is going to all that trouble to background check us then the tip is likely to be good."

I sighed. It was a promise of a lot of extra money. "I'll need to speak to my dad." Fact was, my father would be looking forward to a break, too. I spent my days looking after rich, entitled guests, but he spent his days looking after my twenty-five-year-old disabled brother. There was no escape for him, no days off, and he certainly didn't get paid.

"I need an answer today. I have no doubt this will be a challenging charter, but if anyone can think on their feet and make the weirdest requests work, it's you." Captain

Moss stood, our conversation over until I'd made my decision.

"Thank you. I'll make the call now."

I excused myself and headed back to the sleeping quarters. A forty percent raise and my own bedroom would have ordinarily had me busting out the champagne, but the last five months of the Caribbean season had taken its toll. I'd been so looking forward to a break, and the thought of going straight into another five-month season, the first eight weeks without a day off, sounded exhausting.

I scooped my phone from my nightstand, lay back on my bed and dialed my dad.

It stopped ringing but no one answered. "Dad, it's Avery," I said. "Can you hear me?"

"Yes, honey, I just dropped the phone." He sounded breathless.

"Were you running?"

"No, I just came in from the kitchen."

My heart squeezed. The man used to toss me in the air as if I were a football, and now he was breathless walking from the kitchen into the living room. How long was he going to continue to care for my brother?

"How are things in Sacramento?" He hated when I fussed, and he'd have a fit if he knew how hard it was to call him every day when our hours on duty were so long and the guests were so demanding. But hearing his voice

made me feel less like I was abandoning him.

"Not as sunny as Florida."

Despite being sixty-seven, my dad still hadn't retired—couldn't with my brother's medical bills—but since I'd started taking on a lot of the expenses, he'd gone part time and no longer worked Fridays. "Did I wake you?"

"No, we're just having breakfast."

I grinned at the thought of them at the kitchen table. Right after the accident, Michael couldn't move his arms and had to be fed, but after some time and with physical therapy, he'd made a lot of progress above the waist, although he still couldn't walk.

"You do anything nice yesterday?" I asked.

"We kicked back and watched the game."

I shook my head and smiled. Watching baseball, hockey, even football—it was the only time I saw the light back in my brother's eyes.

"Did you order pizza?" I asked.

"Of course we ordered pizza."

I rolled my eyes. Of course they had. "You've gotta try to stay healthy, Daddy." I loved to cook for them when I was at home. Things like going grocery shopping, making soup, even watching sports with my family became special, something I craved when I was at sea, so far away from home.

"I'm as strong as an ox," he replied.

I grinned as I imagined him standing straight, puffing out his chest. "I just want you to stay that way."

"Stop your fussing. The Walker men are just fine. Tell me about what's going on there with you. How many rich, spoiled asses have you wiped today?"

I laughed. "All the guests left yesterday."

"Nice, so you doing a little sightseeing or sunbathing today before heading home?"

"Something like that. Did the physical therapist come yesterday?" Michael had someone come to the house three times a week to work with him.

"She sure did. He's building up his muscles in his legs nicely—the weights help." My dad sighed.

"What is it?"

"Oh, she's nice and everything. It's just she's always

talking about how more sessions would help and if Michael wants to make progress then . . ."

Michael mumbled something in the background, probably telling us to quit fussing.

"More therapy sessions? Like how many more?"

"I don't know, honey. She was talking about having six months of six days a week. But I told her there was no way we could afford that. The insurance won't pay."

Michael wanted to walk again. My dad and I wanted that for him, and I'd gone into battle with the health insurer on more than one occasion about physical therapy. It was why he still had three weekly sessions even now, so long after the accident. I knew they'd never agree to six sessions a week.

"She thinks it will make a difference?" I asked.

My father didn't respond and the scrape of a chair and my father's slight groan as he stood echoed down the phone, indicating that he was moving rooms so Michael couldn't hear him.

"She said that if Michael had six sessions a week, after six months she'd be able to tell us whether it was realistic to believe Michael would walk again, and if it was possible, we'd be able to see the progress in that time."

My brother's accident seven years ago had changed things completely for my family. My mother had abandoned us shortly after, unable to cope with a life that revolved around her newly disabled son, and soon after the bills had started to pile up.

I'd been planning to start UCLA that fall, but suddenly my family had needed me, and I'd needed to earn money, fast.

A friend of a friend had spent a summer in Miami as a yachtie and came back after her first season with a Louis

Vuitton bag. It seemed like a quick and easy way to earn a lot of money that didn't require skills or experience. I'd been partly right. It *was* quick. But life on superyachts, catering to the rich and occasionally famous, was far from easy. I missed my dad. And my brother. But I couldn't complain. I wasn't stuck in a wheelchair, my whole future snatched from me.

Michael just wanted to walk again. And if I took the charter Captain Moss was offering, I might be able to give him that. Or at least find out whether it was possible.

"Six months of an additional three sessions a week?"

"Yeah, it's completely impossible. I told her."

I did the sums in my head. At a rough guess it was north of ten thousand dollars.

My stomach dropped.

"I was about to head to the airport, but Captain Moss has offered me a last-minute charter," I said, then explained about being personally recruited.

"That's an incredible compliment," my dad responded. "Not that I would expect anything else from my amazing daughter."

"I don't know what to do. I was really looking forward to seeing you and Michael."

"We were looking forward to seeing you too, honey. Come home. We complain about it, but we miss your fussing."

I knew my dad was grateful for the financial help I provided, but I also knew it was hard for his ego to swallow. So we both liked to pretend that my job was more glamorous than it was.

"It's a lot of money, Dad. It would pretty much cover the additional therapy." I'd call the therapist to see if we could get a discounted rate, but I might be able to cover it.

"But it would mean I didn't get to see you for another five months."

"If you don't want to do it then you should say no. I want you to live your own life, honey. You don't need to worry about Michael and me." Dad said it as if worry was a tap I could just turn off. I was damned if I did or damned if I didn't. More money meant better care for my brother but going home meant respite for my dad and a month of normalcy for me. It was lose, lose.

"I think I should take it," I said. That would be the sensible decision. The one I could live with. I wouldn't be able to live with myself if I'd had the opportunity to help my brother walk again and not taken it. No matter how tired I was. No matter how much I wanted to sleep in my own bed, have drinks with my girlfriends and cook for my family.

"I think you should do what will make you happy."

I stared up at the bunk above me. I'd be happy in Sacramento, but providing for my brother was the most important thing to me. Although earning the money this charter would provide wasn't exactly happiness, it came close.

"I just wish I were closer to you and Michael."

"You're a good daughter and sister, Avery. But you need to worry about yourself more. Let someone fuss over you for a change. You've sacrificed an awful lot for your brother and you deserve a break."

"I'm perfectly fine. I think I'm going to take this offer, but I'm going to miss you."

"Are you sure? You sound tired and we miss you."

"Did I tell you that I'd get my own room?" I had to focus on the positive. My own room was a huge win. "I'll be able to video chat with you whenever I like."

"Just to make this old man happy, promise me that if you decide to do this, you'll find something just for you when you're in Europe. You spend far too much time looking after everyone else."

Like what? A trip to Zara was never going to happen now. A date? Dating was impractical and finding someone to love was impossible. Guests were strictly off-limits and relationships with another crew member never lasted long after my feet hit dry land. I didn't want casual.

Just like I didn't want to be heading to France in two days. But it looked like that was how life was panning out.

"I promise I'll find something nice to do." I rolled my eyes. Maybe a bowl of pasta and a new bottle of fake tan would qualify.

"That's my girl. And try not to work too hard."

Hard work came with the job, but I still had a few days off. I'd book myself into a nice hotel. Perhaps a couple nights' sleep and a few days of room service would make up for another five months alone at sea.

THREE

Avery

Another day, another blue sky, another superyacht. As I reached the main deck of the *Athena*, carrying a glass of champagne and a glass of orange juice, I glanced across at the Saint Tropez marina in the distance and took a deep breath to calm myself. I was usually well rested for the first charter of the season, and May was usually a beautiful month in the Med, but I still carried the exhaustion of the previous season with me. On top of fatigue, the lack of information that we'd been given about the first eight-week charter meant I was unprepared for this guest and it made me more than nervous.

We arranged ourselves into the welcome line. Captain Moss first, me next to him, Eric the bosun, then Chef Neill and the rest of the crew, excluding the engineers who disappeared back to the engine room rather than meet our guest.

The tinny sound of the tender grew louder from behind us, and from the corner of my eye I caught my stewardess, August, craning her neck to look. "Eyes forward," I said. I hated riding my crew's ass. Some of the chief stewardesses I'd worked under enjoyed wielding their power, but that wasn't me. I just wanted the job done, the guests delighted and the tips huge.

The sound of footsteps headed up the stairs toward us. I plastered on a smile, careful to keep the tray I was holding steady.

As our guest appeared, I drew in a breath. He was young—around thirty, no more than thirty-five—and handsome with dark brown hair and wide shoulders. This guy wasn't anything like the normal charter guest. But then this was nothing like a normal charter. He was tall—well over six feet. Sharp cheekbones framed his face and led down to a perfectly smooth, square jaw. His eyes were dark and serious. If his nose hadn't been a little crooked, as if it had been broken at some point in his past, I might have even described him as pretty, but the unevenness tipped him toward handsome. It suggested there was a little rough beneath the oh-so-smooth.

I swallowed. I'd never found a guest attractive before. Not even a little bit. But then again, we never had charter guests who looked like this guy. When I first got into yachting, I'd expected to be surrounded by rich, beautiful people all the time. And while there was plenty of wealth, the attractive guests tended to be women. Although I was pretty flexible about a lot of stuff, I was strictly dickly when it came to my fantasies.

He strode toward Captain Moss and they shook hands. "Good to meet you," the man said in a deep, gravelly voice that seemed to make my whole body vibrate.

"Good to have you on board," Captain Moss replied.

"I'm Hayden Wolf," he said, turning to pin me with a

stare so intense it was as if he were getting some sort of psychic reading. "Avery, right?"

How did he know my name? Maybe the background check had given him a photograph. And the way he said it—my name shouldn't sound that different in a British accent, but the way he enunciated every syllable, coupled with the deep timbre, somehow made it sound important. "Yes, sir," I replied.

He nodded and smiled. My nipples tightened. *Fuck.* Thank God I was wearing a t-shirt bra.

The first rule in yachting was never cross the line between personal and professional. Some crew found it difficult, especially when the guests were laid back and wanted the staff to join in the fun. Sometimes the lines got blurred, but never for me—it was the easiest way to get fired. I'd never seen a guest as anything other than the person responsible for my tip and the reason why I could send money home to my family.

But Hayden Wolf?

There was something about him that erased the line completely, and all of a sudden I was imagining him naked and sweaty. *Shut it down*, I told myself.

"May I offer you a glass of champagne or orange juice?" I asked.

He shook his head. "No, thank you."

My heart, which had been skipping in my chest, suddenly sank to the floor.

Please God, tell me he drinks.

A sober charter guest was the worst. I'd take someone who demanded all his sheets flown over from Italy and his whiskey from a distillery in the remote islands of Scotland over a guest who didn't drink.

"You've disabled the Wi-Fi?" Hayden turned to ask Captain Moss.

"As you requested," Captain Moss confirmed.

The Wi-Fi was disabled? Usually it was the other way around. Guests were always asking for a better connection, failing to understand that when you were afloat, there were things beyond our control—like the freaking ocean.

"Okay, I'm going to need everyone's mobile devices," Hayden announced. "Phones, tablets, laptops."

No one moved and I glanced across at Captain Moss, but he wore his normal impassive expression. Were they being checked for something?

"You heard our guest," Moss said. "We'll be waiting."

We all filed back inside the yacht and headed to our sleeping quarters, where the few personal things we had on board were kept. We were unusually silent as we collected our devices, unclear on why our guest was demanding our personal things.

"Is this everything?" Hayden asked as Chef Neill, the last person to emerge, placed his computer and phone on the teak table that would be later set for lunch.

"It's vital to me that nothing leaves this boat. No pictures, no phone calls, no emails, nothing," Hayden said.

Privacy was rule number two in yachting. We all knew how to be discreet. No one on a yacht gossiped about their guests outside of the yacht. Well, that wasn't true. We all gossiped about the guests, but we never mentioned names. We never attributed the outrageous stories that we collected during our careers.

"I understand that it might be a challenge, so as an additional layer of security, you won't have access to your communication devices during my stay," Hayden said.

The entire charter without our phones or laptops? He

had to be kidding. August gasped beside me, and I fisted my hands, trying to keep the smile on my face.

"Nothing for eight weeks," the captain confirmed, and I could tell the entire crew were desperate to complain but no one would want to embarrass Captain Moss.

The third rule of yachting was the guest gets what the guest wants. I was used to outlandish requests, but no phone or internet for eight weeks wasn't just inconvenient. If I'd known this before the charter started, I probably wouldn't have said yes.

"Please, may I clarify?" I asked. Ordinarily I sucked up everything a guest asked for—went above and beyond what they'd hoped for—but I couldn't hold back. "We're not going to be able to contact our family for two months? Some of us have personal situations—"

"Not from this yacht," Hayden snapped. "I have very few requests, but my need for absolute privacy and discretion is paramount. There are no discussions or negotiations about this. You can contact people from the shore, but if you don't like it, then you will need to find a different yacht to work on."

It was as if I'd been thrown against a wall by the force and intensity of his words. The jerk hadn't even let me finish my sentence. I'd dealt with unreasonable guests in my time, but normally I could separate the job from the real me and I didn't care less. I wanted to explode and yell that there was no way I could be without any way of contacting my dad for two months, but I knew I should be setting an example to my two interior crew members, Skylar and August. I had to stay calm and then figure out what the hell I was going to do.

"Thank you for your cooperation," Hayden said as if

he'd asked us not to chew gum or wear pink for the next eight weeks. What a way to start a season.

"Avery will give you the tour," Captain Moss said.

I smiled, trying to focus on something other than Mr. Wolf's almost-perfect face and how I wanted to kiss it and slap it in equal measure. I knew there must be a catch to being that handsome—he was clearly totally paranoid and an asshole. But I was a problem solver. Maybe I could change his mind.

I handed my tray to Skylar, my second stew. "Let me show you to the main salon first. If you'll slip off your shoes?" I asked, pausing at the automatic sliding doors and indicating a shallow basket by the door that I'd left out specifically for shoes.

"Really?"

I nodded. "I'm afraid so. Yacht decks are traditionally unvarnished to keep the color natural, so shoes are likely to damage the teak. Every yacht's the same."

He glanced at my stockinged feet, then bent and untied his shoelaces. I glanced over his broad back. Who wore a suit to the start of a vacation? I needed to know more about this guy than that he was good looking, British and so suspicious. "How was your journey?" I asked. Perhaps he'd relax and in a couple of days we'd have our phones back. I didn't want to have to walk away from this beautiful yacht and the increase in pay, but I had to be in contact with my father. I'd figure it out. I'd have to.

"Fine," he replied, rising from where he crouched, and picked up his briefcase that he'd set down.

I reached for it. "Can I take that for you?"

His knuckles turned white as he tightened his fist around the handle. "That's fine. I have it."

His clipped tone indicated whatever was in the briefcase was important. I just hoped for all our sakes it wasn't drugs. Yachting had a zero-tolerance policy for drug use. If even a trace of illegal drugs were found on board, a captain would be stripped of his license with no second chances. If Hayden Wolf had drugs in that briefcase, Captain Moss would cancel this charter, and we'd all be guestless and without a tip for the next eight weeks.

I glanced up as he towered above me. Despite him kicking off this charter with an entirely unreasonable demand, being this close to him made me slightly giddy, which wasn't an adjective anyone had ever used to describe me. I was focused and diligent according to most, funny and loyal if you asked my family. But I was never giddy. *Shut it down, shut it down,* I chanted in my head.

"This is the main salon. We have a selection of games here," I said, pointing to the chessboard and the card table. Not that he'd be able to play the games by himself.

He slid his free hand into his pocket. "Chess."

I paused, waiting for him to elaborate, but he didn't so we walked the length of the main salon.

The *Athena* was a beautiful yacht, just as Captain Moss had promised: simple lines, elegant and light. The whole interior looked like a Hampton's summer house—clean, crisp and fresh in white, creams and grays. All the furniture had a high-end feel without being over the top. Sometimes yacht interiors could be a little gaudy, but if I had a yacht, I would choose something like the *Athena*'s decoration; it was all understated luxury.

Hayden Wolf made no comment about the decoration.

"We can make up any cocktail you like," I said, indicating the bar in the corner. "Do you have a favorite?"

He shook his head. "Whiskey sometimes."

We had some good whiskies on board, and I was

relieved to hear he drank. Hopefully we could interest him in a tasting. "Do you have a favorite that I might be able to track down?"

He scanned the windows, looking out at the horizon. "No. Whatever you have on hand will be fine."

"And with your meals, Neill is an excellent chef. He'd love to make you what you like. Are you a steak man?"

He shrugged. "Sometimes."

"Fish?" I suggested.

"I'm not fussy."

I smiled while holding myself back from calling him a liar. There was no such thing as an unfussy billionaire. I managed to say nothing and led us toward the stairwell. "We have four floors of guest accommodation, bedrooms are at the bottom, so let's start with the top floor, just above us."

The reflection from the water was almost blinding as we opened the door and stepped outside onto the upper deck. "It's really just the hot tub up here. You can get a little bit of shade as well," I said, indicating the two loungers while avoiding looking at Hayden. As a chief stewardess, I made it my business not to show my emotions and this man wouldn't change that. "Most guests like to use the loungers on the main deck. There's also space at the front of the boat at this level for sunbathing as well." I pointed toward the route to the beds at the top of the boat. I bet he had strong thighs and a hard chest under that suit. Not that I would be looking. "You'll figure out which you prefer."

I snuck a glance when he didn't respond. He just pursed his lips and nodded. It wasn't that he was impolite, he just seemed a little uninterested, as if relaxation would be superfluous to him over the next eight weeks.

"Okay then, let's head to the second lounge and dining room." I led the way down two floors. "This is where you'll eat if it's too windy outside," I said as we reached the living-dining space. I shrugged. "Or if you want a change, the main salon is bigger, but here there's a television and some people think it's a little cozier."

He chuckled, and I snapped my head around in case I'd misheard, but I hadn't. He was laughing. It was good to know he could and it suited him. Made him look younger and less serious.

"I don't think there's much about this boat that's going to make me feel cozy," he said.

He had a point. He was going to rattle around the place. "Are you planning on having any guests? We'd be happy to accommodate additional people."

His smile disappeared. "No."

I'd clearly touched a nerve. I just didn't understand why. I hadn't asked anything controversial. Getting this guy to talk was impossible. "Okay, let's head to the bedroom level."

At the bottom of the stairs, I paused. The space down here was tighter than elsewhere on the boat and there were no windows in the square hallway. He and I were alone in this darkened, small space, just inches between us, and the atmosphere seemed to shift slightly. He sucked in a breath, and I found myself staring at his expanding chest. I glanced up and caught his eye. *Shit.* "Of course you have six cabins for you to use." Hopefully he hadn't noticed.

"And they're all secured?" he asked.

"Yes, privacy is a key feature." I made my way into the second guest bedroom. As Captain Moss had indicated this would be a working vacation, I'd arranged to have all the regular furniture removed and replaced it with a large, white modern desk, a desk chair, two easy chairs and an additional office chair. "I thought it might be useful for you to have this room to work. If you need anything else, just let me know. I wasn't quite sure what you'd want."

"That's helpful," he said, glancing around. "And you have the keys?"

I pulled a key ring out of my pocket and passed it over.

"Thank you." He offered me the palm of his large hand and I caught an earthy, masculine scent. The outside of him —the suit, the hair, even his walk—was smooth, but the way he was so guarded in what he said, so private and measured . I couldn't help but feel there were things below the surface I wanted to know.

I dropped the keys into his hand, careful not to touch him, and he clenched his fist tight.

"I don't want other crew members down here, and no one else has keys to the rooms except me, right?"

I nodded and turned to head out, not wanting to meet his eye. I had another set of keys nestling on my key ring. The captain had mentioned that Hayden wanted to be the only one with keys but there was no way that was going to happen. Moss had instructed me to keep a set. I hated to lie, but I did what the captain told me to do.

"The master suite is next door. I presume that's where you'll want to sleep, but obviously you can choose any of the other four bedrooms." I opened the door of the master bedroom. "Let me show you." It was my favorite room aboard the *Athena*. It was luxurious but felt really fresh with crisp, white linens, a silver-gray carpet and velvet headboard, not to mention the freestanding tub for two and shower that could fit four. It was the kind of room I'd like to disappear into with a lover or my husband for a romantic week away if I were chartering a yacht or if I was a guest of someone like Hayden Wolf.

But I wasn't chartering this yacht and I wasn't anyone's guest. I was the help. A maid and a waitress.

"Shall I unpack for you?" Eric had already placed Mr. Wolf's bags on the luggage racks.

He frowned. "I can unpack my own suitcases," he replied, as if me offering to do it for him was the most ludicrous thing he'd ever heard.

"Whatever you prefer. The closet space is here. If you need anything ironed, just let me or one of the other interior crew know." I didn't feel as if I were doing enough.

"You normally unpack for guests?" he asked as he unzipped his first case.

"Absolutely," I replied. "It would be my pleasure." Surely he was used to that kind of service. Even if he'd not been on a yacht before, he must have stayed at the best hotels. And he was *British*. Didn't rich, British people have butlers and shit?

He turned to me and blinked, his long eyelashes sweeping down and up. "Your pleasure?" The corners of his mouth twitched, and his gravelly tone sent a wave of goose bumps across my skin.

I nodded, trying to keep my breathing even. "Absolutely. I want you to enjoy your stay."

He gave a half chuckle. "I can manage, but thank you."

Was he laughing at me? I ignored his amusement. "Chef Neill is preparing lunch for you. Can I get you a drink in the meantime?"

"I have a call to make. Then I'll come up and find you."

"You can press the buzzer by your bed and—"

"You'll appear in a puff of smoke like my fairy godmother?" He raised his eyebrows.

I started to reply, but before I got my words out he

clasped my shoulder with his large hand. "Thank you. I'm fine. I'm going to make my call."

I tried to keep my voice at a normal pitch. "I'll leave you to it." I slipped out of his room and paused at the bottom of the stairs. My shoulder was still hot where he'd touched me, and I placed my palm over my shirt, trying to retain the feel of his hand. I couldn't figure this guy out. He was incredibly handsome but here alone. Clearly wealthy but didn't seem to be used to being waited on. And worse, he seemed to find my desire to help him amusing.

He might think my job was worthless, and maybe it was compared to whatever he did, but I'd show him how great service could make his life so much easier. This trip might be all business for him, but I knew I could make him enjoy it just a little more than he'd expected to.

FOUR

Hayden

Abandoning my office for eight weeks to float about on the Med seemed counterintuitive. My instincts said I should be back in London, fighting for the Phoenix deal. But my instincts hadn't been serving me well this last twelve months, and here I was preparing for battle from a superyacht.

I unzipped one of three pieces of luggage I'd brought with me and pulled out a satellite phone. Were people really so lazy and entitled that they had someone unpack for them?

I shook my head at Avery's suggestion. Ms. Walker, born in Sacramento, working on yachts for seven years, no college degree despite having an excellent SAT score. She'd been one of a few who had passed my brother's extensive vetting. I knew all of the crew far better than any of them knew me. Avery was attractive, which I hadn't been expecting. In fact, she was more than attractive. She was beautiful and I'd found myself having to catch my breath when I'd first laid eyes on her. My brother had provided photographs with the dossier on the crew, but I had only skimmed them, not taking in Avery's beauty. She had an easy smile and was desperate to make me comfortable which was . . . sweet. Amusing. Sexy. Plus she had a nice arse.

But focusing on what Avery Walker might look like naked was not what I was on board the *Athena* to do.

I punched my brother's number into the satellite phone he'd had delivered to me this morning at my London flat.

"Hayden. Are you on board?" Landon asked.

The first thing I'd done after the Lombard deal fell through was call my brother. I knew I was in trouble, and in a crisis, my little brother was the only person who could help. Paranoid as ever, he hadn't even let me finish explaining what had happened before he'd suggested a face-to-face meeting.

"Yep, just got here."

"How's the weather?" We'd conceived the idea of me going away to complete the Phoenix acquisition while he and his team figured out who was the leak in Wolf Enterprises. When I'd suggested the yacht, he'd given me a lot of shit about me making up a conspiracy just to have an excuse to charter a yacht.

I shrugged. "It's the South of France. How do you think the weather is? I'm here to work, not sunbathe."

"How are the women?"

"Landon, can you focus? I'm not calling to give you a blow-by-blow account of the humidity and how the women look in bikinis." Landon and I always got into trouble at school. They could never fault our academic record—we were both straight-A students. But we were able to get under the skin of the teachers because of our attitude. We were supremely good at covering up how hard we worked and how much we cared about doing well. So despite Landon acting as if catching my leak was the last thing on his mind, I knew he would be all over it.

An exasperated sigh echoed down the line. "You haven't got your mobile on you, have you?"

I rolled my eyes. "No. I might not be ex-Special Forces, but I do have the capacity to listen and follow instructions. I left my mobile in the flat, just as you said." Landon and I had always been close despite our careers—he'd entered the SAS straight out of university to the dismay of our parents while I'd been off trawling the City, looking for a way in, an edge. Despite our differences, right now he was the only person I trusted.

"And you've not brought your laptop or tablet or anything?"

"Nothing electronic other than what was in the briefcase you had delivered."

"Good. So you have a basic phone without web access, some countersurveillance stuff and an airgap computer that's never been connected to the internet—makes it almost impossible to hack." Since leaving the SAS, Landon had set up a private security firm.

"Okay, superspy. Don't you think you might be going a little over the top?" Landon always assumed the worst of everything and everyone, and given that he'd seen the worst of humanity when he'd come face-to-face with the Taliban, I guessed that was his right.

"Trust me, will you? Corporate espionage is the fastest growing part of my business. And there are two reasons for that. First because it's becoming more and more common. Second because I'm great at what I do. And even though you're my brother, and bloody irritating, I'm still going to bring my A game."

I ignored his bluster. I knew he was good. But I wasn't going to puff up his ego any more than it already was.

"And you've taken the mobile devices from everyone on board?"

The crew had not been pleased with my request. "Yes. But I thought we agreed I wasn't hiding. That I should just act like I'm on holiday."

"Absolutely. It doesn't matter if people know you're on board. We just don't want people to be able to record you. If crew have their phones on them, they can be hacked and used as listening devices."

I wasn't sure anyone would go that far to bury me, but anything was possible when it came to James Cannon. "If you say so."

"What did you say to people at the office?" he asked.

"I just said I was taking a working holiday. People asked about being able to contact me. I told them Anita would handle it all." I had hoped I'd out the leaker when I told people and be able to get back to normal, but if I'd spoken to the mole, they'd not made it obvious. Although I'd been running my assistant's reaction through my brain since I'd told her I'd be leaving. "Anita asked me if everything was okay. In the decade she's worked for me, she's never asked me a single personal question."

"What did you say?"

"Just that everything was fine." I hated how the situation I was in was making me doubt everyone around me, had me doubting myself and my judgment. I couldn't wait to get started—buy Phoenix, have Landon find the leak and then get back to life as normal.

"I'll have her under surveillance so we'll see if it was genuine concern or not. I've got taps on all the phones of your senior team—personal and work. And I'm going to analyze their finances, check out any suspicious deposits. And on your end, I have a team on the ground to see if anyone's watching you. You'll need to check for surveillance gear on the yacht. Do you have the RF device?"

I pulled out the countersurveillance sweeper Landon had given me. "Yeah. But no one knows I've chartered this yacht—you arranged it, remember?"

"Agreed. Just make sure you do a check where you're working and sleeping, and don't take any phone calls anywhere else."

I blew out a puff of air and locked the bedroom door. "Okay. I'll do that before I unpack. And you'll report to me daily on your progress on tracking down the leak?" Even if I did manage to acquire Phoenix, there was no point in resuming business as usual until whoever it was who was selling my corporate secrets was cut out of Wolf Enterprises like a disease.

I could almost hear him rolling his eyes. "I might just keep that information to myself."

"Okay, whatever." I twisted the venetian blinds, the room darkened and I picked up the torch Landon had given me along with the RF device.

I depressed the button, creating a beam of light that illuminated the bed.

"Make sure you do the inspection with the torch first. People skip that step but it can pick up things the more sophisticated stuff doesn't," Landon said. "You're checking for the reflection of a camera lens or the blink of a recording device."

"I'm on it." I moved through the room with the light, scanning the walls and the ceilings, even the blinds and the pictures.

"And I'll let you have more as soon as I do."

"I'm going to check this place for bugs and then get to work."

"And, you know, take advantage of the fucking yacht you're on. Only for you could trouble end up looking like a luxury holiday for the rich and famous."

"If it makes you feel any better, I'd rather be back in the City."

"You're an idiot."

"Shut up and get to work." I hung up and threw the phone on the bed as I worked my way around the room.

My pulse steadied when my initial inspection found nothing. I checked the switches and sockets to see if any looked as if they'd been tampered with recently. I moved on to the smoke detector. Nothing. Apparently air fresheners and mobile phone chargers were often a prime place to put surveillance devices but nothing was plugged in where it shouldn't be.

I changed out of my suit and into a shirt and shorts. It would be the first time I worked a deal in casual clothes, or from a sun lounger, or while being served cold drinks by a woman as beautiful as Avery Walker. None of that mattered. Nothing and no one was going to distract me from saving my business and weeding out my hidden enemies.

FIVE

Avery

The crew had gathered in the galley and their focus turned to me as I wandered in after showing Hayden Wolf down to his room. "He seems happy" was all I could say in response to their obvious anxiety about such an unusual charter. He'd seemed to relax a little when we were downstairs. My skin still tingled from where he'd touched me, as he tried to reassure me that I needn't fuss. My family always told me off for fussing but guests normally enjoyed it. They paid for it, after all. "I'll get him a drink when he's finished unpacking."

"No fucking phones or computers, Avery," Neill said.

"Right," I replied. There was nothing I could say. Neill and I had worked a few seasons together and he knew me well enough to know that I'd be pissed about the lack of phone, but I wasn't about to lose it when August and Skylar were around. We needed to focus on the positive. "He might calm down after a couple of days. Otherwise, I'm sure the inconvenience will be reflected in our tip." I would just have to go to shore regularly to call home.

"Something's off with this guy," August said as she polished a wine glass to a high shine. "I mean, who comes aboard a yacht in a suit? Even if he did look hot as hell."

I stared at her and placed a finger over my mouth. We were in the galley, which was only a few feet away from the formal dining room. I could normally hear guest footsteps a mile away, but I was taking nothing for granted where Hayden Wolf was concerned.

"What?" she whispered. "You've got to admit he's weird. Hot, but weird."

"He's just British," Skylar said. "Right?" She turned to me for confirmation. "They're all a bit stuffy, but let me tell you, they can normally drink like they're going for gold at the liquor Olympics."

"Husband material?" August asked Skylar.

"Maybe. I mean he's off-the-charts hot. And he's rich so that's two out of three," Skylar replied.

"He's not husband material," I interrupted. "Because he's a guest. And that trumps any list of husband qualities."

"Skylar wants a rich, good-looking husband who isn't an asshole. The guy's not going to *live* on the yacht. Surely guests are fair game once the charter's over," August said.

"No one should even be thinking of guests in that way," I interjected. "Let's focus on the job." I wasn't sure if I was trying to convince them or me. "Speaking of the job, he did tell me he liked whiskey." I tried to catch Neill's eye as he pulled vegetables from the refrigerator.

He'd been in a bad mood since the captain announced that Hayden Wolf wasn't going to be filling in a preferences sheet setting out what he liked in terms of food, drink and activities, and I thought the news that Hayden liked to drink would cheer him up.

"Did he say anything about food?" Neill asked.

"Just that he sometimes like steak and sometimes fish."

Neill rolled his eyes and went back to sorting through the vegetables that were on the counter in front of him.

"I get the impression he's not fussy," I said.

"Bullshit," Neill muttered. No doubt he'd had food sent back too many times to believe any guest on a yacht wasn't fussy.

"We'll figure it out." I was totally bullshitting. Usually the preferences sheet gave a lot away about how demanding or fussy guests were going to be. Some ran to fifty pages. Others were just ten but in seven years of yachting I'd never been without one completely. "I'll ask him again when I get him a drink later."

"Ask him to fill in the freaking preferences sheet," Eric chimed in. "He clearly thinks he's too good to do paperwork and expects us to read his mind."

Crew tempers always flared during a season—it was inevitable living and working in such close quarters and being under so much pressure to please demanding guests. Yachting could make a jerk out of Jesus. But we were usually a few charters in before signs of strain began to show. We hadn't even started yet and I was already wondering how I could last the next five months.

"And I don't get why we couldn't pick him up at the marina. Why did he come in from an obscure harbor? Is he Batman or something?" Eric asked.

"The privacy thing, I guess," I replied. They were being unfair to our new guest. I'd had people come in on tenders before.

"Yeah, but only allowing you and the captain on the

bedroom floor is one thing, but did you know that we can't have provisions delivered to the yacht? Not fresh vegetables or flowers or anything?" Neill sliced into an onion as he spoke. "We have to get someone to collect it every time."

"Really?" I asked. That was unusual. "Even though we're going to be moored offshore for the entire eight weeks of this charter?"

I cringed as I spoke and Neill started to laugh. I shouldn't have brought it up because Eric had been mad as hell when he learned that we wouldn't be going into dock for eight weeks, and I didn't want to aggravate him. He and his team were going to have to do overnight shifts on anchor watch to ensure the anchor didn't drag and we didn't crash into anything.

Eric just muttered and folded his arms.

It really wasn't a great way to start a season.

"We'll loosen him up." August grinned and I shot her a look. I'd gotten used to sizing new crew members up quickly. August was clearly a girl who liked to have fun. I just hoped she understood where the line was.

"I know," she said, rolling her eyes. "No touching. No thinking about him in the wrong way. Doesn't mean I can't flirt a little though, right? I mean we want a good tip, don't we?"

August and Skylar were complete opposites, but both beautiful. August had boobs I would die for, raven black hair and a very loud voice. Skylar, on the other hand, was calmer with nearly white-blonde hair, a button nose and a wide smile. I'd seen pictures of her Norwegian family taped up on the wall by her bed and they were all impossibly good looking.

"I think we just need to concentrate on service rather than flirting," I said.

"Maybe flirting is part of the service," August said, and she and Skylar laughed.

"Excuse me," a male voice interrupted.

I whipped my head around to see Hayden Wolf de-suited, though I didn't let my eyes take in whether he was every inch as hard bodied and bronzed as I'd imagined he might be. "Sorry, sir. What can I get you?" I was all business.

"Is it possible to get some water? Tap is fine."

In my seven years in this business, no one had ever asked me for tap water. He could probably have had perfectly pure water from an arctic glacier flown in if he'd wanted. I found I kinda liked the idea of an unfussy guest. It would make a change. "Can I get you ice and lemon with that?"

"However it comes," he said and he turned and headed back toward the dining room. There was something compelling about him clearly having so much money but not expecting his every whim catered for. What had made him that way? Did he have a family that kept his feet on the ground or was it something else that made him . . . modest?

"Wow, he's so good looking," August said. "And you were flirting with your 'yes, sir' and 'can I get you lemon with that,'" she said in a ridiculous voice. "So why can't I?"

"I was not flirting. I was being polite. There's a difference." I reached for a highball from the cupboard above the counter. Had I been flirting? Not consciously, but I'd never had to worry about my reactions to a guest before. I'd have to watch myself with this guy. My friends had always teased me for having quirky taste in men, but I'd never liked traditionally handsome guys. I truly believed that what was on the inside shone through, which was why I couldn't figure out why I'd found myself drawn to

Hayden when he arrived. Maybe there was more to him than a pretty face and there was something deeper pulling me in.

I took a step toward the sink and ran the tap, ensuring the water was cold. The boyfriends I'd had in high school had won me over with their sense of humor or passion. Hayden Wolf had me noticing him. It didn't make any sense. I knew nothing about him and the little I had picked up left me with more questions than answers.

After adding ice and a wedge of lemon, I took Hayden's drink up to the sundeck where he had settled on one of the loungers with his laptop and a notepad.

"Tap water, with ice and lemon," I announced as I set his drink on the side table and then felt ridiculous. I wasn't serving up a three-star Michelin meal.

He pushed up his sunglasses and squinted at me, smirking. "Thank you."

"You're welcome. Is there anything else you need?"

His gaze flickered down to my mouth and back up to look at me. "I'm good, thanks." He held my gaze a little too long and I looked away and over the water, facing the May breeze, hoping it would cool the blush I could feel creeping up my face.

"It's going to be a beautiful day. Let me or one of the deck crew know if you want a Jet Ski out or . . ." What was this guy going to do without any friends?

I glanced back at him and he was still watching me, almost as if were analyzing me.

"Thanks," he said as he blinked and then pointed at his laptop. "I have plenty to do."

Crap, had I been interrupting him? "Of course." I turned and left him to his mobile office.

As I got into the main salon, Captain Moss was waiting

for me. His hands in his pockets, he coaxed me over with a nod of his head.

"I want you to check out the bedrooms if you get a chance when our guest's not in them," he said. "I want to make sure he's not doing anything he shouldn't be. You know I won't stand for anything that might put my license at risk."

"You think we should be worried?"

Captain Moss shrugged. "Some of his requests are unusual. We just need to take precautions. I'm not going to worry until I have reason."

I slid my hand over my key ring stored at my waist, my fingers finding the keys to his bedroom and office. "I'll go now to do a refresh. He won't have had the chance to get fully settled yet."

"Come find me when you're done."

"Yes, sir."

Captain Moss swept out and I headed back to the galley.

"Can you make a start in the laundry room?" I asked August. "And, Skylar, please set the table for lunch and then find Mr. Wolf in about twenty minutes to see if he needs anything. I'm going to check the bedroom floor now that the suitcases are in." We always refreshed towels, toilets and sinks after guests had freshened themselves up on arrival, so that's what I'd do and then if he caught me, I'd just tell him there'd been a misunderstanding about the key situation.

I headed toward the stairs, my heart thumping. It wasn't as if I was doing anything wrong—the captain had asked me to check things over.

Even if I didn't find anything, I might get a clue as to why someone wealthy enough to charter a boat like this would happily drink tap water and didn't bother to tell us his food or drink preferences. How someone that good looking could be in this Mediterranean paradise alone. Even if he was working, didn't he want to have dinner with someone? I'd never come across rich men who didn't have attractive girls happy to spend time with them.

I grabbed a couple of clean towels and some cleaning wipes from the laundry room. As I got to the bottom floor I held my breath and listened up the stairs to see if anyone was coming. The distant sound of the dryers in the laundry room was the only thing I could make out.

I pulled out my keys and unlocked the door to the master suite. I glanced around and couldn't see anything out of place. It looked like it had when I'd shown him into the room. Except, where was all his stuff? I opened the drawers by his bed. There were a couple of notebooks in the top and some old-fashioned manila files and a tablet in the bottom drawer. I shut the drawer and headed toward the closet. He'd unpacked and hung everything up neatly, including the suit he'd arrived in. I straightened out the hangers, an earthy, masculine smell winding itself around me. He seemed to have yacht-appropriate clothes, so I had no idea why he might have arrived in a suit, even if it did fit him as well as it did. Maybe he'd had a really early breakfast meeting? I checked the drawers and found nothing but his underwear. I lifted the suitcases that were stacked to one side but they seemed empty. After checking the bathroom and seeing nothing that would concern the captain, I swapped out the hand towels, wiped the sink and did a final scan of the room. There was a book by his bed. It wasn't any request from Captain Moss that made me look closer. *The Martian.* An old photograph being used as a bookmark peeked out from the top. Intrigued, I slid my finger through the pages to reveal the entire picture, peering closer. It was a smiling family lined up with their arms around each other's shoulders with some trees in the background. Two teenagers at one end of the picture then their parents. One of the boys was Hayden, his hair slightly floppier than he wore it now, his body a little less filled out but still handsome. He must have been eighteen or nineteen. The boy next to him, who must be his brother from the chin and the nose, wore a crew cut. I couldn't help but smile at the happy scene. There was nothing cold or mysterious about the younger Hayden. Nothing private in his huge smile.

I snapped my head around at a creak from the staircase and held my breath. August and Skylar knew they shouldn't come down here. I replaced the book and scurried to the door to listen.

It must have just been an odd sound of the boat.

I reached out for the door handle so I could leave before I got caught but froze at the sound of a man clearing his throat on the other side of the bedroom door. Shit. We were only a few hours into this charter, and our guest might be about to leave. I glanced over my shoulder. For a second I considered hiding in the closet but that would just get me into more trouble. The jangle of the keys on the other side of the walnut divide meant there was no going back.

I pulled open the door and came face-to-face with Hayden Wolf.

SIX

Hayden

I hadn't been on this boat a full hour and already things weren't working out. I'd given specific instructions that these rooms down here were to remain locked and that I should have the only keys. "What are you doing down here?" I snapped at Avery, trying to stay calm, but my fingernails were digging into my palms.

Avery swallowed and bowed her head in a gesture that in any other situation I might have found arousing, but right now, I wanted answers. "I'm sorry. I was just checking you had everything you needed. Providing fresh towels, freshening up your room. That's all." She lifted her arms to show me the hand towel I'd used once that she was grasping.

"Everything I needed? What I need is privacy—people keeping out of my business." Should I just pack my bags and leave? I glanced behind her at my room. What had she been doing in there? I'd taken so many precautions. "Why are you snooping?"

"Mr. Wolf, it's my job to make sure you have seven-star service on this yacht. I take that responsibility seriously."

"But what I requested was privacy. You told me I had the only keys."

"You do, but of course I have a set. I don't count. I'm invisible if I'm doing my job. I'm here to get you what you want before you realize you need it—to anticipate your desires. I'm not going to wait to be asked to change your towels or empty your trash. I'm not doing my job if you're focusing on anything other than what an incredible time you're having."

I sucked in a deep breath. She might have passion for what she did, but it wasn't what I'd asked for. "I'm going to have an incredible time if I can get my work done privately without having to be worried that the requests I make aren't being adhered to."

She winced as if ignoring the wishes of a guest was actually painful to her. She looked contrite and seemed genuine, but I'd lost confidence in my ability to judge people. "I'm sorry if I've done anything that you didn't want me to, and if it was up to me I would be happy to give you my key, but if you want to stop me from having access to your room then we need to speak to Captain Moss."

The last thing I expected was for her to suggest we go to her boss. "You're saying he insists you change my towels before I notice them?"

"No, he leaves that stuff to me. But he'll have different concerns. He's in the wheelhouse."

She led the way upstairs and I tried not to notice the way her near-perfect bottom filled out her khaki skirt. Any other time in my life, if I'd been faced with a woman as beautiful as Avery Walker, especially one who said she wanted to *anticipate my desires*, she would have been naked and pinned underneath me within thirty minutes of meeting her. I got the impression Avery didn't realize how alluring and sexy she was. It kind of oozed out of her, in every step she took, every movement. But I wasn't about to lose my focus over Avery Walker. I wanted to know what these concerns of Captain Moss were and why the hell my simple request for privacy had been ignored.

Avery knocked, then waited for Captain Moss to answer before opening the door. We might not be in the Royal Navy but there was a very clear chain of command. We took two steps up into a bright, semicircular room overlooking the Mediterranean Sea.

Captain Moss' eyes slid from Avery to me. "Mr. Wolf. Is everything alright?"

Avery clasped her hands behind her back and glanced at me.

When I didn't speak, she explained. "Mr. Wolf found me refreshing his room and is concerned that I have a key," she said, and shook her head, pressing her full lips together.

Captain Moss nodded. "I see."

He either wasn't surprised or was well used to keeping his emotions in check.

"Do I need to be concerned?" he asked Avery.

"Not from what I saw," she replied.

I'd lost the train of this conversation. It sounded as if Avery had been searching my room. "I thought I was clear that two rooms needed to be secure and that I was to have the only set of keys," I said.

"Well, I'm sure you want Avery to be able to do her job. And even if you didn't, there's no way I can be shut out of any room on this yacht. Let me explain," the captain said, gesturing to banquette seating at a small, polished oval table overlooking the ocean.

I took a seat, careful as always not to let my frustration show. Captain Moss took a seat the other side of the table.

"As captain, I'm subject to an enormous amount of regulation. A room I do not have access to—whether that's directly or through my chief stewardess—is not acceptable. What happens on this boat is my responsibility."

"You're saying that you snoop on all your guests?"

"Absolutely not. And it is not our intention to *snoop* on you. As chief stewardess, Avery has a set of keys so she can do her job and ensure you have the best possible stay. I've worked with her before and she's as straight as a die—I trust her completely. But I asked her to see if we needed to be worried about anything. You bring drugs on board this boat and I'm out of a job."

"Drugs?" I asked. Did I look like I did drugs? Was my suit a little too loud?

"As an example. Anything illegal."

"I'm not doing anything illegal."

"Surely you understand how your repeated requests for the utmost privacy go beyond what we've come to expect and as such raised our suspicions," the captain said.

I blew out a breath. I wished I was here to kick back and relax, that I didn't give a shit about the locked doors and couriered packages that I'd begin to receive. Jesus, they'd really think I was dealing drugs when that started.

"And I don't mean I just wouldn't get to captain this boat. I would lose my license and my career would be over. The stakes are too high for me to take unnecessary risks."

I knew that feeling. I was staring at the very real possibility of my business burning to the ground if I didn't make the next eight weeks count. I'd had Moss thoroughly vetted along with all the crew. His reputation was beyond reproach and was the reason I chose the *Athena*. He was just showing me the extent of his integrity. "I'm not here to do anything illegal. I'm here to work. Being as successful as I am makes me a target for people who want to know things before I want them public, and I'm taking every precaution," I explained.

I glanced at Avery, whose whole body seemed to sag with relief, although her expression remained the same. She had a veneer of personable professionalism, but I had a feeling that what lay beneath was worth getting to know.

"I run a financial services business," I continued. "The regulator would shut me down if I took part in anything illegal."

"I understand, but I have to take precautions in the same way I'm sure you do." Captain Moss glanced at Avery. "Rest assured, you're in trustworthy hands. If you don't feel comfortable with anyone else, you can completely count on Avery."

I nodded, understanding Captain Moss's position, but I no longer believed I could completely count on anyone other than my brother, although I wasn't about to say that. "I have nothing to hide from you, but I have good reason to need to keep my business affairs private."

"Perhaps we can reach a solution that works for both of us. As you requested, Avery is the only member of crew permitted on the bedroom floor and the only crew member to have access to keys to the bedrooms. You have my reassurance on that. And Avery's."

Avery nodded. "Absolutely. I've already informed the rest of the crew that I'm the only one to go down there."

"You've vetted her. You know she's trustworthy. If the only thing you don't want her to see is your computer and some papers, I can assure you that she's not going to be looking at anything like that. When cleaning, she won't touch anything on your desk and you'll be able to tell if she does, right?"

Captain Moss seemed reasonable and he was right, everyone on this yacht had been vetted by Landon. I could definitely leave my papers in a way that it was obvious to tell if they'd been disturbed and I really didn't have anything else to hide. "I want to be clear that she doesn't touch my desk. At all. Not even to clean it. If anything's moved then I'll be extremely disappointed." I could leave highly sensitive things in my briefcase.

"I won't touch a thing on your desk, Mr. Wolf. You can be assured of that."

Her breathy voice and her desperation to please me was too much and I found myself softening. "And I want you to have the key on you at all times. No setting it down where someone else could pick it up," I said, trying to keep my tone terse.

Avery nodded. "No problem. I always keep it attached to my belt." She pulled out a jangle of keys from her waist that seemed to be on a retractable key ring.

"Well, that's agreed then." I patted the table with my palm before standing. "I don't want any deviations from this plan without my express permission."

"Absolutely and thank you for your understanding," Captain Moss said as he shook my hand.

I liked the loyalty and trust Moss had shown Avery and the mutual respect they clearly had for each other. It seemed genuine, and I knew it was hard to find. That had me taking a risk on them. I hoped this time I was right to trust my instincts and put my faith in Avery Walker.

SEVEN

Avery

"You expecting it to do a little dance?" Chef Neill asked, lifting his chin toward the boiling kettle.

I'd been staring into space trying to figure out how I was going to make it to shore as often as I could to call my dad. I snapped back to reality, grinned at Neill and poured hot water into the French press. "Clearly taking my time waking up this morning," I replied.

"Shame our guest doesn't have the same problem."

"Right? What time did he come up?" I asked, nodding my head at the door of the galley toward the main deck where Hayden was sitting.

"No idea. I got here about ten minutes before you. He was on his laptop already by then."

He wasn't kidding about it being a working vacation. "I guess that's what sober guests do."

Neill groaned. Hayden had drunk half a glass of wine with dinner, but there'd been no tempting him with more, and he'd declined an after-dinner whiskey.

"At least there were no complaints about the food," I said. He'd cleared his plate and I kinda liked the lack of fuss. I imagined him and his brother around his parents' kitchen table doing the same thing when his mom served up meatloaf or something. It must be his family that kept him grounded.

"There weren't many compliments either." Neill, like most chefs, was sensitive about the dishes he prepared and as his friend I hated seeing him lack confidence because his cooking was amazing.

"Honestly, he is British and you know they can be more reserved about this stuff. And I think maybe he's not focused on food." Given Hayden Wolf's insistence that he didn't have any food preferences, I was pretty sure that Neill could serve up mac and cheese and Hayden Wolf would be happy with it. He didn't seem like the typical spoiled millionaire who would order lobster or caviar just because they could, then inevitably waste it because they were too drunk, which led to them grabbing my ass, also just because they could.

I pushed down the plunger of the cafetière. Mr. Wolf didn't seem as entitled as most guests. Wasn't interested in exercising his power by telling us all how high he wanted us to jump.

"It just makes my job so much harder."

I was going to try to coax a little more information from our mysterious guest so I could keep him and Neill happy.

"Do you want me to take that?" August asked as she came into the galley, tucking her polo shirt into her skirt.

"No, it's fine. I've got it," I replied. I was more than happy to take him coffee. Maybe he'd decided to take off his shirt. Not that I'd check him out or anything.

"He's such an asshole. Thank God there's only one of him and that he didn't bring any friends," August said.

I didn't like the way the rest of the crew were so hard on him. I knew we always were with guests, but Hayden had done little to deserve it. He wasn't making our lives hell in the way that some guests did.

I raised my eyebrows. "What's got you in such a bad mood?"

"Nothing. I just heard he shouted at you yesterday," she said.

I glanced up at Neill. Had the two of them been gossiping? The galley was the center of the boat and the chef always knew more than anyone else about what was going on.

"It was a misunderstanding," I said. I knew Hayden's frustration wasn't directed at me personally. It wasn't him being spoiled.

"If he shouts at me, I'll shout back," August replied in a singsong voice. "I don't care how rich you are, you should treat people with respect."

I tilted my head. "If you shout at a guest for any reason, I'll fire you." Hayden Wolf hadn't exactly shouted and even if he had, he had a reason to be pissed.

She rolled her eyes. This was August's second season and frankly, I wasn't sure she had the even temper required to be interior crew on a superyacht. Hopefully, if I led by example, I'd be able to knock some of the rough edges off her.

"I'm serious, August. The guests who can afford yachts like this tend to be under a tremendous amount of pressure. If they lose their temper from time to time, it's our job not to react."

She shrugged but didn't argue.

"Get started on the laundry, please" I said, picking up the tray of coffee and heading up the staircase to where Mr. Wolf sat on the main deck.

"Good morning, sir. Coffee, juice, the *Financial Times*, and the *Wall Street Journal*," I said as the doors slid open. I bent and put the tray on the table beside his chair, glancing at him to check his reaction. With his muscular, bronzed legs and slightly curly hair that had seemed straighter yesterday, he looked like any other guest. I couldn't imagine he took much care in shopping for clothes and, given the way he'd reacted to me offering to unpack for him yesterday, it seemed unlikely he had a stylist or someone to buy them for him. Perhaps his expensively rumpled linen shirt, which was still on unfortunately, and French blue shorts had been bought by a girlfriend.

"Because I'm British?" he asked, indicating the *Financial Times*.

Clearly he wasn't a morning person. "No, sir, we have that on board for all our guests."

He slid his laptop to the end of the lounger. "You don't need to call me sir. Hayden is just fine."

"I was wondering," I said, tucking the tray under my arm. "Chef Neill would really appreciate some guidance on your food preferences. Is there anything in particular you'd like to see on the menu?"

"I was serious yesterday when I said I don't mind."

Neill was climbing the walls with this guy's lack of concern about mealtimes, and I hated to see him so stressed. I glanced out over the water. The haze of the sun sitting on the horizon blurred the coastline as though some kind of force field existed between the water and the land. "It's going to be a scorching hot day. What about I get you fruit, yogurt and toast for your breakfast? A chicken, goat cheese and pomegranate salad for lunch and then what about sirloin steak in a watercress sauce for dinner?" I was pretty much suggesting my favorite foods.

A beat of silence passed as I waited for a response. He might think I was being too pushy and get irritated. Some men—I found it was the less confident ones—would react badly to a stewardess trying to steer them in one direction or another.

"I think that sounds like you just read my mind and described my favorite foods."

I wanted to tell him they were mine but that was probably too familiar. "Reading minds is part of the package," I replied, trying not to show how delighted I was at his reaction.

The corner of his mouth curled up and I wondered if he'd be a good kisser. "Good to know. I might have a use for that kinda skill." He paused, almost as if he was going to say something, but then pulled his laptop back onto his knee as I mentally high-fived myself at getting this guy to engage a little, to loosen up. He stopped typing. "And actually, if you can throw in some carbs somewhere, that would work."

"No problem." I was about to walk away but I wanted more for Neill than just today's menu. And it was my job to ensure Hayden Wolf had what he wanted.

"I guess in your business you like working with people who want to give their best. People who give one hundred percent, and are great at what they do?"

Hayden looked up from his laptop, frowning.

"Well, the crew want to do the same for you, and our mind-reading ability only goes so far. We want to give you our absolute best. Neill is a fantastic chef. This boat has amazing facilities—Jet Skis, a pool area that we can set up in the ocean that safeguards against jellyfish. We even have an inflatable banana." I paused. "Although that might not be your thing." It was difficult to imagine Hayden Wolf doing anything just for fun, but I was sure he'd go to his grave without sitting astride an inflatable banana. "We're here to give one hundred percent. And we like what we do. I know you are incredibly busy, but if you could give some thought to your preferences sheet, maybe it will provide you with a little light relief between phone calls." I set down a blank form I'd printed off in the wheelhouse earlier. "This is an unusual charter for us—just one guest, eight weeks." I shrugged. "We would be really grateful for a bit of direction."

He didn't say anything but continued to look at me with his dark blue eyes after I finished speaking. "I'll take a look," he replied eventually.

"Sorry. I didn't mean to go on. I just—"

"I'll take a look." He was done talking.

"Thank you." I headed back to the main salon. It wasn't a promise, but maybe he'd come up with something and at least I had today's menu for Neill.

"Avery."

I turned back to face him.

He didn't look up from his laptop. "I'd like to deal with you as much as possible, exclusively, in fact."

I didn't let my smile drop as heat stirred in my belly. He wanted more time with me? Or did he not like Skylar and August?

"It might make things easier. I don't want to have to fend off small talk from other crew."

I nodded. Of course that was it. It wasn't personal. Just that I was more senior and better able to swallow the thousand questions I wanted to ask him. How had he made his money so young? What had he done to create enemies?

What was his family like? Did he have a wife? I could hold back—I'd make sure I did—but I wasn't so sure about August, so his request made sense. I hoped it at least meant he thought I was good at my job.

"No problem," I replied. "I need to clean your room, if that's okay?"

Hayden exhaled, then swung his legs over the lounger and stood. "I'd like to be there if that's all right."

The last thing I wanted was supervision while I turned his room, but I never said no to a guest. "Okay, but I don't have to do it now if you want to drink your coffee."

"That's okay. I'll fit in around you." He slid his hands through his almost-curly hair. "I can work downstairs as easily as I can up here."

Nothing about this charter made sense—he must understand that I was meant to fit around him not the other way around. But I couldn't fight him on this at every turn, so I decided I would just take his offer at face value. "Careful. I might hand you a mop," I teased, leading the way back into the interior.

He chuckled but didn't say anything.

Once in the bedroom, he opened his laptop and settled at the small table under the window. I set to work.

I'd never felt so much like the help as I did as Hayden Wolf worked while I cleaned. Ordinarily, I didn't mind being the maid of the rich and famous. The guests all seemed to merge into one and I was able to separate who I was from the job I was doing. Maybe it was because Hayden was here alone, or maybe it was because he wasn't that much older than me, but the distance between Hayden and me didn't feel as vast as it did with other guests. And I didn't want him to see me as a stewardess. I wanted him to see the person beyond the uniform as a woman who could have gone to college and done so much more than clean his room and change his bedding.

I kept glancing across as Hayden remained laser focused on his laptop, occasionally frowning or shaking his head. Perhaps I could assist him in some way? It wasn't as if he'd brought a personal assistant on board, which wasn't unusual, although they normally stayed on shore somewhere rather than on the yacht.

"How long do you think you'll be?" he asked without looking up.

Shit, had he seen me staring in his peripheral vision?

I snapped into action, pulling the sheets from the bed. "I'll be as quick as possible, but you really don't need to babysit me. I'm trustworthy."

"Yeah?" he asked, turning to look at me. The intensity of his eyes sent a shiver down my spine.

"Honestly," I said.

Again he looked at me, opened his mouth and went to speak before shaking his head and grabbing his computer. "I'll be next door," he said and swept past me, that earthy, masculine scent following him.

It was probably for the best. The less time I spent in close proximity to this man the better. Normally, I played along when guests told me more than they ever should about their personal business—everything from sexual exploits to dreams for the future. I'd nod, smile and feign interest, but I'd never be tempted to ask for more detail—it wasn't my business and I'd never been particularly interested—always focused on the job and the service I was providing rather than the people I was providing it to. With Hayden Wolf, I found myself having to hold back from following him into the office and asking him a thousand questions. That desire couldn't just be his muscular arms and searching eyes. I'd never been taken in by just the physical before, but with Hayden it seemed as though there was more to him—his family, his drive. The way he looked at me. Yes, it was better that he left me on my own. I'd be able to focus on getting his room fixed rather than the man I was fixing it for.

EIGHT

Hayden

Despite the heat and the rocking of the yacht, I couldn't sleep. My plan had been to spend all night in the office working with advisors based in New York, who I'd selected because they had no public connection to Cannon. Then I'd thought I'd sleep in the day on deck. Working all night was fine. Sleeping all day wasn't. Especially not today. I was due to hear from the lawyers, and I didn't trust Wi-Fi, so I was having to go old school and have everything couriered to the boat in hard copy or on USB sticks.

I checked my watch, noting it was about half an hour since I'd seen Avery Walker. Right on cue, the main salon doors swished open. When she'd been cleaning my room, I'd found her so distracting that I'd had to leave the room. I'd been mesmerized by way her hands gripped the bed linen and found myself fantasying about pushing her onto the bed and my shoving her skirt up to her waist.

"Anything I can get you?" Avery asked as she came out onto the main deck. She made it sound as if she'd just happened to be passing by, but I'd been watching. She was always passing by every twenty to thirty minutes, catering to my every need. Her ponytail swished behind her as she came to a stop by my lounger. How would that ponytail feel wrapped around my hand?

I cleared my throat as I shook the fantasy of her out of my head. "Yes, actually." Nine times out of ten there was nothing I wanted from her, but it was just coming up to noon and I needed her help.

She had an almost permanent smile on her face, but it pulled a little wider, as if my asking for her help was what she wanted more than anything—that was bloody attractive. "What can I get you?"

"Well, first, I want to give you this," I said, pulling out the preferences sheet from beneath my laptop.

She sank her teeth into her full bottom lip as she took the sheet from me and began to scan the papers I'd scrawled over. "This is really nice of you."

It had taken some bollocks for her to ask me to fill this sheet in yesterday. She'd been trying to make her crew's life easier, and my stay more enjoyable, but it would have been easier, less confrontational to have just stayed quiet. From our tour I could tell she was good at her job, but I hadn't quite realized the care and compassion she had for her work and her colleagues. And I enjoyed that she'd called me out—and in such a charming way. She was all politeness on the outside but hinted at her core of steel. I had thought I was being helpful by not caring one way or another about the preferences sheet, but subtly she'd told me I was being anything but and that I had to let her and her crew do their jobs. She'd been confident and clear and my sheer admiration of her and the way I'd been handled meant I had to reward her and if I couldn't fuck her, I could do what she'd asked and fill out the sheet.

"No inflatable banana," I said, not being able to suppress a smile.

She giggled and heat grew in my belly. She had a beautiful laugh. "I thought you might skip that one."

"I don't avoid all fun if that's what you think. But that's a little too much." Why did I care if she thought I didn't like to have fun? I was here to work.

She nodded, smiling. "By the end of the trip, you never know what I might have talked you into."

I raised my eyebrows. I was beginning to think she could persuade me to do a number of things that were against my own best judgement. I cleared my throat, trying to regain my focus. "I'd like you to go ashore and collect a package for me."

"Excuse me, sir?"

Shit, her calling me sir shouldn't be as arousing as I found it. "Please, it's Hayden." I shifted, sitting up on my lounger, trying to distract my dick. "There's a patisserie on Lotissement Château Martin. I'd like you to pick up a cake."

Her smile faded from her eyes but her full lips stayed in place. "No problem," she said.

I pulled out a scrap of paper where I'd written down the name and address of the patisserie while on the phone to the lawyers last night.

"It's only a short walk from the marina." I beckoned her forward and she stepped toward me, closer than we'd been before. My face was level with her pussy and my eyes flickered up over her breasts to her face. Shit. *Shit*.

I stood abruptly and she took half a step away. I had to hold myself back from snaking an arm around her waist and pulling her against me. I didn't know this woman. What was wrong with me? "Please be there no later than two. Someone will meet you and give you an envelope with some documents in it."

"I think I should speak to Captain Moss. I mean—"

"It will be nothing but legal documents in the envelope along with a USB drive. I just don't want to send or receive anything electronically."

She nodded. "I understand, but I should just mention it to Captain Moss. It's protocol if we're picking up something from the shore."

"Do you have a concern about my request?"

"I just need to run it by—"

"Tell me your concerns, or what the captain's concerns might be and perhaps I can allay them. I'm going to be very disappointed if I can't get a simple package delivered to me here. With no Wi-Fi, I'm having to rely much more on hard copy documents."

"I understand and I'm sure it won't be a problem. Leave it with me."

Avery wasn't being unreasonable. I was irritated because the documents I wanted her to collect were important, and I wanted her to know that I wouldn't be asking her to do anything that wasn't legitimate. "Just make sure you put the envelope in your handbag so no one outside sees you carrying it and walk out with the pastry."

She took a breath as if she were going to speak. I understood why she wanted to question me, but I really had nothing to hide. She was trying to walk the tightrope between her duty to the captain and her duty to me and completely irrationally, I wanted her to trust me. To know that I wouldn't do anything to compromise her. To want to do anything I asked.

I pushed my hands in my pockets to stop myself from

reaching for her and providing her with some kind of physical reassurance. "Honestly, it's just legal papers that I have to read. You can trust me."

She *could* trust me. She was smart to be cautious, but she didn't need to be cautious of me.

"Okay." She checked her watch. "I'll have to leave soon. Eric will have to take me, though. Can I tell Eric or am I pretending to buy you a cake?"

I smiled at her desire to do the right thing by me. Was it because it was me or because I was a guest? Obviously it was because I was a guest—one of hundreds she'd fulfilled requests for during her career.

"You're just collecting some documents for me—this isn't *Mission Impossible*."

She glanced down at the piece of paper I'd given her. "I'd better get going then." She turned to leave, but I reached out and caught her arm. She gasped and the sound sent a jolt of lust right to my cock. Her gaze slid from where we were joined to my eyes. She pressed her lips together as if she were stopping herself from saying something. I blinked, trying to fight off the attraction I was feeling.

"Thank you," I said.

She nodded, then headed back through the sliding doors. I'd gotten used to her easy smile and professionalism far too quickly, felt comfortable with her far too easily. It was inexplicable. I was in a state where I was suspicious of everyone, questioning everything yet as Avery Walker disappeared, I imagined smoothing my palm down her naked back and whispering all my secrets to her.

NINE

Avery

The wind cooled my warm cheeks as the tender headed toward the coast. I sat in the back while Eric steered, trying to calm my racing pulse. I turned to see Hayden Wolf leaning on the railings of the main deck, facing in this direction. Was he watching me? When he'd grasped my arm earlier, had he meant to? Was it concern, thanks or something else he was trying to convey with his touch? Perhaps it was because he was the only guest and I was the only person he spoke to onboard, but I'd begun to feel an affinity, something more than physical attraction, a pull toward him. I wanted to help.

I turned back to face the shore.

As Mr. Wolf had predicted, Eric didn't question me further when I said I had to pick up some documents from the shore, even though I'd made up some elaborate story in my head. I guess we'd all seen far wilder requests from guests.

"Do you want me to come with you?" Eric asked as he steered us into the marina.

I took his hand as I stepped off the boat. "No, you stay with the tender. I won't be long."

"You don't even have your phone with you—you know the way?"

My French was basic but good enough to ask for directions if I got lost. "I'll be fine. If I'm not back in an hour, send out a search party."

At the end of the jetty, a paparazzo with a camera hanging around his neck leaned against the railing. It was a little early in the season for celebrity sightings, but there was always the odd exception.

"Hey, beautiful," he called over in a British accent.

I smiled and kept walking. Without the breeze from being at sea, the temperature had notched up. I wanted a long, cold drink. And maybe a pool.

"You work on the yachts?" he asked, following me.

I ignored him and headed up the street, the yachts on my right, surrounded by tourists trying to peer inside to a world inhabited by the rich and famous. A hodgepodge of different buildings screened the other side of the road in chalky pinks and yellows, housing restaurants and ice-cream bars sheltering from the heat under awnings.

The photographer followed. "Hey, you shy? Don't speak English?"

During high season, it wasn't unusual to be approached by paparazzi asking who was staying on which yacht. Sometimes they even offered a little money in exchange for information, but they were easy to ignore. "I'm just trying to enjoy a few hours off."

"So you are yacht crew. I knew it." He punched the air

as if it was some huge victory. Maybe this guy was new. "Anyone interesting on board?"

"Nope," I replied. I was pretty sure a picture of Hayden Wolf wasn't going to earn this guy any money.

"Not Leonardo DiCaprio or JLo?"

"Sorry to disappoint you," I said, seeing the road split off in two and the promise of a restaurant table with shade farther up.

"Give you a hundred bucks if you tell me who's on your boat."

I stopped and turned to him. Like a hundred bucks was incentive for anything. It wouldn't even cover a single physical therapy session. These paps needed to understand that the tip was a much bigger incentive to keep quiet. "No one you would be interested in, but I did hear that man-child Leonardo is going to be in Nice later in the season." I hadn't heard anything about Leonardo DiCaprio that I hadn't read on Page Six, but maybe if I gave this guy something he'd beat it.

"What if I gave you two hundred bucks?"

This photographer wasn't getting it. I just shook my head and started to walk again.

This time he didn't follow me, and I headed into the backstreets away from the chatter, laughter and popping champagne corks of the busy waterfront. Hayden had said I needed to be at the patisserie by two, so I still had some time to call my dad.

Glancing around, I spotted a public telephone kiosk up the street. I grinned at the thought that I could unload a little—be the girl from Sacramento who had her whole life in front of her instead of the woman who was looking after her family by yachting in Saint Tropez.

"Daddy, it's me," I said when he answered, excited to get to talk to him away from everything.

"Hey, kiddo, we were just talking about you."

"I wish I were there," I said. "I miss you guys."

"Well, you not being around means Michael and I get complete control over the television, watch sports all day and eat what we like. Isn't that right?"

I grinned as Michael yelled abuse in the background.

"You miss me, you know you do."

"Of course we do. What are you up to? Been peeling grapes for your guests?"

I laughed. "Not today." Hayden had still been in his office when I got on shift at seven this morning, which meant he'd worked all night. Grapes were the last thing on his mind.

"Guests aren't being too handsy, are they?"

Early on in my career I'd made the mistake of giving my dad too many details about the things guests got up to. Now he worried.

"Not at all," I said, trying to reassure my dad, though I thought back to Hayden touching my arm. It hadn't been disrespectful. Just familiar. The fact it caused my body to heat and shudder was my problem—Hayden hadn't been out of line. "I'm running some errands for the client."

"Always busy running around after everyone else. You need someone to wait on you for a while. Treat yourself."

"You don't need to worry about me." I liked to be busy.

"I know you've told me it's difficult to date on yachts, but maybe you could find another way to think about yourself, carve out a life for yourself. You're a generous girl and I worry you're giving up too much of yourself."

I rolled my lips together, trying to block out what my

dad was saying. "You know that I want to take care of Michael."

"And we both appreciate it. But it isn't the only thing you should be doing. You have your own life to lead as well."

Was I just becoming a vessel for other people's needs and desires? Was I not my own person anymore? It was true that yachting had supplanted any ambitions I'd had before Michael's accident. But that didn't mean I didn't want to take time for myself. I just didn't have many opportunities. I guess I could take up knitting.

"I'm in the South of France. How bad could life be?"

"Well, as long as you're taking time to do what you want to do. It's okay to be selfish here and there. It's okay to enjoy yourself."

I'd not been particularly adventurous since I started yachting. Most of the crew I'd worked with spent time at the end of each season exploring and getting to know the country they'd been sailing around. I'd always wanted to get back home.

"Okay, Dad, look, I've got to go." I was nearly out of minutes, and I didn't have long until I had to get to the patisserie. "Tell Michael I love him. And go easy on the pizza, you hear me?"

"Love you, honey."

"Love you, Daddy."

I hung up and as I headed to the address Hayden had given me, I tried to remember the last time I'd done something selfish or reckless. I could drink tequila with the best of them. It wasn't like I was afraid of fun. But it always took place within very carefully drawn parameters.

I'd always wanted to spend more time in Italy, so maybe I'd take a few days at the end of this season and be a tourist instead of going right back to Sacramento. I'd at least think about it even if it was just for a day or two.

I reached the patisserie so quickly I was almost disappointed. It was a large shop with glass counters running around two sides, with a dozen tables and chairs for people who wanted to enjoy their pastry on-site. I scanned the customers but didn't see anyone with a brown envelope or who looked like a lawyer.

Hayden had told me that his contact would find me, so I focused on the rows of desserts, so many that I couldn't imagine how many customers the shop got each day. There were big cakes and individual cakes. Some had fruit, lots had cream and all varied in color and shape. I should remember this place for my next charter—it would be a good place to send guests who'd never been to France before. Hell, it would be a good place to bring August and Skylar after this charter finished. We could eat cake for breakfast and move on to the bar for lunch.

"*Bonjour*," one of the servers behind the counter said. "Can I help you?"

I was always slightly depressed when I was in a foreign country and they realized I wasn't a native. I guess with my polo shirt and khaki skirt, it was clear I was a yacht worker. "I'd like a Gâteau St. Honoré," I replied. I'd only had one once, but it had been beyond the most delicious thing I'd ever eaten. "Do you have them?"

"*Bien sûr*. Large or small?"

"Two large, please."

I followed the assistant along the counter as she made her way toward the section with the large cakes.

She pulled the tray toward her and chose two towers of profiteroles, caramel and cream. It might just be the best thing I'd ever laid eyes on in my life. I should order ten.

"Ms. Walker?" a quiet voice asked from behind me. I snapped my head around to find a petite girl with mousy brown hair clutching a brown envelope.

"Yes."

"This is for you," she said, lifting her chin at the brown envelope in her arms.

I glanced back at the assistant, who was busying herself making up a box for the cream concoctions I'd just ordered. I unhooked one of the handles of my tote off my arm. "Thanks," I said.

She glanced around and then slipped the thick envelope into my bag and scurried out the door. Jesus, the girl looked as guilty as hell.

Loaded with cake and more questions, I headed back to the tender.

"You got it?" Eric asked as I handed him the two boxes before climbing back aboard.

"Sure did. And a treat for us as well."

He smiled. "It's weird that documents are the first thing this guy requests. I mean, usually it's the wine with this type of guest."

"He's a workaholic." I shrugged, then took a seat at the back of the boat.

"I've offered to get out the toys a couple of times, but he's always said no. I guess it's weird going down the water slide on your own." He untied the line and cast off.

"I think he just wants to kick back, relax and work uninterrupted. I'm sure you've had worse guests. I know I have." This charter was unusual but it wasn't difficult.

"I guess. I just wish he wasn't here for eight weeks. If nothing else, I'm going to get a little bored, especially without my computer."

It was true; there was a lot less to do when we only had

one guest who didn't seem to do anything but work all night and sleep or work all day. "Let's finish off the schedules. That way, we can keep the rest of the crew motivated if they're working toward time off."

"Good plan." Eric started the engine and we headed back to the *Athena*.

We'd been gone nearly an hour and a half. Would Hayden have asked Skylar for anything while I was gone? I sort of enjoyed how he insisted on dealing with me as if I was special. The way he'd reacted to me asking him about the preferences sheet—another guest might have lost it, but I liked that I'd read him well enough to know I was okay to bring it up and I liked him even more for filling it out. He understood and respected we had a job to do and he didn't seem to look down on me—that was unusual. Now here I was wondering if anyone else had noticed that instead of just making sure my hair was neat, now I tried to make sure it looked glossy. Lately I'd worn a little more makeup than usual. Hell, I was running out of fake tan. It was stupid. Hayden didn't see me like that. To him, I was staff.

TEN

Hayden

I exhaled, trying to beat back the panic pushing through my veins. I straightened out the *Financial Times* and read the feature again in more detail. It was all about the performance of private companies and how success was so closely tied to their leadership. The article went on to detail companies that had gone belly up when their CEO left or retired. Phoenix Holdings was highlighted as being at risk as their CEO and owner was coming up for retirement.

This article couldn't have come at a worse time. Negotiations between us were tense. We were in the stage where I asked lots of probing questions, and because the CEO was the major shareholder, he wasn't used to it.

But it was all information I needed in order for me to complete the acquisition. However much I wanted Phoenix, I wasn't going to buy it blind.

Part of me wondered if Phoenix were responsible for the article. It was bound to get people sniffing around. And the CEO would know I'd see it. Whether or not it was planned, it increased the pressure on me to get this deal done.

I leaned back in my chair and picked up my satellite phone.

"I need you to do something for me," I said the second Landon picked up.

"Nice to hear from you, Hayden. How am I? Fine, thank you very much. Work is good."

Sarcasm was my brother's primary skill.

"Like you have time for social niceties any more than I do."

"True. What can I do for you?" he asked.

"I want to know if Cannon and Phoenix have a connection." I went on to explain the article.

"I don't get it. You think Phoenix had something to do with the article being in the paper?"

"I happen to know that Cannon have strong links with the *Financial Times*. They could have fed the article to them easily."

"But if Cannon knew Phoenix was on the market, wouldn't they be making their move already?"

My mind was whirring with reasons why Cannon might want me to buy Phoenix. "Not if they're setting a trap for me." I opened the drawer in my desk and dropped the pink newspaper inside. "This article might be designed to attract other buyers and put pressure on me to sign before I've done my due diligence. I want to make sure every rock is overturned and I've seen every skeleton in every closet. I won't be rushed into signing this deal."

"Are you sure you're not being paranoid?" he asked. "You need to be focusing on getting your deal done and the leak in your office."

"I don't want to do this deal if it's not right."

"So focus on getting your due diligence done before it can get thrown off track. Don't borrow trouble."

Was that what I was doing? Getting distracted by my own conspiracy theories? Maybe. The thought of someone working for Cannon in the business I'd built, someone trying to destroy me from the inside, wasn't any easier just because I wasn't in the office.

"Okay, you have a point. I just want this leaker found," I said.

"From what my team on the ground tell me, no one's tracked you to Saint Tropez. And I've not seen anything unusual back in London, no phone calls from your senior team to any Cannon numbers and no meetings between them either. They're not making it easy for us. But we'll figure it out."

Landon and I hadn't discussed the personal connection between our family and Cannon. But we both understood what was at stake. We'd experienced the aftereffects of the destruction of our father's business, so we knew what they were capable of.

"If my digging doesn't work, we'll have to try to draw them out—we can brainstorm some ideas in a few days if I don't find something before then."

"Hang on," I said as someone knocked on my office door. Who the fuck was bothering me? No one other than Avery was supposed to be down here.

I rounded the desk and swung open the door, coming face-to-face with Avery's big brown eyes.

She glanced at the phone I was clutching in my hand. "Sorry, I just brought you some fresh coffee as you seemed to want to be back at your desk so quickly and I know how you like a lot of coffee in the morning." She lifted up a cup of coffee, which was just what I needed in the absence of a slug of whiskey.

I took the saucer out of her hand and our eyes locked for a second. She really noticed everything. I prided myself on reading people, on building relationships and by remembering small things about people I met throughout my career, but this woman could give me a run for my money. "Thanks. I appreciate it." Whether she knew it or not, the times I saw this woman were fast becoming the most enjoyable parts of my day.

"My pleasure," Avery said and then shook her head slightly.

I was pretty sure I caught a slight blush in Miss Professional's cheeks. Perhaps it was wishful thinking, but that didn't stop me wondering what her real pleasures were.

I lifted my eyebrows and grinned at her and she shut her eyes almost as if she were trying to regain her composure. Then without another word she turned and I watched her and her fantastic arse climb the stairs.

My brother calling my name caught my attention and I lifted the phone to my ear. "Sorry, it was just—"

"Someone catering to your every need? Must be tough."

I shut the door, put the coffee on my desk and collapsed back in my chair. "I'd prefer to be back in the office, making deals, but you're right, if I've got to disappear, there are worse places to be." Just having Avery around was like breathing pure oxygen, adding color to my otherwise taxing days. If she weren't so bloody professional, I'd have had her bent over my desk by now but she was better than that. Worth more than a quick fuck. She was the kind of woman I'd have to take my time with.

"And you're dealing with the lawyers okay?" Landon

interrupted my train of thought. "Annie said the drop went well yesterday."

"Yeah. I spent the night working through the documents —thanks for arranging that."

"No problem. You're paying me."

"I am?" I chuckled.

Landon rarely talked about money, but the fact that he'd paid cash for his penthouse in Kensington told me business was booming for him.

"It's not like we're family or anything. You'll get my bill at the end of this."

"You better be worth it."

"I'll remind you of this conversation when you sign the Phoenix deal."

"If you're sending me a bill anyway, can you dig a bit deeper into the crew here? I just want to make sure everything thoroughly checks out." What I wanted was more information about Avery. What drove her to be so good at what she did? What had made her become a yachtie and not go to university? I'd seen glimpses of the Avery underneath the professional façade, and I wanted to know more.

"I've done thorough checks—there's nothing to worry about."

"Do me a favor and the next time we do a drop, give me everything you can find on Avery Walker."

"The chief stewardess?"

"Yeah, that's the one."

"Is something making you suspicious?"

Only the fact that I trusted her and didn't know why. Wanted to fuck her but hadn't made a move. It was weird. Not like me. "Nothing I'm ready to share. Just an instinct."

"Okay. I'll do some follow-up work on her."

"Now, get out of here—I've got to go and catch some

rays." I hung up and grabbed my laptop. Sunbathing and relaxation was the last thing I needed, but I found I quite enjoyed my interactions with Avery and so working from the main deck, knowing she would pass by intermittently tending to my every need, wasn't an opportunity I was going to pass up.

ELEVEN

Hayden

All I got from my lawyers were invoices and bad news. "Fuck," I spat as I hung up my satellite phone.

This deal had started off like clockwork and then out of nowhere the wheels had fallen off and I was stuck in the middle of the Mediterranean without an assistant or my email. I wished to God Landon had found the leak, so I could get back to London.

There was a rap at my door. "Come in," I said. If it had been anyone other than Avery, I wouldn't have answered but she was so dedicated, always knowing what I wanted before I did, not to mention she was fucking beautiful. She was basically kryptonite for me.

"Hey, I just brought you a coffee, but did I come at a bad time?"

I sighed as I sat back in my chair. "Thanks. On this deal, there's never a good time."

She winced, placing the large cup of coffee in front of me. I caught the scent of her—all sunshine and summer flowers, as though she just came from a better part of the universe than I did. "Anything I can help you with?"

"Unless you can explain to me why people decide to clam up on me and make outrageous demands then I'm not sure you can help."

She transferred her weight onto one leg, and her hip pushed out to the side, creating a delicious curve I wanted to trace with my fingertips. "What's happened? Someone's stopped talking to you and has started demanding stuff? A customer?"

"It doesn't matter."

"I know it's all super top secret and everything, so don't tell me anything you shouldn't, but sometimes just talking out loud can help shuffle stuff around in your brain and a solution appears."

A grin tugged at the corners of my mouth. She made it sound easy and if I didn't know better, I'd have believed her.

"I see your skepticism." Her eyebrows darted up. "Try it." She lifted her shoulder in a half shrug. "You never know, I might even be able to help."

I sighed. Avery's presence was calming and I wasn't ready for her to leave. "I'm trying to buy a company. And it was all going according to plan and then the seller just starts making crazy requests in the legal documentation and he's not answering his phone. And I don't have email so I can't email him. It's bloody frustrating."

"You think he's gotten a better offer and he's stalling?"

She was smart. That was my suspicion but if he was after the best price, he'd have put the company up for auction. "Maybe. I feel disconnected from the process out here. If I were back in London I think I'd figure it out. It's like I have one hand tied behind my back."

"And you can't get back to London because you don't want anyone to know you're buying this company."

I didn't deny it—she didn't know which company and she'd been vetted. I needed to stop being so paranoid, as Landon had said. "Something like that."

"So you're out of your comfort zone but that doesn't mean you're in a worse position. If you were in London, what would you do in this situation? I mean if it's so secret, I guess you couldn't just have a meeting with this guy and ask him outright what the matter is?"

I reached behind my neck, pressing my fingers into the knotted muscle. "Right." What would I do differently if I was back in London? "Seeing people is the easiest way to figure out what they put a value on. It's pretty easy to read people."

"That's for sure. Mainly. Although not always. Some people are tough to figure out. Especially those who don't care if they're eating oysters or fish sticks."

I narrowed my eyes. "You trying to make a point Ms. Walker?"

She laughed in such a completely unaffected and genuine way, I couldn't take my eyes off her. She leaned on the side of the desk and I shifted my chair around so I was pointed toward her. "Seeing people definitely makes it easier to read them, but what do you already know about this seller? Is it a corporation? A family? What?"

"A guy in his mid-sixties. He started the business nearly fifty years ago. He's selling up and retiring." I was probably telling her too much but I trusted her, trusted Landon to have vetted her.

"Oh wow. Fifty years. So he's gotta find it tough to let go."

I chuckled. "I'm not getting it for free. He's going to

retire a very rich man. He could live on one of these for the rest of his life and his kids are still never going to have to work again."

She drew the edge of her thumbnail across the desk, dividing the space between us and I imagined her delicate wrists circled by my hands and pushed up over her head as I kissed her. "But that's not it. If his company's that successful, he probably could have sold a long time ago and never worked again, right?"

"Absolutely. He's crazy to have waited until now."

She nodded as if what I was saying completely made sense. "So that's it then. He's deliberately placing obstacles in the way of the sale. So he doesn't have to let go."

I sat forward, almost crossing the invisible line she'd created, and she lifted herself off the desk and stepped back. Was she concerned I was going to touch her? I could read women pretty well, and I was more than sure this attraction I was feeling was mutual.

"No one gets that successful without being driven by the performance of the business. Of course it's about the money for him."

"Is it all about the money for you?"

I took a breath. I wasn't about to confess to Avery that it was important for me to be successful and for people to see me as such. I wasn't about to tell her how I wanted my father to feel some sense of satisfaction from me building up a business more successful than Cannon. "I'm not sure I'm the right comparison. Most people in my business are driven by pounds and pence." I wasn't convinced by Avery's theory. Greed was the guiding force in the City.

"I'm not saying that he will give his company away for free. But that money represents something for him. I bet you a hundred dollars that this is personal when you get down to it."

"A hundred dollars, huh?" I grinned at her. I liked the way she stood behind what she was saying and didn't back down.

I sat back in my chair. I'd heard rumors of several abandoned attempts at a sale over the years. Was it less about the cash and more about Harold not wanting to see his legacy belong to someone else?

"Yes, a hundred dollars. How would you feel if you'd built something up for fifty years and a perfect stranger was going to take it over? The people he works with are probably like family to him and then he's got to decide what to do with all the time he normally devotes to his work."

"It's possible. But I'm not sure it helps. If he doesn't want to let go, he doesn't want to let go."

"Really? So you just give up? I can't imagine you made the kinda money you need to make to rent a yacht like this for eight weeks by just surrendering."

I laughed. "You pretend you're all sweetness and what-can-I-get-for-you but in fact, you're actually kinda pushy. A fighter."

She shrugged, trying to hold back a smile. "I have both sides to me. Most people don't get to see beyond the sweet."

For a long second we held each other's eye, on the edge of acknowledging that she'd confessed I knew her better than most. I liked that I did. I liked her and both her sides.

She looked away first and backed toward the door. I stood and shoved my hands in my pockets.

"I think you might be on to something. I need to figure out how to get this guy comfortable with selling to me, and it's not going to be about what's in the legal documents."

"Sounds like your brain rearranged. I hate to say I told

you so but . . ." Her voice was higher, less conversational than before. Sweet Avery was back. "I should get back to it. Can I get you anything else?"

I shook my head, smiling at her, keeping my gaze fixed on her as she slipped out of the office. I wasn't sure if it was because she was the only woman I'd been physically close to in weeks, but my cock was twitching, and I'd been seconds away from reaching for her. Sweet, funny, sexy and smart—Avery Walker had it all. And as much as I might not want to fuck her quickly, bent over my desk. I definitely wanted something more from her.

TWELVE

Avery

"I owe you, Avery Walker," Hayden said, turning from where he was leaning against the balustrade facing the sea. He grinned as the sliding doors of the main salon closed behind me.

"You do?" I set down his coffee on the side table near his usual lounger. I wasn't quite sure what he meant but his British accent, softened a little by the sun and that wide grin, felt overfamiliar.

"You were right. He was getting jittery about letting go," he said, striding toward me.

As he leaned to pick up his coffee, I caught his scent—a combination of ocean breeze and forest floor, clean and masculine.

"That's so great," I said, moving away from him, trying to keep my distance, trying not to notice how his face had bronzed in the sun and his hair was smattered with licks of gold. "It was just a suggestion."

"It was a good one. Really good," he said, looking me

straight in the eye. My heart began to pound. Was he making a pass at me? No, this man was all business. He was clearly just grateful for me talking to him. Yes, that was definitely it.

"What did he say?" I asked.

He blinked, his long eyelashes sweeping up his face. "I left him a voicemail talking about his people and suggesting he continue to have a role on an employee committee. He called me back. He'd wanted to know that the business was more than a balance sheet for me."

"I'm glad. People are my business. It's my job to spot what could make them unhappy and head it off before it happens," I replied, trying to stay matter-of-fact.

"I see that. I can't imagine anyone being unhappy with you around." He narrowed his eyes and my heart began to flutter against my ribs.

I didn't know how to respond. I'd never known a guest so focused on business on a yacht. But this lighter, and definitely flirtatious, side of Hayden that snuck out here and there had me in a spin. And I knew I shouldn't encourage it, but I enjoyed this side of him and wanted to see it more.

A beat of silence passed between us and I went to walk away before he spoke. "I bet you've seen a lot. People with money can be . . . colorful." It was as if he were trying to prolong our interaction, just to talk about nothing in particular.

"It's amazing what money can buy," I replied, also wanting the conversation to continue. Most of the time I just saw people's behavior as indulgent but every now and then I found the excess too much.

"Drugs?" he asked.

I flipped my tray under my arm. "No way. That's a pretty

hard line. I mean, I know it happens on boats used by the owners, but not on charters. There's too much to lose for the captains, though the alcohol tends to more than make up for it."

"I bet. I've never really been much of a drinker."

Of course I knew that about him already. "Too much of a control freak?" I asked, then inwardly cringed.

He smirked. "You noticed?" He sipped his coffee as if we were two colleagues or friends having a chat. "I think I've always been too ambitious, too focused. Even at university I was scouring the financial pages at 5am when everyone else was passed out with a hangover."

I understood that. I'd been working long hours away from home when all my friends from high school had been drowning in Jell-O shots. "Yeah. I never did the college experience thing either."

"It seems we have that in common—we both take our work a little too seriously," he said.

Pleasure bloomed in my chest at him acknowledging my job. I did work hard, and I might not make millions but that didn't mean I wasn't committed and focused. "Yeah. The hours are long and it's nonstop all day."

"We both probably should have a little more fun." His eyebrows pulsed up suggestively, so different from the intense, focused, private man I saw most of the time. Was he intimating that we have fun together or just generally? If any other guy had said that I would know they were coming on to me, but Hayden was . . . different. Interesting. Confusing.

"We have plenty of tequila on board," I said. "And then there's always the inflatable banana."

Hayden let out a roaring laugh and leaned back on the railings. "You were right about me when you said I wasn't the banana boat kind of guy. Like you say yourself, you read people well."

"Sometimes." *Not with you,* I thought. I should have excused myself. I should have made an excuse about towels or something, but I wanted him to tell me more, give me more. "You must have some vices even if inflatable bananas aren't among them."

"Don't we all?" He paused, holding my gaze, his tongue darting out to catch the dot of foam that collected at the edge of his mouth. "Women, for one."

I nodded slowly. Of course he was a womanizer. I wasn't even into guys like him and I was completely attracted. My stomach swooped and my breathing echoed off the deck, mixing with the hard syllables of what he'd just said. Did he mean to be provocative? It was as if he'd hypnotized me with his stare—I couldn't look away.

He smirked and took another sip of coffee. "But work has always been my drug of choice."

I couldn't help but wonder what drove him to work so hard. It couldn't just be about the money even though he might say different. It must go beyond that. "I can tell."

"What about you?" he asked. "You can't be quite as perfect as you seem to be."

"I seem perfect?" I scrunched up my nose. Was that how he saw me? Did that mean cold and officious? "I'm anything but. It's my job to ensure whatever I'm thinking on the inside doesn't reflect on the outside."

He trailed his thumb over the scruff of his beard. Today was the first time I'd not seen him clean-shaven. It suited him. "I thought I had the best poker face in town, but you put me to shame."

"I'm well practiced. Some of the things we're asked

for . . ." I exhaled, glancing into the interior. I should have left, gone back to the galley. "It would blow your mind."

He raised his eyebrows, waiting for me to elaborate.

"You get the usual stuff—caviar flown in from Russia, unusual wines, that kind of thing. And then people who want certain types of bedding or special doggy menus. I once got a request for white kittens for a six-year-old. We had to go and buy cats for this kid." I shook my head. "That kept her entertained for twenty minutes and then we had to rush around finding homes for them all. And then last season the whole crew had to call some guests 'Your Majesty' and curtsey whenever we addressed them."

"Wow." A smile flirted at the corners of his lips and the sun seemed to shine just a bit brighter for a few seconds.

"And last year I had a guest ask that wait staff serve their final dinner in a thong."

Hayden frowned. "Topless?"

I laughed. It had been such a ludicrous request. "Yeah. A black lace thong and nothing else."

"Wow. I didn't realize that was an option. I should have taken more notice of that form you had me fill out."

I glared at him and then laughed.

"Did you do it?"

I held his gaze but shook my head. "No, but you can never say no, right? I had the deck crew guys turn into waitresses for the night. They took their shirts off and wore a thong over their boxers. The guests had a sense of humor about it, at least."

"Can't say no?" he asked. "Because the client is always right."

"Of course." I curved my mouth into my usual, at-your-service smile. It felt as though he was digging for something.

I just wasn't sure what. "I just try to focus on the job. Isn't that what you do?"

"Put the work first? Absolutely." He held my gaze. Seconds ticked by, and I felt as if I were being pulled toward him, the barrier between guest and crew dissolving in the heat.

"I should go." I couldn't handle the weight or intensity of his stare. It was almost as if he were willing my deepest, darkest secrets to the surface.

"I enjoyed talking with you, Avery."

The way he said my name, the pronunciation, was so different, as if he strung out the syllables to make the sound last. It was so unnerving that my skin scattered with goose bumps. "I enjoyed talking with you too."

"I mean it," he said, scanning my face before he brought his hand up and swept his thumb over my chin, just below my mouth. My legs weakened under his heat and I blinked slowly, desperate for time to slow down so I could take in every sensation. "About you being perfect." He withdrew his hand and took another sip of coffee as if touching me like that was no big deal. Maybe it wasn't. To him. This wasn't a friendly grasp of my shoulder or a squeeze of my arm that I could dismiss as him being tactile—this was intimate and flirtatious, and I needed to leave before he saw how much I wanted it to happen again.

THIRTEEN

Avery

Despite it being days since Hayden had touched me, the heat of his fingers still echoed against my skin every now and then. Particularly when I was alone and trying not to think of him. This early in the morning, the entire boat was silent and, attempting not to make a sound, I made my way up the spiral staircase and out through the main salon to the deck. The outside lights were on but dimmed and the sea was particularly still this morning—a sheet of black silk beneath us. A ribbon of fiery orange trailed across the horizon as the sun threatened to burst into the sky. It was beautiful. I leaned against the railing, breathing in the fresh air that would become almost stifling by mid-afternoon.

In moments like these, yachting was worth it. But they were fleeting.

The sliding doors behind me whizzed as they opened, and I stood straight and twirled around as if I'd been caught doing something I shouldn't have been.

"Good morning," I said as Hayden appeared, his hair

rumpled and gray half-moons settled under his eyes. I was more pleased to see him than I should have been. I spread my arms, presenting the horizon, which was threatening to burst into flames. "The sunrise is putting on a show."

Hayden glanced from the sky to me. I was probably grinning a little too widely and looked like a maniac, but I couldn't help it. It was so beautiful.

The corner of his mouth twitched.

Was he laughing at me? "These moments have to be enjoyed, that's all."

He strode toward me, reached out and squeezed my upper arm. "You're absolutely right."

His touch momentarily paralyzed me before I found my voice. I needed some space, some distance. "Can I get you a juice while you enjoy the view?" I asked, stepping sideways toward the door.

He turned away from the sky to look at me and frowned. "Stay. This is a moment to be enjoyed, to share."

I knew I shouldn't stay. "I have a lot to do. I need to—I should really . . ."

"Stay." He said it so simply, so finally, there was no arguing with him. I stepped up next to where he leaned against the rail, watching as the orange edged into pink and bled into the black.

"Sunrises aren't something that should be witnessed alone," he said after several minutes had passed.

We stood facing forward and he turned his head to me. I glanced at him, as the beginnings of the day caught the sharp edge of his jaw.

My body relaxed and I leaned forward next to him, our elbows just an inch apart.

"Thank you—this was just what I needed." Did he mean he needed the sunrise or me staying to watch it with him? He unclasped his hands and shifted closer, our elbows touching as he trailed his knuckles over my hand as if to reinforce his gratitude. I glanced down to where our skin touched, then back up to find his eyes fixed on mine.

Though it was just his hand against mine, the gesture belied the nature of our relationship: guest and stewardess. We weren't lovers or friends. Maybe it was the ocean air or the magnificent sky, but the more time I spent in this man's orbit, the more I thought maybe I *wanted* to be friends with him, know him a little better, understand his changes in mood and temperament, know what drove him.

"I'm glad," I whispered, our arms still close enough I could feel the heat of him. If he was happy that meant I was doing my job. Although the way my heart swelled, and my cheeks heated, it felt less like a job and more like a calling. Or fate. Something bigger than I'd known before.

Yachts and boats on the water and the shapes of buildings and trees along the shore began to come into focus and everything filled with color as the sun crept out from behind the horizon. The whole coast seemed to yawn and stretch as it slowly came to life.

A flock of geese flew overhead, breaking the comfortable silence, and we tipped our heads back, trying to drink in every sight and sound.

"I'm normally at the gym by now," he said as he settled his gaze back on the skyline. "I'm not sure I notice whether the sun has risen or not when I'm in London."

"I know what you mean. Sometimes it's easy to miss the beauty in the everyday."

Hayden's gaze dropped to my mouth and back up. "That's my biggest fault. I don't make enough of each moment."

I felt the same. I was so focused on the job, on the tip, on taking care of my family, being in this beautiful place barely registered. It was almost as if I hadn't let myself enjoy it. As if I were punishing myself. "I can't remember the last time I watched the sunrise."

Hayden shifted so he was facing me, still leaning on one elbow against the aluminum balustrade. "But surely that's why you're here? To take advantage of the setting?"

I shrugged, self-conscious under the full force of his attention. "The job can be a lot. Sometimes on my days off, I just sleep."

"I assumed that people who worked on these yachts did it because they loved the traveling."

"Some do." I knew some people took the job to feed their wanderlust, but for me it had only ever been about the money.

"But not you. Do you get a lot of time to explore?" he asked as if he were trying to nail down my motivations, as if he were trying to get to know me.

"We get a day or so between charters." I tried to concentrate on the view but all I was conscious of was Hayden Wolf and how close he was and how my skin set alight every time he touched me.

"How long do those usually last?" he asked as his eyes followed a strand of my hair, set free by the breeze.

"A few days to a couple of weeks."

"So eight weeks is a long charter," he said, almost to himself.

"Usually there's a month's break between the Med season and the Caribbean season. That's when most people do their traveling."

"Usually?"

"This charter was a little early, so I flew straight in from

Miami, not that I had travelling planned. Unless you count Pavilions Mall in Sacramento."

He laughed. "I don't think you need a *Lonely Planet* guide for that. So you're doing two seasons back to back. It doesn't show."

"I have good lighting," I replied as I pointed at the sun. "And a good crew. And one unfussy guest."

"I can be very demanding," he said, pinning me with a stare. "You haven't seen all of me yet."

My pulse throbbed in my neck as his gravelly voice echoed through me. Heat rose up my body, and I snapped my head around to focus on the water.

Silence pulsed between us as I concentrated on keeping my breathing steady. I should go but I wanted to see what was next.

"Where would you take this boat if this was your charter?" he asked eventually, the heat between us having cooled to a simmer.

Was he interested or being polite? I wanted to tell him everything.

I smiled. "Italy is beautiful. Taormina in Sicily is as breathtaking as it gets. I've only ever been for an hour here or there but from what I've seen it's desperately . . ." I stopped myself from finishing my sentence, from telling him how romantic I'd found Taormina the twice I'd managed to set a foot on dry land there.

He inhaled and stood, and I could only focus on how his chest expanded and his body seemed to take up all the space around me.

"Do you vacation a lot?" I asked, wanting to prolong our interaction, and still unclear why we hadn't left the spot we'd started in two weeks ago.

He chuckled. "Hardly." He leaned back on the railing, facing away from the view that had brought us here.

It was strange that he was my guest and yet here we were both working. I should be trying to lighten his load. "Have you thought about changing your surroundings a little? You could at least watch the sunrise light up a different coastline." He'd enjoyed the sunrise and he might enjoy a different view. If I could do anything to make his experience on the *Athena* better, I would.

He frowned as if he hadn't really contemplated the idea, but Captain Moss would have talked him through the options.

"Just a thought." I sank my teeth into my bottom lip. "I know relaxation—the food, the wine, the ambience—isn't your priority here, but in the nanoseconds that you allow yourself to relax, it could be nice to have a different view."

He nodded, and I stared out over the water, as he focused on something that wasn't the view. For a moment I wondered if I was the only one who felt the link between us. It was as if we were being drawn toward each other by an invisible current—I wanted to stop swimming against the pull and let myself drift toward him, but I knew that wasn't an option. And anyway, he'd be gone soon enough.

"I'd need someone to share those sunrises with," he said.

Before I had the chance to respond or to analyze what he'd said, a crash in the kitchen brought me back to the moment. I straightened and checked my watch. It was a few minutes after seven, which meant Neill had started to prepare breakfast. It also meant Hayden and I had been admiring the Med for almost an hour. "I'm officially on shift," I said, taking a deep breath as if it would magically transform me from tourist to waitress. "What would you like for breakfast?" I asked, knowing the answer would be eggs.

Hayden stood and ran his fingers through his unruly hair. I pulled my hair into a ponytail while Hayden watched, his gaze flitting from my face to my hands, down my body and up.

"You've been up all night," I said. "Maybe you should sleep rather than eat."

"You're probably right." He stretched, the edge of his shirt lifting past his waistband to reveal a bronzed ribbon of skin—my own personal sunrise.

I squeezed my eyes shut, trying to block him out. "I'll ask Neill for some eggs." I turned and headed toward the sliding doors.

"Thank you," he called after me.

I turned my head to smile. He was watching me, and the warmth that rose in my belly shouldn't have been there. Perhaps I shouldn't have suggested he catch the sunrise. I definitely shouldn't have stayed to watch it with him, and I was certain that this feeling of connection I had to him was one-sided.

And it needed to end. Fast.

Hayden

The squawk of seagulls pulled me from my nap and as I opened my eyes, even though I had my sunglasses on, I had to shield myself from the glare of the sun. I checked my watch. I'd been asleep four hours, ever since I'd slumped on my lounger after breakfast. I glanced at my laptop, which was firmly closed beside me. It was just coming up to one local time, so the U.S. wasn't even at their desks yet. I'd not missed anything.

"Mr. Wolf," the captain said as he came through the sliding doors of the main living space.

I stood to shake his hand. He checked in with me daily to ensure everything was okay and to ask if I wanted to pull up the anchor to go somewhere else. I'd always insisted I was fine where I was, but now I was in the mood for a change of scene. Avery had been right about so many things. She'd helped me set the Phoenix acquisition back on track, after all, so how could she be wrong about changing up the scenery? And if she liked Italy, then Italy was where we were taking this boat.

"I was thinking we could make our way down the Italian coast over the next week."

Captain Moss nodded, probably relieved he was going to get to do something. "Absolutely. Do you want to leave today?"

"At your convenience," I replied.

"We can get going this afternoon. The weather is good, and the winds are low."

"I thought we could end up in Taormina."

"That's a great spot. No problem at all."

He turned to leave, but I added, "I'm aware that this is a longer charter than most, Captain."

"Yes, but we're delighted you're on board." I was used to recruiting people for their skills, not their charm. I wasn't a man who reveled in pleasantries and small talk. I preferred to cut to the chase. Captain Moss had a similar temperament, but I appreciated the effort he made.

I nodded. "But I am here alone and require very little looking after. I appreciate that the crew might need to blow off some steam, after all, I've already been on board two weeks. I'd like to drop anchor somewhere and give the crew the night off." I got the impression I was less demanding than most, but the crew shouldn't be expected to work eight weeks without some time off. I might have been betrayed by a senior employee, but I still believed treating people with respect produced their best work. And their loyalty. Most of the time. People labeled me a generous employer, but I was motivated by self-interest—you got what you deserved most of the time.

"That's not necessary, Mr. Wolf. The crew are assigned enough free time."

Of course he'd push back, but my mind was set. "I appreciate when we're not in dock I can't be the only one left onboard, but I'm sure most of the crew can be given the evening off. Shall we say tomorrow from six?"

Captain Moss hesitated. "That is more than generous. Rest assured I will be on board at all times along with one of my engineers."

"As you wish." I shook his hand.

"I'll get us moving as soon as I can."

"Excellent. Thank you."

I'd been selfish by insisting I deal only with Avery, and I hadn't even realized until I'd seen her with her hair down watching the sunrise this morning, trying to steal a few moments for herself. I wanted to be the one who gave her those moments. She'd earned it—talking through the issues I had with Phoenix had genuinely helped. I could get stuck in the numbers, but she'd been right—this deal was all about people. Watching the sunrise with her, where she'd let joy replace her professional veneer, had been breathtaking and infectious. I was pretty sure I'd enjoy watching a traffic jam if I was watching it with her.

For a few moments, as we'd faced the new day together, we'd been just two people enjoying the dawn. I'd remembered what it was like to feel free from the pressure of my whole world on the brink of collapse.

It had been over all too quickly, and we'd both returned to our respective pressures—although she was far too professional to give away that her long hours were a problem. But she'd clearly not had the break between seasons she normally did, and that was down to me. While I couldn't relieve that pressure again so easily for me, I could do it for Avery. Giving her and the rest of the crew the night off meant I could reimagine her and that easy manner she had when she wasn't on duty. Even if I wasn't there to witness it, it was reward enough to know she'd leave her hair loose and wear that warm generous smile somewhere ashore.

Avery Walker deserved the night off. And it felt good to be the one who could make that happen for her.

FOURTEEN

Hayden

"How's paradise?" Landon asked as he answered my call.

I pushed my chair away from my desk and rested my right leg on my left knee.

"It's fine." Why did we have to go through this rigmarole of Landon trying to point out that I lived a charmed life? I rolled my eyes, desperate to get down to business. "I've asked the captain to take us down the Italian coast over the next week or so."

Landon cleared his throat as he stopped giving me shit and became the focused professional he was with others. "Not a problem. I have contacts all over that area who can make drops if you need them and I have a mobile team following you. I'm glad you called, actually."

"Why? Your bear-baiting skills need sharpening?"

I could almost hear his grin at the other end of the line. "Well, yes, as it happens. But I also wanted to let you know that I finished tracing the finances of your senior team."

"And?" I asked, gripping the phone a little more tightly.

"There's a few things that we need to follow up. One with Anita and one with your finance director."

"Anita? There's no way she's the leak."

"We need to do some investigating. But she opened a bank account just over a year ago and there have been chunky payments into that account that total just shy of a hundred grand."

My heart began to knock against my ribcage. Anita was the one I trusted over everyone. It couldn't be her. She'd worked for me for ten years and been part of the team before we had seven figures on our balance sheet. But what Landon had found didn't sound good. Anita and I didn't share anything personal, but I assumed she and her husband didn't have a lot of money. From what I'd heard when my office door was open, she was putting two kids through university and was finding it tough. I'd given her a ten percent pay rise when I'd heard that, although she'd never asked for a raise in the whole time she'd worked for me. Perhaps her kids' education had been her Achilles' heel. Had Cannon found her weak spot?

"You're talking about my assistant, Anita? Fenton?" I asked. Perhaps Landon had mixed up the names.

"Yes, Anita Fenton. The bank account activity is unusual. But I need to trace where it's coming from. We're on it."

"Okay, well let me know as soon as you can, please. I can't imagine it's her, but if it is . . ." The woman had access to everything I'd ever touched. I kept nothing from her; I trusted her implicitly. If she wanted to, she could cause chaos back at Wolf Enterprises.

"We'll find out what's going on."

"I might call her. Check in." I'd not spoken to her for a few days, and I could tell she was uncomfortable with me being away from the office. She'd tried to be respectful and not ask too many questions, but I could tell she wanted to know more about what I was doing.

"Don't set off any alarm bells. Don't try to question her."

"I'm not an idiot." That wasn't conclusive right now. And if Anita was the source of the leak, I was pretty sure I'd be up for Idiot of the Year. "Did you say something about my finance director?"

"Actually it's not the director. It's his reports. The controller and the treasurer."

"What's the deal there?" Jesus, it sounded like Landon was investigating the entire company. Perhaps Cannon had more than one person on their payroll. It was clear they were coming for me, just like they'd come for my dad all those years ago.

"I'm not sure. A couple of calls to unregistered mobiles. An account in the Cayman Islands that one of them holds."

"An offshore account? Why would anyone working for me need an account in the Cayman Islands?"

"It's actually not that unusual for finance professionals. I see it all the time, especially if they've spent part of their career abroad. But it makes my job harder."

I swallowed. Landon never admitted he found things difficult. It wasn't his style.

"Also, I don't think I asked you, but who's the newest member of your team?"

I'd poached all five of my executive team from positions in other companies—I'd handpicked them—none of them had applied for the job. "My strategy director was the last person I recruited." Sally'd been on the other side of a negotiation and she'd done her best to kick my arse. I'd decided I'd rather have her inside my tent pissing out than the other way around. "But that was over two years ago."

"What about other women?"

"There's Jean and Helen."

"I don't mean other people on your executive team. I mean *women*."

Was he five? "You mean girls I've fucked? Well, you know the score there."

"Are you still as prolific as you've always been?"

I chuckled and amusement sliced through my anxiety. It seemed so odd that my brother was asking me personal questions in a way that was clearly meant to be professional. I was used to a different side of him. "Prolific? Jesus, I bet locker room talk was boring when you were in the SAS. I fuck a lot of women, but they never come back to my place. I don't take them to dinner or talk about my day with them."

"So it's just shagging. No pillow talk?"

"You want details? Okay, well if you must know, generally I like to start with getting my dick sucked. I like women to take their bra off for that but leave their knickers—"

"Shut the fuck up. I don't want to hear about how bad in bed you are."

Given how differently our lives had turned out, it always surprised me how quickly we reverted to our teenage selves around each other. There were lots of upsides to being successful, but there were downsides too. I didn't get to kick back with the guys much. I didn't have many friends. They'd been abandoned along the route to the success. And at work I was the boss—a leader. I was deadly serious and laser focused. Landon was really the only person in my life I could joke with.

"Think about it. Is there anyone you've shagged over the last couple of years you changed your MO for? Maybe she turned up to your place, naked, wearing just a fur or maybe you've fucked some office junior—"

"Hey, that's enough. I've never taken advantage of a junior member of my staff. Like I said, there's no one. I'm not saying there aren't girls, but I *never* bring them back to my place and I *never* discuss work with them." I fucked to forget about work. It was my release, the way I disappeared from the stress of the day.

"Calm down." Landon paused. "If you're sure then we'll put all our efforts into the office. I just want to make sure we're not missing anything. I expected it to be easier. Whoever it is has covered their tracks."

"When I call Anita, I could ask her to arrange for me to be sent a couple of IMs and have her send them to me on USB."

"IM?" Landon asked.

"Information Memorandum—the sale particulars of a company."

"Sounds good. It could help flush someone out. That way if Cannon swoop in and buy any of the companies whose sale particulars you've requested, we'll know Anita is the source."

"Right, Einstein." I hated to consider the possibility that Anita was the leak but if she was, I needed to know sooner rather than later. She had too much access to too much information. More than anyone, she had the ability to destroy me and I wasn't going to let that happen.

FIFTEEN

Avery

There was no end of lobster, steak and chocolate on a yacht, which meant I craved the most basic things. It might not be everyone's idea of a perfect meal but as far as I was concerned, carbs and cheese were as close to heaven as it was possible to be while still breathing, and *combining* them was just the best invention outside of tampons, the internet and lipstick.

"Hey, what are you doing?" Eric came into the galley as I was shredding the perfect strength cheddar, which I knew Neill stocked just for me.

"Making myself a cheese sandwich, or changing a tire—delete as appropriate."

He checked his watch. "But we're heading to the restaurant in like twenty minutes, and are you grating cheese to go in a cold cheese sandwich?"

I shook my head. "First, with August in your party, you'll be lucky if you make it out within the hour. Second, I don't see how I can join you."

He drew back as if I'd whacked him in the face with a frying pan. "What do you mean?"

I shook the grater, small curls of yellow tumbling onto the board. "I don't see how I can? I mean, is the captain going to make Hayden a coffee if he wants one?"

"Captain Moss said himself that Hayden had given us all the evening off. Neill's prepped some food and left it in the refrigerator. Wolf knows there won't be any crew on board."

"I know but it doesn't feel right." It did go against my instincts to leave a guest on board, knowing there was no crew other than the captain. But the reason I was still in my crew uniform was more complicated. I'd enjoyed watching the sunrise with Hayden the other morning. No one else had been awake and we'd had the boat to ourselves. I could pretend for a moment that he wasn't a guest and I wasn't a stewardess. And although I knew it was stupid, reckless even to think like that, I wanted that feeling again. Maybe that was a good reason to go ashore.

"We're in Italy, dude. You have to come ashore."

I smiled. Not at anything Eric had said but at the fact that after my conversation with Hayden and my suggestion at moving the yacht, he'd done exactly that.

"Don't be such a martyr. You've got to come. Neill's told me how much tequila you can drink. I want to see it for myself," Eric continued.

Neill and I had had a blast in Greece last year. And there'd been far too much tequila between charters. A night out with Neill was guaranteed fun and my dad's words about me taking time for myself rang in my ears. Maybe I should go, but the problem was I didn't want to. I swept my hand down my body. "I'm not dressed for it anyway. I really should stick around in case Hayden needs anything."

"Did Moss say you had to?" Eric asked just as Skylar wandered into the kitchen.

"You're not changing?" she asked, her gaze flitting down my body.

"Moss ordered her to stay," Eric said.

I cut my sandwich in half and put it on a plate, then set about cleaning the mess I'd just made. "Captain Moss has done no such thing. I'm chief stew. It's my job to put the guests first." It would have been nice to go out tonight and have fun, dance a little, drink a lot. Maybe find a hot deckhand from another yacht to kiss. But it wasn't a deckhand I wanted a kiss from. Just Hayden's touch covered my skin in goose bumps and heat. I couldn't imagine what his lips might do.

If I was staying because of the thought of Hayden's mouth on mine, perhaps going ashore would be the safe option.

Skylar slumped on the banquet. "You've gotta come. It won't be the same without you. Please. Who will help me find rich, single men who have husband potential?"

"These guys will look after you," I said, lifting my chin as Neill came into the galley.

"Cheese sandwich?" he asked and I nodded. Although no one was allowed to heat anything up in the kitchen—chefs were territorial—we were all permitted to make ourselves cold food.

"She's saying she's not coming tonight," Skylar said.

"*She's* right here," I said, pointing to myself.

"Why don't you just come for an hour? I'll bring you back," Eric said, his expression pleading. "Or I can stay and once he locks himself in his office, we can head out. You know he never comes out once he's gone in there for the night. You won't see him again until tomorrow."

I could easily go. Eric was right. Hayden had been the person to instigate our night off. He didn't need looking after. But I didn't want to leave. "I'm not doing it."

Neill blew out a breath. "Save your breath, Eric. I've tried to talk her out of it, but you know how dedicated she is."

"I'm dedicated to my tip." I laughed and took my plate to the dining table, tucking into the banquette next to Eric and Skylar.

"You're dedicated to the job," Skylar said. "I'm never going to be a chief stew if this is what it takes. I'm always going to choose husband shopping, vodka and dancing over a guest."

"It's really not a big deal, guys. It's one night. We'll have plenty of fun times this season when this charter is over." The problem was, I knew if it were any guest other than Hayden Wolf, I could be convinced to go ashore.

"I'll drink your share if it makes you feel any better," Eric said.

"Taking one for the team." I winked at him and a slight blush crept over his baby face.

"Always. I'm all about the sacrifice," he mumbled.

"You're going to miss the fireworks," Skylar said.

"Fireworks?" I asked before taking a bite of my sandwich.

"Yeah, some festival or other. Maybe you'll catch them from the boat," Neill added.

It was dumb, but I really did like a good fireworks display. Especially from the water. "I hope so. That would be cool."

"That's if you're not running around after the Wolfman," Eric said.

"The Wolfman?" We didn't call the guests nicknames

because there was too big a chance for them to overhear. Not until the charter was over anyway. And Hayden had been nothing but courteous to all the crew as far as I was aware.

Eric just shrugged.

"Like you said, he'll go down to his office and I won't see him all evening. I doubt I'll be running anywhere."

"Then why don't you come ashore with us?"

I tilted my head, encouraging Eric to drop it. My mind was set. There was no point having this discussion.

"I think they'll have them over the water, so you're bound to see them," Skylar said.

For a second I thought about taking some photos to send to my dad and Michael, but then I remembered we didn't have our phones. My dad loved to see beautiful pictures from different parts of the world. I think it reassured him that I was having fun. "I think so too. So, you see, I'll hardly be missing out at all. But it's very sweet of you guys to be concerned."

"Concerned about what?" August asked, appearing in the doorway.

I groaned. I wasn't about to go through it all for the ninetieth time. "You look pretty," I told her, trying to throw her off the scent. "Come on," I said, standing. "I'll see you guys off."

"You're not coming?" August asked and voices began to murmur. I ushered everyone out of the kitchen and down to the tender.

"Seriously, it's a full day of work tomorrow, so not too much alcohol. I'm not picking up your slack." I eyed August in particular.

We trailed down the stairs and everyone piled onto the tender. I untied the bowline and threw the rope to Eric then waved them off. It was good to see everyone in such high spirits.

Giving them the night off was a nice thing for Hayden to have done. I glanced up to the main deck, still smiling at all their excitement, and locked eyes with Hayden. He looked far from happy, his face was like thunder and fury burned in his eyes. Was it his work that had caused that or was he mad I hadn't gone with them? My stomach churned and my skin prickled with heat. I hated the thought that he might be angry with me.

SIXTEEN

Hayden

I wasn't used to my instructions being ignored. I'd had money and power for long enough that people rarely said no to me. I'd been clear when I'd spoken to Moss that the crew should have the night off. I accepted he'd have to stay on board, but I'd told him I wouldn't need anything from anyone. I threw my pen across my desk. My concentration was shot. I didn't know if it was the lack of sleep, or the overnight working, or just the irritation of being ignored by Avery, but tonight, I couldn't focus. It was Saturday night and I'd just dismissed the lawyers. At least they'd have the afternoon and evening with their families.

I knew I was working too hard. And I knew I was working my team too hard. I just wanted this deal done as soon as possible.

I leaned back in my chair and glanced out the window—just blackness with slivers of silver when the water caught the lights of the boat. It was almost nine and I was hungry.

And I could do with a whiskey. If I couldn't work, then perhaps a drink would send me to sleep.

As I entered the formal dining room, Avery appeared from the galley, her professional smile fixed to her face. "Can I get you anything?"

I narrowed my eyes. "Why didn't you go with them?"

She blinked several times, as if riffling through possible answers. "I just didn't—"

"Did the captain say you had to stay?"

She placed her hand up to her throat. "No. Not at all. I just wasn't feeling too well . . ."

I stepped toward her. "Then you should rest."

She exhaled and her shoulders dropped. "That's not true."

I crooked my head. She'd lied? And if so why had she immediately confessed? "What about? That the captain didn't stop you from going ashore or that you're not feeling well?"

"I feel perfectly fine."

"I like the truth, Avery."

"I'm sorry." Her shoulders drooped a little, as if her professional veneer was slipping. "The guys gave me a really hard time about staying. And I just don't want to go through it again. Can we drop this, and can I get you something?"

"The whole point of me giving the crew the night off was so you didn't have to fetch and carry for me." I stepped closer, and she had to tip her head back to still look at me. Her delicious throat, temptingly exposed, trailed down to her full breasts. "And I'm not dropping anything. Tell me why you didn't go ashore."

"I . . . I . . . I don't know. I just . . ." Her cheeks bloomed pink and I realized. She was embarrassed because she'd *wanted* to stay.

I just wasn't sure if it was the pull of me or her job that kept her on board tonight.

"I'm hungry," I said, half whisper, half growl. Hungry to taste *her*.

Her eyes widened and her eyelids fluttered in confusion before she gasped. "I'll get you something." She spun around, headed back to the interior.

I'd been a tenth of a second away from pulling her into my arms and exploring that polite mouth of hers. Had she not scurried away, I wouldn't have been able to hold myself back. Maybe that's why she'd disappeared inside. Something was holding *her* back.

I followed her into the galley, watching her skate around the kitchen as I leaned on the doorjamb. She worked quickly, uncovering dishes of various meats, cheeses, pickles, bread, fruit, and then carefully rearranging any that weren't exactly perfect. Picking up two dishes, she smiled and nodded toward the door.

"Can I take those?" I reached for the dishes but she stepped back.

"Please let me. This is what I do. This is what I'm good at. You're happy to eat outside?"

I nodded and waited for her to leave. She hesitated, presumably expecting me to go with her but I didn't. As soon as she was out of sight, I picked up two more platters and made my way upstairs.

When she saw me, her expression was unguarded. I wasn't sure if it was anger or hurt I could see in her eyes.

"I'm just trying to help. It's senseless for you to make an additional trip while I follow you with nothing." I wanted to tell her how she was good at more than carrying plates, how I imagined she could be good at anything she wanted to be.

She pressed her lips together before taking the plates from me and placing them on the table. "Can I kindly ask you to take a seat?"

I pushed down my smile. It was more than a little satisfying to see her so frustrated with me but trying to hide it. "I will take a seat if—when you've collected whatever other accoutrements you need—you'll join me."

She paused before straightening the platter. "I want you to enjoy your meal in peace."

"And I've asked you to join me. Now, please do as I say, and bring a plate for yourself." I pulled out the seat on the side of the table facing the water and made myself comfortable.

She opened her mouth to argue, and I simply raised my eyebrows and she flitted back inside without a word. For whatever reason she was uncomfortable joining me, but for me the thought of her company overrode my need to be fair.

She returned with my place setting. I enjoyed her needing to be so close—the two of us just centimeters apart so she could slide the placemat in front of me then set the cutlery down. Without saying a word, she folded the white linen napkin in a triangle and placed it in my lap.

"Can I create a plate for you?" she asked, taking a half step back.

My hand was just inches from the back of her thigh, temptingly close. I nodded and she set about placing a selection of food onto my plate and then poured my glass of wine.

She clasped her hands in front of her after she'd set the bottle down in the ice bucket. "Anything else?"

"Sit," I said, taking a forkful of jambon and slipping it into my mouth. I nodded at the empty chair at the end of the table, next to me. I never took the head of the table—not in boardrooms, not around a dining room table. I always thought it betrayed a lack of self-confidence for anyone to have to proclaim themselves as the leader, the most important, the most dominant, by sitting at the end of the table. I preferred to prove it through my words, actions and presence.

She transferred her weight from one foot to the next, trying to decide if she was going to do what she was told, and I didn't rush her. Tentatively, she pulled out the chair I'd indicated and took a seat, sitting forward uncomfortably.

"Have you eaten?" I asked.

"I have, actually."

Of course she had.

"What did you eat?"

Her eyes narrowed, and I couldn't figure out whether she didn't want to tell me because I had no right to ask or if she was simply avoiding sharing anything, not wanting to take the next step because we both knew there was a next step.

"A cheese sandwich."

I picked up my bread roll. "Like this?" I was basically having a ham and cheese sandwich, which worked for me.

"Grated cheddar."

I nodded, taking another mouthful, wanting her to say more.

"Bread and cheese is . . ." She looked dreamily out over the ocean and sighed.

I chuckled. "Well there's plenty here. And you have a plate," I lifted my chin at the extra place setting she'd set in front of her as I'd asked. "Join me."

Her mouth twisted as she fought the need to remain professional with her desire to do exactly what a guest wanted her to do. She didn't take any food—for now—and I didn't push. Our exchange on the deck below had sent her running and I wanted her right next to me. I didn't want to frighten her off.

"What else?" I asked.

"What else?" she questioned me back. She knew I was asking for more than just a rundown of her dietary habits. I wanted more of her.

"*What else* do you like to do in your free time when you're not eating bread and cheese?"

She shrugged. "During the season there's not much free time. So dinner and dancing with the crew is about as far as it gets." She sat back in her chair.

"And between seasons when everyone else goes exploring, what is it you do?" Did she have a boyfriend? Maybe even a husband waiting for her?

A smile curled at the edges of her mouth. "The first night, sometimes I like to check myself into a really nice hotel. I know it's extravagant, but it's my treat to myself—one night when my bed's made, my dinner is served to me, and my drink is made by someone else." She ran her fingers down the wood grain beside her fork.

"I can imagine that's nice after running around after guests all season."

"It is, but it's more than that, too. It's about being me again—Avery Walker."

"And you're not Avery on the boat?"

She pulled her lip into her mouth as she thought about her answer. I enjoyed these pauses she took, the thought she put into what she said. I appreciated the effort she made to think about what I'd asked her.

She glanced at me and sat back in her chair, adjusting to this arrangement between us. "Yacht crew are invisible but available on charter. We blend into the background. Generally guests aren't rude, but they are guests, right? I mean, this is my job. I'm not here to have fun. As a crew member, we're here to ensure the guests enjoy their vacation. So we're part of the package, just like the fresh sheets, the good food, and the strong cocktails."

"But you're not a thing," I said, uncomfortable at the idea she thought she was an object and that I may share that view.

She squinted. "Not exactly, no, but if we're doing our job well, we're invisible when we need to be, and helpful when it's required."

I regarded her while I continued to chew, wanting to hear her talk more, to know more about the Avery behind the professional gloss.

"And that night at the hotel—it's like I come back into focus. I become Avery Walker again."

"And then?"

"Then I go back to Sacramento."

"California." For some reason it was hard to picture her anywhere but on this yacht. "And you're invisible again at home?" Why did she need that night alone? Who did she belong to that she wasn't vibrant and authentic when she was sleeping in her own bed?

"No," she snapped, a little too quickly. "I didn't mean that." She reached out to take a pickle from one of the serving plates. I grinned—she was relaxing.

"I like being home. It's less . . ." She peered at her lap and then shrugged.

"You live alone?"

She shook her head and my pulse began to throb in my neck.

"Nope, with my dad. And brother. I'm only there a couple of months of the year so it doesn't make sense to have a place of my own." The way her words tumbled out, she sounded well-rehearsed. I wasn't sure if she'd said it out loud a lot or just in her own mind. "I like spending as much time as possible with them when I'm back. So it works."

My pulse faded back into the distance in response to her answer. No husband and no mention of a boyfriend.

People observing from the shore wouldn't see how much Avery and I had in common professionally. She worked hard, took pride in what she did and went above and beyond what any reasonable person would expect. She didn't deserve to be invisible. I couldn't imagine not noticing her.

I wanted more of the woman I'd watched the sunrise with—her loose hair and warm wonder. She pulled me in despite doing her best to be invisible but available to me. I wanted to fill in the gaps, get to know the real woman, not the shadow who was always around in case I needed something. "How old's your brother?"

"A year younger than me."

I'd put her at twenty-five, though I bet she'd look the same for the next decade. She had a timeless beauty about her—the small waist, the high cheekbones and perfect arse.

"He's twenty-five."

"I had you down for twenty-five."

She grinned. "You were close."

"I'm thirty-two," I said. I wanted this to be a conversation between us but I guessed she wasn't going to feel comfortable asking me questions.

"I know," she said, popping another pickle in her mouth. "I Googled you when I went on shore that first time."

"You did, huh? What did Google tell you?"

She poured herself a glass of water from the bottle of San Pellegrino on the table that I'd not touched. "Not a hell of a lot, unfortunately." She leaned back in her chair, for the first time acting as if she might stay more than a few short seconds, and smiled. It was Avery Walker's smile, rather than the grin of the stewardess on the *Athena*.

"I'm quite careful about what's out there about me," I said.

"Shocker." Her eyes widened teasingly. "I just like to personalize the guest's experience, you know? I thought I might find something useful."

"I filled out my preferences sheet. Because you asked me to." I probably would have ignored anyone else. But she'd caught my attention—shown me that I was being a pain in the arse by not doing that. And I respected that. I didn't expect servitude from the people around me but the more successful I got, the bigger the gap between me and those in my orbit.

"I shouldn't have. I don't know what got into me. I should have just accepted there was no sheet."

"I liked that you did."

Our eyes locked and she didn't reply.

Eventually she looked away and over the dark waves that were lapping at the boat. "The crew was grateful. As you would say in England, it caused great consternation not having the information."

"I'm not sure anyone says that in England, outside a Jane Austen novel."

She laughed. "I suppose not."

"I'm just not that fussy about things like that."

She scrunched up her nose in the most adorable way and I couldn't help but smile at her expression. "I think if I were rich, I'd want the things I like. Otherwise, what's the point?"

"I agree, but I just don't care about the water I drink or the sheets I sleep in."

"Why?" Leaning forward, she rested her chin on both hands, and I couldn't help but notice the way the movement pressed her full breasts together under her top.

My dick twitched and I blinked, trying to force myself back to our conversation. "Because that's not what matters. We have to focus on the important stuff, like people. *You* reminded me of that."

Her lashes swept up as she blinked, almost in slow motion as if I'd said something profound she had to give weight to and assimilate. Damn my dick needed to behave itself. But that pink in her cheeks, the wisps of hair that had escaped her ponytail—I wanted more of *that* Avery.

I put my knife and fork together and leaned back. Talking with Avery was far more fulfilling than food. "It's not like I'm slumming it." I glanced around, indicating the boat.

She laughed. "I guess not." She checked her watch. "It's coming up to nine. There are going to be fireworks on the shore. We should be able to see them, but the view will be best from the upper deck." The way her eyes lit up, she didn't just want me to see the fireworks because I was a guest, but she was actually looking forward to them. "Are you finished?" She pushed her chair out and reached out to take my plate when I nodded.

I didn't want her to wait on me. Not tonight. I wanted

to encourage her to see me as a man not a guest. "Let me. You were supposed to have the evening off."

She closed her eyes and shook her head. "Please don't. That would make me really uncomfortable."

That was the last thing I wanted to do, but I didn't want her to be invisible either.

"I'll make you a deal," I said.

She rolled her eyes. "You're all about the deal."

"It's who I am. I'll head to the upper deck now and leave you to this if you join me with a bottle of champagne and two glasses."

"We don't drink on charter," she spluttered almost before I'd finished my sentence.

"So for an hour you won't be on charter. You were meant to have this evening off anyway."

She shifted her weight onto one leg. "I don't know . . ." She scanned the horizon as if looking for something external that would resolve the conflict inside her.

I knew she could feel this pull between us. I could tell now when she was being polite and when she was being real, and I knew she wanted to say yes but her dedication and sense of duty held her back. "Isn't it your job to fulfill a guest's request?" I shouldn't abuse my power, and if I hadn't thought that Avery and her big brown eyes wanted to continue our conversation over a glass of champagne, I wouldn't have pushed it. But she did from the way her body shuddered on the few occasions I'd touched her, to the way her cheeks pinked when I grinned at her—I could feel the attraction no matter how hard she tried to hide it.

"Not every request," she replied.

"You're right." Again, she'd pulled me up and I just wanted her more because of it. "I don't want you to join me because I'm a guest. I want you to watch the fireworks with me because the Avery Walker that exists off this boat wants to."

Avery

It would be easier if I didn't *want* to join Hayden. If another guest had asked me to watch the fireworks with them I probably wouldn't have resisted so hard. Tipsy guests would often encourage us to join them in their revelry and we'd smile and join their conga line, sing karaoke or line up their shots. But I fought against Hayden's invitation, albeit half-heartedly, because I knew I'd want more from our encounter than I was supposed to. There was no doubt that Hayden Wolf was attractive physically, but the more I got to know him, the more I liked and admired him. From the way he wasn't so prideful that it stopped him from taking advice about his deal and he was prepared to admit it to the way he used a family photograph as a bookmark. My draw toward him was . . . unusual, dangerous, frightening.

I released the cloth, dropping it over the ice, and scooped up the bucket, resting it on my hip. I picked up the two champagne glasses I'd set on the counter and headed to the upper deck.

I'd resisted because the transparent but very clear divide between crew and guest, which was always in place, even when we were dancing and singing along with them, I felt crumbling when I was with Hayden. I'd want him to tell me things guests shouldn't tell crew—personal things about his family and life. I'd want him to look at me and think that I was beautiful. I'd wanted to forget I was crew and paid to serve him.

And more than anything else, I didn't want to join

Hayden and be disappointed that that barrier between us disintegrated for me, but stayed in place for him.

But I'd lost this battle. I wanted to please him, was a little drunk on the attention of this rich, charming man who seemed to be so different to anyone else I'd met who was in his position. But even more, I wanted this for me. I'd never felt such a strong pull to someone and I wasn't ready to let go. I never did the wrong thing. I was always caring about my family and my job but right now, I just wanted a few more minutes of feeling as special as I did when Hayden looked at me, searching and fascinated.

As I got up to the upper deck, Hayden was facing the ocean. His untucked, white linen shirt rippled in the breeze, threatening to lift to reveal his hard, tan body. He turned at the sound of me setting down the ice bucket and strode toward me.

"It's almost nine," he said, pulling the bottle from the ice and removing the foil and the cork. There was no point telling him I'd do it. Something had shifted. He'd asked me to join him as the Avery Walker who wasn't a stewardess and that's who I was in that moment.

As we stood silently in the dark, the low, orange light from the external lamps and the heat left over from the day making the outside feel like the inside, Hayden released the cork like a professional and poured two glasses.

He handed me a flute and raised his own. "To you, Avery Walker."

He couldn't make a toast to me—it felt wrong. I wasn't the girl who was ever the reason for the toast. "Let's hope the fireworks are good," I said, raising my glass.

He shook his head and I wasn't sure if it was because I'd ignored his toast or because of my expectations of entertainment from the shore. Outstretching his arm, he guided me to the portside, which was closest to the shore.

"It's beautiful without the fireworks," he said, and when I glanced at him he was looking right at me.

My heart thundered under his attention, and at the possibilities of his intentions. "And different from the South of France, right? It's only a few miles away but you can tell it's another country."

He nodded. "Do you get to go ashore a lot?"

"In Italy? Not much. You end up with time off where you're picking up your next charter—which is usually Saint Tropez or Monaco. The French Riviera, mainly. But I do volunteer for trips ashore during charters down the Italian coast. You know, if guests need anything. Do you like Italy?" I was babbling, trying to hide my desire for him. My eyes flitted across to him. I wanted to see his reaction, to study him, to know what he was thinking.

"Yeah. I've been to Milan for business countless times. And I've holidayed in villas in Tuscany."

Boom.

The first of the fireworks exploded in the sky—an umbrella of bright pink followed by white raindrops—stark against the black backdrop. I turned to him. I loved it. He smiled back at me and I had to look away his stare was so intense.

Boom. Boom. Boom.

The sky exploded into a shower of orange and blue stars as if we were in our own, alternative snow globe.

"I like this smile."

I turned back to him and realized his eyes had been on me the whole time.

"*This* smile?"

"The Avery Walker smile. It's different to the stewardess smile I normally get. They're both beautiful, but I prefer this one."

Boom. Boom. Boom. Boom.

I wasn't sure if the noise pounding in my ears was the fireworks up above or every atom of my body thundering in unison.

I glanced down at my glass, hiding my blush.

Another burst of light pulled our attention back to the sky and we watched for a few minutes in silence.

"Michael would love this," I said to myself, watching the colors surge and retreat. One of my first memories was Fourth of July fireworks with Mom and Dad and Michael. I'd missed that annual family outing since I'd begun yachting. Since Mom left.

"Michael?"

"My younger brother."

"You're close?" he asked.

Though I shouldn't, I took my first sip of champagne. I had to be up early tomorrow, would probably have to pick up the slack from August and Skylar because of their hangovers. "Yeah. Kinda." I didn't see him that often and although I spoke to my dad every day, Michael and I didn't shoot the breeze or say much at all to each other unless I was at home.

"But you want him to see the fireworks?"

I exhaled, my shoulders dropping. "He had an accident. There were spinal injuries. Head injuries. He doesn't walk anymore. But he loves sports on TV and he would love this." I wished I could transport him here, show him how beautiful this place was. But he was unlikely to ever leave Sacramento, let alone the United States.

"I'm sorry," Hayden said, sweeping his knuckles over

my cheek as though it was the most natural thing in the world.

I shook my head and pulled my shoulders back. "It was seven years ago. And he has excellent medical care. And he and my dad eat too much pizza and watch far too much TV." I smiled at the thought of the two of them pretending to like my stir-fry or the vegetable casserole that I made whenever I was at home.

"Is that why you wanted to work abroad, to escape what was happening back home?"

It was such a personal question—prying and invasive—but I wanted to tell him.

I leaned against the railings, holding the stem of my glass with both hands. "Nope. I'd prefer to be with my family. But medical bills mount up, you know?"

He closed his eyes in a long blink as if what I'd said pained him. "I get it," he said, settling next to me, like we had been when we were watching the sunrise. "I have a brother. Younger. I'd move mountains for him if he wasn't more than capable of moving them for himself."

Tears misted my eyes. "That's what family does, right?" My mother hadn't felt the same.

"Not always," he said, as if he were reading my thoughts. He took a sip of his drink and turned so his body was facing me side on. "What would you do if the medical bills didn't exist?"

I paused, watching the sky burst into greens and purples. "I don't think about that. There's no point." At least I tried not to think about it. It wasn't as if I had options or choices. "Michael really wants to walk again. That's what we're all focused on."

Another boom echoed across the sky, bringing with it another glitter of color.

"There's always a point in having hopes and dreams—ambitions—isn't there?"

I kept focused on the sky. "I really want Michael to walk again." If I could have that, if my yachting career did nothing else but make that happen, every dream of mine would have come true.

"My brother was in the special forces," Hayden said a few minutes later and I faced him, wanting to hear every word he was saying. I'd assumed his brother would be a lawyer or a doctor. The military seemed so removed from Hayden and what he did, but it explained the crew cut in the photograph I'd seen. "SAS. I hated it when he joined up. Partly because I knew I'd miss him and partly because I wasn't going to be able to look after him where he was going."

I tried hard not to, but I reached across and curled my fingers around his wrist, wanting to provide some comfort. Hayden Wolf wasn't a man anyone would assume would worry over his younger brother. But maybe we weren't so different. "Maybe that's part of the reason why he did. So you didn't have to," I replied.

He let out a breath and I released his arm. "I'd never thought of it like that, but you might be right. He came back different. Which of course he was bound to because war changes you but also he just didn't need me as much. Maybe that was his plan."

Hayden sounded like he wanted to be needed by his brother. Would I miss it if I didn't have Michael relying on me?

The fireworks continued and we watched, commenting every now and then on how beautiful they were, our confessions to each other settling like foundations of a building.

"I was angry with you for not leaving the boat this

evening," Hayden said out of nowhere. "You deserved a break. When I gave the crew the night off—I meant for you to go with them."

"It's my job to be here. You're meant to be on vacation. If anyone deserves a break, it's you. You've not stopped since you came aboard." I wasn't sure he was going to make it a full eight weeks. He was barely sleeping and working through the night every night.

"But that's my choice. I'm trying to save my business."

"And yachting is *my* business. You take your career seriously and so do I. I'm not leaving my guest without a stewardess on board. What if you needed something?"

"Is that the only reason you stayed?" he asked.

I'd never been a good liar, but with Hayden I found myself revealing parts of me I'd kept completely secret. "I don't know," I replied. It was only half the reason. I could hardly confess the rest.

He paused. "You're beautiful," he said, and my heart thundered in my chest.

"Because I care about my job?" I teased, trying to lighten the moment.

"Exactly." He narrowed his eyes and the air all around me pressed against my skin, making me aware of every part exposed to the warm breeze.

He turned his entire body toward me. "I want to kiss you." My heartbeat got louder, mixing with the booms of the fireworks. I could make a joke and move away; it was what I would do if any other guest made a pass at me. I could excuse myself. I could run.

But I didn't. I didn't want to avoid anything. So I stayed, looking at him, my gaze flickering to the faded sky. "I can't kiss a guest," I whispered. I'd never wanted to before. Never even been tempted. I'd assumed that would always be the case, that I'd always care about my job above any fleeting moment of . . . whatever this was. But right then, it felt like a choice between my job and my *soul*. Like I fundamentally *needed* this deep down inside. Needed him. Maybe it was what my dad had said about having something for myself. Maybe it was just that I'd gone so long without a man touching me, but I didn't think so. It was Hayden Wolf and the way he kept constantly blowing my expectations of him out of the water, his lack of entourage, his moments of humor and his dedication to his business despite the fact that he probably didn't have to work again given his obvious wealth. It was the way he'd given the crew the night off when there was no reason to. He was a good man. A man so beautiful I caught my breath every time I saw him, and a man I wanted to kiss.

"But you want me to kiss you," he said, plucking my glass from my tightened fingers and placing it on the table behind him alongside his.

I couldn't argue—I wasn't a liar.

"The blush across your cheek . . ."

He stood right in front of me, so close I could feel the heat rolling off his body. He reached behind me and pulled my hair free from the tie, slowly, deliberately as if he was savoring some kind of transformation. "The way your nipples tighten when I'm close. The way your pussy is aching right now . . . it all tells me how much you want me to kiss you."

I pulled my bottom lip into my mouth and glanced at my feet. I couldn't move, couldn't contradict the dirty things he was saying. I wasn't sure if it was because he was right, or because his words were just so damn filthy, but I couldn't remember ever being so turned on by a man who'd barely touched me.

His thumb swept across my bottom lip, coaxing it free of my teeth, then

he tilted my head up to face him. He stared into my eyes intently as if he were communicating, telling me he'd stop if that was what I wanted.

But I didn't.

I wanted to forget he was a guest and I was a stewardess.

I wanted to forget I was putting my job on the line at that precise moment.

I wanted him to kiss me.

He stepped forward, his thighs scraping against my hips as he cupped my face in his hands, sweeping his thumbs across my cheekbones.

I sank against his body, needing more of him, desperate for his lips on mine. He sighed and closed his eyelids lazily before pressing his lips to mine. My skin began to buzz. I wasn't sure if it were in warning or pleasure, but either way, I didn't care. I was right where I wanted to be, selfishly enjoying the man in front of me. He snaked his arm around me, pressing his huge palm into the small of my back, pulling me against him.

I opened my mouth with a groan and he slipped his tongue into my mouth. He tasted masculine, like heat and earth, as if he was the center of everything, and at that moment he was. He was solid. I could trust him. He'd look after me and protect me and a long-buried part of myself burst into relief. My knees buckled, but he kept me upright. His arms felt as if they were exactly where they were meant to be—around me.

I'd kissed men before—of course I had—but I wasn't sure I'd ever *been* kissed, not like this, not with Hayden's possessive, perfect way.

I slid my hands up his chest, heat against heat, his heartbeat hammering against my palm. He pulled back for a second, narrowed his eyes and dived to my neck, pressing kisses into the dip between my collarbone, then trailing up, nipping and sucking before pulling away again, looking at me as if I was some kind of prize he'd never thought he would win and didn't think he deserved, then hungrily found my lips again.

He was right, my pussy was tight and hot. I arched my body against him, trying to give it some peace. He moaned into my mouth, grabbing my ass, sliding his hand down the back of my thigh and raising my leg as he pressed his erection against my belly.

The heat between us winched up, higher and higher, with no telling when or if it would stop or explode.

My sounds were getting louder and I knew I needed things to stop before . . . before I became incapable. I couldn't lose control. I was so close to not caring about anything but this moment, about anyone except Hayden and me.

The breeze carried laughter from a nearby yacht, echoing into the quiet night now the fireworks had stopped. If we could hear them, could they hear us, see us?

I pushed my hand against his chest and he pulled back, looking me right in the eye. I shook my head. "We have to stop this." I wanted him to keep kissing me. I wanted to feel the heat coursing through my body for just a few more minutes, but I had to end this now.

"But you don't want me to stop," he murmured, scraping his scruff-covered cheek against mine.

"You're right. I don't," I whispered, need spreading across my skin, but I managed to resist him and stepped back, out of his arms. "But I need to go." I should never have come up here. I knew it would lead to trouble, however sweet it might feel in the short term. It was too risky. There was too much at stake. My brother's care and my career were never going take second place to any man. But the choice had never felt so difficult, had never stung quite so painfully, as it did when I turned away from Hayden Wolf.

SEVENTEEN

Avery

Everything was on its ass. Last night I'd kissed Hayden Wolf, which I absolutely should not have done. And this morning when I'd gone ashore after breakfast, I couldn't get hold of my dad. I was five seconds away from freaking out.

So far this charter I'd managed to get ashore at least every other day to call my dad. Today was important. Michael got a physical therapy report every month from his therapist and it was due yesterday. The report set out Michael's progress and was required by the insurer, but it also lifted all our spirits. Despite Michael's accident being so long ago, the fact that he was still making progress gave us all the drive to move forward and especially Michael. It kept his goal of walking again at the forefront of his mind. Michael had just started his additional therapy, which my forty percent pay raise was paying for, and even though it was unrealistic I was hoping it would have already made a difference and the report would reflect that.

"Avery, Avery, this is Neill. Mr. Wolf is looking for

you." My radio rang out from my waist and I sighed. Hayden still insisted on dealing with just me. August and Skylar weren't complaining, and usually neither was I, but right then I wanted to focus on finding an excuse to go back on shore so I could call home again.

I hooked my hair into a ponytail and straightened my skirt, checking my reflection in the floor-length mirror on the back of the door. "This is Avery. I'll be right there," I said into my radio and I headed to the galley. Last night I'd forced myself back to my room. This morning I could still feel the press of Hayden's thumbs over my hips, still feel his teeth against my neck, and I wondered how long the memories might last, how long I could keep remembering our kiss. I wanted to etch it into my brain as the most perfect one I'd ever had.

I'd tried to avoid his eyes as I served him breakfast this morning, and he had seemed amused at my embarrassment. But he wasn't the one who'd risked everything for a kiss. And although I was sure my guilt was scorched into my forehead, no one had said anything. And why would they? The only one who'd been onboard last night was Captain Moss, and if he'd seen anything, I'd have a plane ticket in my hand and my suitcase packed already. No one else knew.

"Where is he?" I asked Neill as I got to the kitchen.

"Pacing in the dining room." He lifted his chin to the galley entrance. "This isn't fair to you. August and Skylar are perfectly capable of being at his beck and call. It puts too much pressure on you."

Why was Neill acting as if Hayden was being unreasonable? We'd had guests who were much more demanding. "I don't mind," I said, heading out.

"Just be careful. I've seen the way he looks at you."

I paused in the doorway, my heartbeat shifting up a level, and turned around. "What?"

Neill shrugged. "He's clearly got a thing for you."

I frowned and hoped it covered my blush. "He does not. He's just intense about his privacy."

Neill stopped slicing whatever it was on his chopping board and fixed me with his stare. "Look at you," he said, glancing at me from head to toe in the way only a gay man could get away with without being a sleazeball. "Of course he's got a thing for you."

I opened my mouth to speak, not quite knowing what to say, but before I could respond he continued.

"Look, you know I think you're an amazing stewardess and a kick-ass tequila drinker. You also know I can pick up on chemistry a thousand miles off. It's my superpower."

Had I been flirting without knowing it? Had Neill picked up on the fact that me staying on board last night had something to do with Hayden? "I don't know what you mean. Hayden has only wanted to deal with me since he came on board—"

"I also know you're a terrible liar, so I'd prefer you didn't say anything." My stomach crashed to my knees. If Neill had picked up on something between us, then who else had? "Don't let him take advantage."

"As if," I replied, trying to shrug off his comments as alarm bells began to ring in my ears.

"Hayden's good looking and charming. I get it," he continued. "But ask yourself if he's worth losing your career for. Worth you not being able to help your family. You have a lot at stake, Avery, and I really want you to be happy. Just be careful."

"I have to go." I waved my hand in the air and spun to exit the galley before the weight pressing on my chest stopped me from breathing. I didn't want to have this discussion with Neill. Hayden might be a paying guest, but he hadn't pressured me to do anything I didn't want to. He could read me—he'd known I wanted him.

Shit, as if I didn't have enough to worry about not being able to speak to my dad, now Neill was talking about my chemistry with Hayden. If Neill could sense something then I needed to be more careful with how I interacted with Hayden before anyone else came to the same conclusion. And I definitely shouldn't be kissing him or watching sunsets with him.

"Hayden," I said when I almost bumped into him as I reached the dining room.

"I need you to collect something for me," he said. His words were clipped and his jaw tight. What had happened since breakfast?

I exhaled and nodded. "Okay. That's not a problem." I could call my dad again on shore. We were moored off Marina di Andora, a small port in Northern Italy. From what I'd heard from the crew, there wasn't much going on ashore but at least there was a pay phone.

"Where do you need me to go?"

He went to speak and then paused as he scanned my face. I looked away, unnerved by his ability to read me. I didn't want him to see how much last night had affected me. How much I wanted him to slide his arms around me and pull me against him. He blinked and then cleared his throat.

"There's a yacht supplies shop on Via St Michael. If you could pick up something from there, my person will find you."

I was used to doing all sorts of things for clients, and fetching and carrying wasn't unusual, except I was more accustomed to finding the nearest Gucci dealer and bringing back half a dozen bathing suits for clients or a specialty liquor store for some exclusive alcohol. Brown envelopes or boxes of documents weren't the normal pickup. "Okay."

"It's just the latest versions of the legal documents. This draft will be crucial. I'll be able to tell a lot about how easy it will be to conclude this deal."

I took a step back from him. "No problem."

He reached out and pressed his hand against my forearm. "Thank you."

I froze, trying not to react to his touch, trying to block out the way his fingers felt on my skin.

He released me. "Can you go straight away?"

"Sure."

Neill said he wanted me to be happy, but the only time I'd been truly, butterflies-in-the-stomach, grin-I-couldn't-control happy on this charter was when I'd been with Hayden. Distance, even for a little while, was what I needed. Distance from the bad decisions I'd made last night. Distance from those damn butterflies and the pull in my chest every time I set eyes on Hayden Wolf.

I DIALED AGAIN and then checked my watch. Where were they? Despite the expense I'd tried my dad's cell and Michael's but still nothing. I glanced back toward the tender, knowing I should get back.

Hayden was desperate for whatever was in the envelope I'd collected from the woman in the yacht supplies shop. It had been the same girl who had given me the envelope in Saint Tropez. She must be following him down the coast. I just wasn't going to go back to the yacht without having spoken to my dad. It could be another two days before I got to speak to him again.

Our house voicemail clicked on and I hung up. I'd already left three messages. I dove into my tote and pulled out my address book. Luckily for me, I still used the small, pink address book I'd been given on my eighth birthday for all my important phone numbers and hadn't had to rely on the numbers in my cell that I didn't have. I'd call my aunt. She lived three blocks away, and I could get her to go around to check on my dad and Michael.

With the receiver tucked under my chin, I held my address book open with one hand while I punched in the numbers.

It felt like an hour and a half passed before the line finally connected. It rang and rang. Nothing. It was Sunday. They should be reading the paper and Michael should be on his Xbox. There was no reason for people not to be answering the phone.

Concern morphed into panic. What if something was wrong? What if Michael had collapsed or been told he'd never walk again and everyone was too upset to pick up?

Still the phone just rang and rang.

I flipped over the page in my address book and found my aunt's cell number.

I hung up and dialed again. She always had her phone on her.

My heart boomed in my chest. I was getting stressed out for nothing, I told myself as I waited for an answer. Maybe they'd gone grocery shopping or to get gas.

My knees almost collapsed when my aunt answered.

"Hello?" I said.

"Avery?" she answered.

"Can you hear me?" I yelled into the phone. *Please, don't let the line fail.*

"Yes, Avery. Don't panic. Are you okay?" My aunt was a lot like my father—calm through the stormiest seas—but I knew her well enough to know that if she was telling me not to panic, then I had good reason to do the opposite.

"I'm fine. Why aren't I panicking?" I held my breath, not wanting to make a sound so she wouldn't have to repeat herself.

"We're at the hospital. It's your dad."

I stumbled backward, almost dropping the receiver. "What happened?"

Hayden

What was taking her so long? I stuffed my hands into my pockets as I paced the main deck.

"Skylar," I called just as she was heading back through the sliding doors after silently collecting my empty glass from beside my lounger.

She turned, a huge smile on her face. "Can I get you another? Or a snack, maybe?"

She was probably shocked I'd even spoken to her. Avery had done her best to be the only member of her team I had anything to do with, which was exactly what I'd wanted. Maybe I'd asked too much of her.

"Do you have a pair of binoculars?" I wanted to see if they were on their way back. Perhaps the tender had engine trouble and Eric was trying to fix it.

"Certainly. I'll just get them for you."

I scanned the shoreline, trying to see where the tender had docked, but it was just too far away. I wanted my documents and the fact I couldn't just open my email and have them appear was driving me nuts. This was my future that was taking so long to arrive.

"Here you are," Skylar said as she returned and placed two pairs of binoculars on the side table, one larger than the other. "They focus automatically, but let me know if you need any help."

"Thank you. And actually, you could get me a glass of water, please."

Her grin grew wide as if I'd just promoted her. Maybe I had. Avery was working around the clock. Perhaps it was time I let Skylar take some of the burden. Avery waiting on me didn't seem right after last night.

I took out the binoculars, focused on the marina and caught sight of the tender with Eric at the helm. I jerked the binoculars up and Avery Walker filled the frame. She was wearing her yacht uniform, her bronzed legs shown off by her mid-thigh khaki skirt, her hair in a ponytail and large sunglasses that made her look like a movie star. Eric reached out to help Avery onto the boat. As they touched, a shot of jealousy seared through me. Did he have a crush on her? Of course he had a crush on her. The woman was a goddess—elegant, poised, wise and kind—not to mention the most beautiful woman I'd ever laid eyes on. Had they kissed? Had he held her like I had last night?

She'd disappeared after our kiss like Cinderella fleeing before the clock struck midnight. I was so used to being in control with the women I was with, I couldn't recall a time when I'd felt abandoned. Maybe it was because Avery and I hadn't fucked, because neither of us had gotten release, but I knew it was more than that. I got the distinct impression I'd never be able to get enough of Avery Walker. She was equal parts tough and vulnerable. Loyal and trusting, hard-working and driven. I couldn't remember admiring someone as much as I did her.

Avery sat at the front of the tender, facing me and away from Eric. Ridiculously, a sense of satisfaction circled in my gut. Was she looking for me like I was looking for her?

She pushed her sunglasses to the top of her head and covered her face with her hands. Was she shielding herself from the wind? No, it was as if she were crying. Surely not. I lowered the binoculars, trying to think of reasons she might be upset. Had someone seen us on the yacht and disciplined her? She'd said that guests were strictly off-limits for crew. Had something happened while she'd been ashore? Had she been mugged? No, I'd seen her bring her tote back on the boat.

I picked up the binoculars. She wiped under her eyes with the back of her hands, then slipped her glasses back on. She took a deep breath, smiled and then turned back to face Eric. She'd thought she was having a private moment. And I'd intruded on that when I had no right to. I'd been spying on her, invading her privacy, but now I had to know what was wrong. I was constantly asking too much of Avery. Had she felt pressured last night into kissing me? Was she upset because of what she'd done or was it something else entirely? I set the binoculars down.

"Shall I just set this on the table for you?" Skylar asked as she appeared with my glass of tap water on a tray.

"No, I'll take it," I said, reaching for the glass. "I'm going down to my office. Can you ask Avery to come and find me as soon as she gets back? It's urgent."

She smiled and almost did a little curtsey. I would have chuckled if I hadn't been so concerned about why Avery was upset. "Certainly. No problem," she replied.

I headed back downstairs to my office to wait for

Avery. She'd be back in less than five minutes, but it wasn't quick enough. I heard the deck crew tying up the tender and I had to stop myself from bellowing upstairs for her to get a move on. Christ, I was an impatient, unreasonable bastard.

When I finally heard her footsteps on the stairs I took a seat and watched the door, willing it to open.

Avery knocked, then entered when I called for her. I had to clear my throat. I hadn't imagined it. Her eyes were puffy and red. She'd definitely been crying. I shot to my feet. "Avery." I didn't know what to say, didn't know how to navigate this situation. This was a woman I wanted to strip naked and kiss head to toe then fuck through to next week, but she was also a woman I didn't want to see cry. I wanted to make it better for her, whatever was wrong. Before I had the chance to question my own instincts, I'd moved around my desk and pressed the door closed with my palm, locking it with my other hand.

"Sit."

"Please, I need to go." Her voice quivered as she set the thick envelope of papers on my desk. "I have a lot to do."

"Sit," I repeated, and she relented, sinking into the chair, her limbs heavy and her eyes sad. I leaned against the desk, our legs almost touching. "What is it?"

"I have to organize lunch," she said. "Then—"

"Please don't make me repeat myself. Why are you upset?"

She took in a deep, jagged breath and shook her head. "It's nothing."

I didn't reply but I wasn't going to be fobbed off. She was going to tell me what was wrong and then I was going to fix it.

She wrung her hands and avoided my gaze, but I stayed

silent, despite the way my muscles twitched, desperate for action. I wanted her to talk to me.

Eventually she spoke. "My father was taken to the emergency room last night."

Shit. I clenched my hands, wanting to reach out and touch her, but after last night, I didn't know where we stood, what I should do. I just knew that I wanted to do something —anything—to soothe her pain.

"He's okay. They thought it might be a heart attack, but apparently it wasn't. They're doing tests." She glanced up at me, her face filled with sadness, and I hated myself for not being able to fix it immediately. I wanted to pull her into my arms and tell her everything was going to be okay, but I couldn't make this better for her. Wealth and power meant nothing in a situation like this. "Jesus, I'm sorry. Do you need to leave?"

She exhaled. "God, my father would never forgive me. He's . . . a proud man. Would hate for me to make a fuss." She shook her head. "He only accepts the money I send for Michael's sake. No doubt he's making the nurses' lives hell at this precise moment."

It wasn't enough information. Did her dad have a heart condition already?

"My aunt is staying with my brother."

Where was her mum? I didn't ask in case she got more upset. Thinking back, Avery hadn't mentioned her at all.

She pressed her palm against her forehead, as if trying to cool herself, and I found myself wanting to be that momentary relief for her. "I should have seen this coming. He's getting older and it's too much for him to be working and looking after my brother. But trying to get either of them to accept a caregiver when my dad's at home is impossible. My dad says he doesn't like strangers in his house when he's there."

I reached for her, my need to provide her with comfort overwhelming, but she recoiled and stood, shaking her head. "Don't," she said sharply and then looked away as if her own tone had shocked her.

"We can't. We never should have in the first place." Her voice started to falter again. "I'll have to insist my dad accepts more help." Her gaze flitted about the room as if she were going through her options, making a plan. "We'll need more money. Maybe even a full-time nurse."

She looked me straight in the eye. "My job is more important than ever. I should never have—last night—I just can't."

A dull ache looped in my stomach. It was unfamiliar. I couldn't remember a time when a woman had evoked that feeling in me, as if I was missing out on something by not having her close, by not knowing her.

"I'm sorry."

"You don't need to be," I said. "But I would never allow you to lose your job over me, you know that?" I was careful not to touch her, despite how much I wanted to. I didn't want her to feel uncomfortable, but more than that, I didn't want to have to suffer her rejection again.

"It's not up to you." She glanced at her feet. "It's Captain Moss's decision. And in any case, gossip runs riot in this industry. An affair between a crew member and a charter guest would get out and I'd never find another position." She paused. "It's not that I don't . . . There's just too much at stake." Her eyes welled with tears. "I feel like I'm being punished. Last night—I should have never. And now my dad and I'm thousands of miles away, with no way to contact them. I'm not going to find out the test results until God knows when. I just wish I could be there."

"But you can call, every hour if you need to, surely. The captain doesn't ration the phone, right?"

"We don't have access to the satellite phone. The calls are too expensive."

I stood and rounded my desk. "Then use mine. In fact, stay in here today. And you be on the phone the entire time if you need to." Thoughts of the legal documents she'd brought with her had faded with her desperation. She was driving chaos into my priorities.

She looked up at me. "Really?"

"Of course." I hated to see her upset and I could easily work in any of the countless other rooms on the yacht.

She shook her head. "I shouldn't use your phone. I think it would be frowned upon. I mean, I really shouldn't have told you all this. It's unprofessional." She pushed her shoulders back, but her eyes still glistened with tears.

"Avery Walker, I will be offended if you don't use this phone." I checked my watch. "I'll need to use it at three fifteen New York time, once I've read these documents. So make the most of it."

She shook her head.

"Avery, I am a paying guest. I thought guests always got what they wanted?"

She paused and exhaled. "Thank you," she said, her voice quivering. "You're a very nice man." I winced at how formal and awkward that sounded and as if she agreed, she frowned. "And a very good kisser. I just—"

I shook my head and tried to bite back my grin. "Shhh. You don't have to feel bad. My heart is intact." I dipped, trying to catch her eye, and she nodded, reaching out to place her palm on my shoulder.

I smoothed my hand across her back. "Sit down. Call your aunt." I guided her around my desk so she could take a seat in my chair.

"I need to keep busy," she said. "But I don't want everyone asking me why I'm upset."

"So stay here. Tell people you're helping me with filing if they ask."

"I can't believe I'm having a meltdown on a guest."

My stomach pinched at her referring to me as a guest. "Being away from your family when they're vulnerable is tough," I said. "I understand."

Talking about personal stuff wasn't something I did often. In fact, I couldn't remember the last time I'd spoken to anyone about anything other than business. I'd talk a little to the women I slept with but only enough to get them into bed and never anything personal. I found that the ultimate seduction technique was to listen. Or at least pretend to.

I leaned on the desk beside her. "I told you that my brother was in the special forces. During his deployments, it was . . ." I swallowed, remembering the time he went missing for three days in Afghanistan. "It was difficult. Not knowing what's going on is the worst part. But your father's doctors have ruled out a heart attack—that's good news. I'm sure you'll feel better when the test results come back and you know what you're dealing with." I swept my thumb under one eye and then the other. "Save your tears until you have more information." It was what I'd said to my mother when we heard Landon was missing.

In the days Landon had been unaccounted for, anger, not fear, had been my primary emotion. Anger at the armed forces. Anger at his decision to enlist. Anger at my inability to do anything. My mother's tears had represented a lack of hope, so I'd channeled my fear into anger.

"Do you want me to call the hospital to see if I can speed things up?" I asked.

"No, but thank you. My aunt is a lioness. She'll be all over those physicians, riding their asses. But I appreciate it."

I stood and headed out to leave her in peace. "If there's anything I can do, just say it."

She gasped. "No, I'm meant to be doing things for you. I just—"

"Avery," I said, warning her as she put her hands on the arms of the chair as if she were about to stand. "Stay there. I've already had Skylar bring me some water."

"You did?"

"Yes, I've been too demanding of you—"

"I don't mind." Her eyes went wide—open and honest—her professional veneer long since gone. "I like to be busy."

"Stay there. I'm a grown man and I can fend for myself with the rest of the crew on board running around after me."

She surrendered and sat back. Even if I couldn't mend everything that was broken, at least I was able to provide her with a way of contacting home.

This was Avery Walker—all emotion and kindness. It was a raw, more honest version of the yacht stewardess. They were both beautiful, but I preferred this girl a lot more. This was the woman I'd held, kissed and was still desperate to devour. But now she was also the woman I wanted to cloak from sadness and protect from pain.

EIGHTEEN

Hayden

I dialed Landon's number and caught a strain of Avery's perfume. It was sexier and more complex than her professional gloss would indicate—it hinted at the woman beneath the mask. I shook my head, frustrated at the way my thoughts slid to Avery more and more. I had enough to think about with Phoenix and the leak at Wolf Enterprises, but somehow Avery had taken up residence in my mind, day and night. In the days since the evening of fireworks and our kiss, we'd reverted to what we had been when I first arrived on the yacht—guest and crew. Perhaps that was really all we ever had been. Since her tears in my office, she'd only confided in me enough to say that her father had been discharged and that everything was going to be fine. I was relieved, but also disappointed that she'd shut down. I liked her. I enjoyed her smart mind and generous heart, but now all I got to see was the yacht stewardess.

"Any news?" I asked my brother as he answered the phone. Due diligence on Phoenix was uncovering opportunities rather than issues, the risks were as expected and the contract negotiations productive. I'd been on this yacht nearly four weeks and if things continued like this, I might be leaving early. But before I got back to the office—or bought Phoenix—I wanted to understand who'd been betraying me to Cannon all these months.

"Yes, I'm fine, thanks for asking. I had a great weekend, took a woman out for a second date on Saturday which went well, though disappointingly I didn't get laid, and then on Sunday I played lacrosse."

"Lacrosse? Since when?"

"Oh, so you do take some interest in my life beyond whether or not I've found your mole."

"Not really, but if you're going to demand attention like a five-year-old, I'll indulge you a short while. You are my little brother, after all."

"Christ, you're a dick."

Landon no more wanted to share details of his weekend with me than I wanted to hear them, but he liked to make it sound as if I was the less emotional and the more uptight of the two of us. But we both knew there was no way he could have done the job he had without being able to put aside everything other than the moment at hand. We had that in common. Most of the time, at least. "Do you have any news about the leak?"

Landon sighed. "Nothing. You getting Anita to request the information pack doesn't seem to have tipped Cannon off. According to my intelligence, they haven't placed a bid or so much as a made a phone call. But still no clue as to where that additional money came from that she has in her new bank account."

I should be more relieved than I was. Anita was smart. And if she really was the leak, which even after hearing about her newly acquired nest egg, seemed impossible, she'd understand that if she was the only one who knew about the company I was looking to buy, she shouldn't pass that information to Cannon.

"Right, and what about the finance team?"

"The treasurer is clear. We're still digging around the financial controller."

"So, no real progress?" The thought of having to go back to the office, knowing someone was betraying me, wasn't something I relished. I wanted to leave this boat a winner, not still under threat.

"We're eliminating people, which is helpful, and there is one thing. Looks like there's been an attempted break-in at your building."

"In my flat or the building?"

"The building."

"Okay, well that happens from time to time. They weren't trying to get to me, were they?"

"Difficult to say. A panel of glass was removed from the ground-floor windows but apart from that no one is reporting any damage or disturbance. CCTV from the street shows two masked men enter and leave but the building security cameras don't show anything. I'm following up."

Surely this wasn't connected to Cannon. Bribing someone for information was one thing, but breaking and entering? It all seemed to reek of some kind of underground, criminal gang. James Cannon was a pig, but his collar was white. Perhaps it was graying in his old age.

"It could be nothing. But I'm going to check your flat and we're going to check it for surveillance devices."

"Jesus, Landon. This sounds like it's getting out of control. Should the police be involved?"

"I'm on it. I'm probably being paranoid because of what that guy did to Dad, but I'm not taking any chances." We hadn't talked much about James Cannon being at the helm of Cannon. The man who'd tried to destroy my father and succeeded in many ways. We didn't need to go over old ground. Landon understood how serious the situation was. We'd lived the aftermath of James Cannon our whole lives.

"Thanks, Landon. I appreciate it."

"Okay, well I'm too busy to chat like sisters, so fuck off," Landon said.

"Actually, there was something else I wanted to talk to you about. I want to get off this boat." Even saying the words lifted my spirits. Avery still used my satellite phone periodically, and she was in the office and my bedroom to change sheets and towels, fiddle with the loo paper, folding it into shapes and whatever else she did. Her perfume surrounded me at every turn. Everywhere I looked on this boat, there was a shadow or a memory of her—a sign she'd been there and would be back soon. If I couldn't have her, I needed a break.

"What do you mean 'get off the boat'?" Landon asked.

"Like, experience dry land for a day or something."

I wasn't used to not getting what I wanted, and I wanted Avery Walker. I respected Avery's decision, but it didn't make it any easier.

We arrived in Taormina tomorrow and Avery still hadn't had a day off. If I offered the crew the evening off as I'd done before, Avery wouldn't go with them. She might even think I was trying to engineer some alone time with her. I might be a manipulative bastard in business, but I wasn't about to trick a woman into letting me kiss her again. I reckoned the only way Avery would take a break would be if I wasn't onboard. If I was ashore for the night then she'd have no possible excuse to keep working. And she needed a break. I couldn't give her much, but I could give her that.

And I could give myself a break from wanting her. Maybe even find an Italian woman to seduce and bury myself in. Perhaps that would push Avery out of my mind.

"Are you fucking crazy? Everything is working. You're making good progress with your deal, Cannon haven't figured out what you're doing and we're eliminating potential leaks. Why would you jeopardize that?"

Why indeed?

"I'm not suggesting I come back to London," I replied. "I'm just feeling a little stir crazy. I want to go ashore. Overnight." True, but it was only part of the story.

"What? Stay in a hotel or something?"

"Yeah. Maybe get rid of my sea legs. I've been on this thing a month and I just want to get back on dry land for a few hours."

Landon was right—I was in one of the most beautiful places on earth. As well as trying to make things easier on myself, maybe I could enjoy it if I was away from the yacht and everything connected to the Phoenix deal. I had a day or two while I waited for the lawyers to review everything. I could afford to catch my breath. I wanted to see the place Avery was so keen to visit.

"You mean you want to get laid," he said. I didn't respond. I had no desire to discuss my need to fuck Avery Walker out of my system with Landon. "I don't know. We'd need some time to set it up. I'd want to check out the hotel before you got there, and you'd have to do a full sweep for bugs when you got back."

"I do a full sweep twice a day on the yacht anyway so that's not a problem. And I won't do any business on shore or make any calls. I want you to set this up."

He sighed, and I could almost hear the cogs in his brain trying to process what I was saying, trying to find a solution. "I could send in someone to conduct surveillance while you're there. You never know, if we get lucky someone might be following you."

"Lucky?" My brother was a twisted fucker.

"When were you thinking?"

"Day after tomorrow."

I could almost hear the eye roll.

"Okay, leave it with me. I'll find a hotel. I'll also get some security for the boat while you're ashore. It's a good job you've got money. This is going to cost you."

I chuckled. "Just stop whining and make it happen."

Hopefully my being ashore would ease Avery's burden. She'd told me she'd always wanted to explore Taormina—now she'd get the chance. Perhaps it would take her mind off what was happening at home. And maybe I'd stop thinking about her.

Landon could organize this without any consequences for the Phoenix deal, couldn't he? If I didn't conduct any business on shore then the only risk would be someone planting a listening device on me while I was on dry land and me taking it back to the boat. But I could scan anything I brought back. This shouldn't be a problem, and my little brother wasn't the type to not tell me when he thought I was being an idiot. An overnight trip would be worth it. I could distract myself and make Avery happy. Not that the chief stewardess of the *Athena*'s happiness was on my agenda at the moment.

Definitely not.

I was just going stir crazy. I needed to find something else to think about.

NINETEEN

Avery

Nothing made me happier than my dad cracking jokes about the Sacramento Kings' shitty defense. It meant he was feeling better. And I got to hear it because of Hayden's generosity in letting me use his satellite phone. He couldn't have been more thoughtful or concerned. I'd also called my aunt and between the two of us we'd arranged for some additional care for my brother to ease the strain on my dad. He'd been diagnosed with atrial fibrillation and although apparently it was easily managed with the drugs, I wanted him to take it easy.

"All crew, all crew in the mess—five minutes," the captain announced through my radio on my nightstand.

I groaned and peeled myself off the bed. All-crew meetings mid-charter were rarely a good thing. Usually it meant there was a serious complaint or an unexpected change of plans. Surely Hayden would have told me if something was wrong? He'd started to ask Skylar for things here and there, but I hadn't seen him properly interact with anyone other than me and I kinda liked it that way. It was ridiculous but I didn't encourage him to ask Skylar for things. I liked to be the one who got him what he needed. It was my job to ensure guests had everything they wanted, and he was the only guest on this charter, so it made sense I would be his main point of contact. I was the chief stewardess. He was a guest.

A guest, so I shouldn't be kissing him on the top deck while watching fireworks and sipping champagne.

A guest, so I shouldn't be playing our kiss over and over again in my mind.

A guest, so I shouldn't be wondering if he'd ever kiss me again.

I blew out a breath, smoothed my hair back into a ponytail and headed to the mess.

"How's your dad?" August asked as I appeared at the doorway.

I slipped onto the banquette. "All over the Sacramento Kings and their shitty defense, apparently."

She laughed. "Sounds like he's getting back to normal."

Neill high-fived one of the engineers while Eric tried to explain why the joke he'd just told was funny. With twelve of us in the tiny space, it was loud but good-natured.

"Settle down," Captain Moss said as he appeared. He was only ever in the mess for mealtimes and meetings, so the crew often hung out here when we were on break or off shift.

Everyone quieted, and the banquette filled with five others while everyone else leaned on counters and against doorways.

"We're switching things up a little," Captain Moss said.

People exchanged glances and murmured. There hadn't been many changes this charter.

"Mr. Wolf is going ashore tomorrow and staying overnight in a hotel," he continued.

It wasn't unusual for a guest on a longer charter to go ashore overnight, or to stay at a particularly nice hotel or a friend's villa. That wasn't what had my heart thumping in my chest. I just didn't understand why Hayden hadn't said anything to me. I saw him regularly throughout every day. He'd discussed business with me, he'd kissed me but didn't mention he was going ashore overnight? It didn't make sense.

The room grew quieter as everyone waited for Captain Moss to continue. There were two possible scenarios when a guest left the boat. We could end up detailing the yacht from anchor to radio mast, or we could be getting time off. It all depended on how decent the captain was.

"As a result, we all get a day off," Captain Moss said.

Everyone whooped and cheered and despite the uneasiness spreading through my body, I couldn't help but smile at their joy. Even the corners of Captain Moss's mouth threated to curl into a smile.

"Settle down or I might change my mind," the captain said.

The whooping calmed but the excitement was still palpable.

"Tender leaves this boat at ten tomorrow morning and collects Mr. Wolf from shore at nine a.m. the following day. That means you have to be back on this boat, sober and ready to work by eight. Do I make myself clear?"

Everyone grinned from ear to ear, nodding their agreement, and tossed the occasional "Yes, sir" into the excited atmosphere for good measure.

Twenty-four hours in Taormina? That was twenty-three more than I'd ever had before, and if I could have chosen the one place in the Mediterranean to have a day off, Sicily would be the place.

"I want this boat perfect before you go, so get your Q-tips out," Captain Moss warned.

I elbowed August when she groaned. When she'd first started, I'd told her that the bathrooms needed detailing and explained I wasn't joking when I said every inch needed to be cleaned with Q-tips. She'd nearly passed out, but she'd done a good job. She might be a bit flighty and a little too noisy, but she worked hard and that was what mattered.

"Captain," I called as he made for the exit. "I'll stay if you—"

"No. I'll be on board. You're to have the day off with the rest of this lot."

I glanced behind me. The crew had already begun to plan the following day, the boys talking about the bars, the girls, the beaches and cocktails.

"But I don't mind—"

"Take a freaking day off to relax, Avery. This is a gift. Take advantage of it." Conversation over, he swept out.

"Avery," Skylar called. "Isn't Taormina your dream destination? This is fate. There's bound to be a ton of rich, handsome men waiting for me on shore." She squealed and turned back to the table.

Taormina was the place I told everyone about. I'd only managed an hour on shore a couple of times and always yearned for longer. The idea of a whole day there was almost too good to be true

For a split second I remembered my conversation with Hayden about always wanting to come to Taormina. He wouldn't have remembered that, right? This wasn't about me, was it? In another lifetime, we'd go together, explore the narrow streets and the amphitheater, sit in the piazza with the beautiful people while being overlooked by Mount Etna. But that wouldn't be this lifetime.

"The boys are just going to drink all day, aren't they?" Skylar came up to stand beside me and we watched them plan which Italian beers they were going to order.

They'd been weeks without alcohol. I was sure they'd make up for it. "I'd say so."

"I want to lie on a beach. Dinner and drinks in the evening. Somewhere glamorous. Where the beautiful people go," Skylar said.

"Should we get a hotel?" Eric called out to us. "Then you don't need to worry about us wrecking the boat if we come back hammered."

There was no way I was going to book a hotel room. I needed to save every penny.

I put on my best, professional grin. "I don't need to worry about you wrecking the boat because you know if you do I'll kick your ass so hard you won't sit for the rest of the charter."

Eric's smile faltered, but he nodded and turned back to the table. "I think we should *definitely* pay for a hotel."

"Sounds good. Then we can order drinks from the beach. And we have somewhere to change for the evening," August said. "I want to eat pasta in Italy. I'm sure it must taste different, right?" she asked, turning to me.

I smiled. Eating pasta in Sicily sounded just about perfect, even if it was at a table for one. Maybe with some Chianti while people-watching in the piazza, even without Hayden. I tried to hold back a smile, not wanting to get too excited in case Captain Moss came back and told us he'd made a gigantic mistake.

"Ready to top up your tan?" August asked as she came toward Skylar and me, grinning like a Cheshire cat.

I could totally understand why the girls would want to laze on the beach for the day, but I wasn't going to waste the opportunity I had to explore even if I had no one to share it with. I was going to take my dad's advice and take some time for myself, be a tourist, get waited on in a restaurant. I was going to think about nothing but the sun and the buildings and how beautiful everything was. And then Hayden kissing me under the fireworks would no longer be the best thing that had happened to me in seven years.

TWENTY

Hayden

I couldn't remember the last time I'd had nothing to do.

I'd left the tender just before ten with a small overnight bag that included my satellite phone and my bug sweeper. Once I'd checked into the hotel, worked out in the gym and had a shower, my skin had started to itch from boredom and boredom led to more thoughts of Avery. Maybe this hadn't been such a good idea. I'd come ashore to escape Avery Walker and here I didn't even have work to distract me.

I wandered into the lobby, scraping a hand through my still-damp hair. I'd go and explore Taormina, pick up a newspaper, have a coffee, keep my options open—it wasn't like I had plans.

"*Signor* Wolf," the porter addressed me as I strode through the lobby. "Any plans on this beautiful day?"

"Just a little walk," I said. It would be nice to stretch my legs and enjoy solid ground. Maybe I'd run into a beautiful Italian girl who would scorch Avery from my mind.

"Don't miss out on our Greek theater," he continued, smiling at me.

Sophocles was the last thing I was after. I'd come here to relax, and although I might be bored and in need of distraction, I wasn't in the mood for a Greek tragedy. I smiled and continued on my way. The porter followed.

"Turn right, up the hill just a few steps and it's right there. It is a very beautiful view," he said.

I frowned. A panorama wasn't the first thing a theater was ordinarily known for, but with nothing better to do, I thanked him and decided to turn right out of the hotel after all. I was already one coffee down this morning and my second one could wait while I investigated a little. Perhaps it would help take my mind off things.

I slipped my sunglasses over my eyes and headed up the hill. The heat crawled over my skin as if it were trying to steal my breath, and I slowed my pace. I'd grown accustomed to the breeze on the yacht and how it took away the stickiness of the humidity. There was no respite now I was on solid ground—it was a different planet.

As I took long, slow strides along the road, I imagined Avery wandering these streets and a sense of pleasure settled in my gut. She'd always wanted to come here, and I'd made it happen. I'd hated seeing her so upset about her father. I'd wanted to bring her smile back, and I'd hoped a day in Taormina would do that.

Avery had been nothing but professional since that day just nearly two weeks ago, but she remained careful to maintain her distance. I understood there were rules between guests and crew, but I was used to exceptions being made for me.

I was used to getting what I wanted.

I *wasn't* used to wanting a particular woman. It never got to that point.

But I wanted Avery.

I wanted to pull the hairband out of her hair, scrunch up her skirt, untuck her blouse and slide my hands over her skin. I'd seen glimpses of the real Avery beneath the professional veneer, but I wanted to pull that wall down for good. I wanted to unravel her, show her how good I could make her feel, hear her scream my name.

Shit.

So much for distracting myself.

Luckily, before me were the ruins of a Greek theater almost erupting out of the ground. I wasn't going to have to endure a play, just take in the ancient stones.

Someone tugged at my shirt and when I turned a short, elderly lady wearing a headscarf waved a book at me. I bent slightly and tried to see what she was offering me. It was a small guidebook with an image of the orange-pink brick structure right in front of me.

I pulled out my wallet and exchanged my cash for her book and she scurried off to the next potential customer.

I paid the entrance fee and stepped through a cave-like corridor back into the bright sunlight and onto the wooden floor of the amphitheater. On my left the wood continued, built over the original brick-and-stone-stepped amphitheater. Modern seats had been fixed to the boxed-in levels. The place was clearly still used. Toward the back the original brick was exposed and the crumbling, dirty, orange walls stood out against a background of bright blue sky. I turned to take in the whole space. On my right was a wooden stage in front of half-remaining Greek columns and more dilapidated brickwork, the sea and the sky filling in the gaps left by age. It was so perfectly decayed it looked as though a set designer had been here, assembling the background, ready for a performance, but the elements and passing time had created this place's background.

I headed up the steps past the modern seating. When I got to the top I turned and instinctively took half a step back, overwhelmed by what I saw—the blue of the sky bled into the warm sea, which dipped and clung to the curves of the land leading up to Mount Etna looking over everything.

It was stunning. Epic.

Something had led me here, as if I'd been meant to see this. To gain this perspective. The people who'd built this beautiful ruin had climbed these stairs thousands of years ago. Mount Etna had looked over them while they'd worked just as it did now as I worked on the yacht floating in the water below. The sun would keep rising and setting over this land whether or not I bought Phoenix. This beauty would still be here, yet I wouldn't have seen it if it hadn't been for Avery Walker saying it was the place she liked most. What else was I missing out on while I fought to keep a business that wouldn't exist in a hundred years?

Thank God I'd done this and not kept myself cooped up on the boat, pouring over documents. My muscles began to unknot, and I smiled. Taking a deep breath, I tried to commit this picture to memory, wanting to press the history and beauty into my soul somehow.

"Beautiful view, right?" a familiar voice said from beside me.

I turned to see Avery Walker, looking out and sharing the same picture I was drinking in, and now she was the only view I was interested in.

TWENTY-ONE

Avery

When faced with the sweeping vista from the top of Taormina, the only thing I wanted to do was share it with someone. Hayden being there hadn't shocked me. It was as if it was meant to happen because the moment was perfect and he made it more so.

"Hey," he said.

I kept my gaze forward, unwilling to tear myself away from the most perfect view I'd ever seen . . . though Hayden Wolf's sugar-brown skin against his white shirt might be a strong contender to the sight of Mount Etna rising out of the landscape.

"Is it everything you hoped it would be?" he asked.

So he hadn't forgotten I'd wanted to come here.

"More," I said softly.

We stayed gazing out in silence for a while.

"Where's the rest of the crew?" he asked.

"The boys are in an Irish pub just off the piazza and the girls are on the beach."

He didn't respond.

"I got a guide," he said, holding up a pocket-sized booklet with a picture of the amphitheater.

I laughed. Hayden didn't strike me as a man who'd pour over guide books. "Did you read it?"

He shook his head and pushed his hands into his pockets. "I was waiting for you so you could explain it all to me."

I narrowed my eyes. "You were waiting for me?"

He shrugged. "Maybe."

It felt as if we were talking in code, but I didn't have the decryption key.

"Well, the place was built in the third century BC. They don't actually know if it's Greek or Roman because the brick suggests Roman but the way it's laid out—"

Hayden turned to me and placed his hand on my arm. "Stop. I'm not really expecting you to be my guide. You're off duty."

I tried to ignore the press of his fingers. "I just want you to enjoy it."

He held my gaze and slipped his hand from my arm and down my back. It was the act of a lover, a boyfriend, a husband. "Now you're here, I couldn't like it more," he said, then turned back to the view.

Despite the heat, I had to repress a shiver.

A few minutes later a cloud passed over the sun, breaking the spell this place had trapped us in. "What's next?" he asked, turning to me.

"Next?"

"Where do we go now?"

The corners of my mouth quivered. "We? I thought I wasn't on duty."

He cupped my face and swept his thumb over my lips. "You're not. Where do *we* go now?" His tone was matter-of-fact, as if he always touched me as though he owned me, as if I shouldn't be shocked he had his hand on the small of my back as he guided me down the steps.

I should have made my excuses and left. I should've done a lot of things. But being there, in that beautiful place I'd wanted to visit for so long, I just wanted to enjoy it. And I knew I'd enjoy it just a little more with Hayden. We'd run into each other by accident, after all, and if any of the rest of the crew spotted us, I could legitimately say that I'd found him and ended up walking around the island with him. I didn't have to tell them if I enjoyed it, though I knew I would.

I puffed out a stream of breath. "Let's walk around, get lost a little."

"Really?" he asked, smiling at me. "That doesn't sound like you."

"Maybe it's the me that you don't know so well." It was my day off. Today I wasn't a yacht stewardess and Hayden Wolf wasn't a customer.

He nodded. "Then that sounds like an irresistible proposition."

We headed right when we got out of the theater and made our way down the hill. The streets were perfectly uneven, part slate-gray cobble, part asphalt, shaded by the buildings either side of the narrow streets. We had to dodge the scooters as they raced up the hill in the opposite direction and children as they ran past us. It was difficult not to get distracted by the potted flowers tumbling from balconies above us and the noise of the rambunctious Italians as they went about their every day.

I stopped outside a shop window crammed with colored pots and plates, so bright it was as if the colors of the Mediterranean originated from this store.

"You want to go in?" he asked. Was Hayden Wolf about to go shopping with me? This titan of industry who was always so focused and serious was about to browse homewares? Perhaps I didn't know all of him yet either, but despite myself I wanted to.

We headed into the store, suddenly surrounded with a riot of primary colors and robust crockery. "I'm not sure this would look right on the *Athena*." I laughed as I picked up a blue plate covered with pictures of sunshine-yellow lemons.

"A different style for sure," he said, looking at a bowl of ceramic oranges.

"What's your home like back in London?" I asked the question before I realized how personal I was getting. The barrier between guest and stewardess dissolved more and more with each second. I'd been here before, the divide between us lowering to the point I forgot myself and risked too much. Desperate to maintain distance from anything that might cost me my job, I'd spent a lot of time and effort putting that barrier back up. But here, with Hayden, it didn't feel so wrong. In fact, it felt completely and absolutely right.

He frowned as if he were trying to remember his own home. "It's more like the yacht I guess," he said, as if he'd never thought about it before.

"Do you like it?"

"I don't think about it."

"Is this you trying to pretend you're not fussy again?" I elbowed him, but he caught my arm and slid it around his back while putting his hand on my hip. The familiar way he touched me caught me off guard. It was as if he knew my body already, understood how we fit together.

"I'm just not fussy about everything. My home office chair was very expensive and is incredibly comfortable, and my bed is huge and handmade." He pulled me toward him. "Some things I obsess over—others I don't notice. But when I decide I want something, I won't settle for less than *exactly* what I've set my mind on, and I won't rest until I have it."

It was meant to be light conversation but what he was saying had weight. It revealed a lot about him and although I hadn't been digging, it was almost too much to know. I twisted, pulling away from him, and headed toward the exit.

"But the huge bed is important because it gets so much action." I wiggled my eyebrows and dipped under his arm as he held the door open, trying to lighten our conversation. I wanted the day to be fun.

"*Grazie*," Hayden called over his shoulder to the store owner, who was reading his paper behind the counter. "You seem to have a poor impression of me," he said, dipping to speak directly into my ear. "I think you of all people know that my bed hasn't been getting much action recently, but it seems I might have to try harder to impress you."

I grinned but didn't respond. Everything about him was impressive.

"Tell me about your work and why you're on the yacht," I asked as we wove our way through a group of children all dressed in school uniform, heading in the opposite direction. Hayden seemed so committed and obsessive about what he did, I wanted to understand what drove him.

"It will make me sound paranoid if I tell you," he said, grinning at me.

"Try me. Maybe I'll like paranoid."

"It's a long story," he warned.

"Just give me a little shove if I doze off," I said, nudging him with my elbow.

He paused before he spoke. "My mother and father fell in love when my mother was engaged to another man."

Was he changing the subject? I'd thought I was going to be hearing about his business.

"They met at a charity gala. Apparently it was love at first sight. The stuff that only exists in fairy tales."

"That's romantic," I said, wondering if the instant pull I'd had for Hayden had been what his mother had felt for his father.

"Yeah, I think it was for them. But she was already engaged to a business rival of my father's, so things were a little complicated. I don't know the details, just that my mother and father ended up together and that pissed off her ex-fiancé."

"I imagine it would. He must have been annoyed."

Hayden squinted and slid his sunglasses over his eyes. "Annoyed was the least of it. He wanted revenge. And he didn't stop until he'd destroyed the business my father had worked so hard to build up. It took a decade, but when I was about seven my father was declared bankrupt."

"And it was your mother's ex-fiancé who caused it?" I slipped my hand into Hayden's.

"I didn't find out the story until years later. I'd never understood why we moved from a comfortable house in a nice street to a cramped flat above a chip shop. We'd just been told that dad had to find a new job that didn't pay as well. Our parents shielded us from the evil there was in the world. But apparently, ruining my father wasn't good enough. He wants to bury me as well."

"Shit, Hayden. So you've come to the yacht so he can't spy on you?"

He squeezed my hand, acknowledging the connection between us. "Yeah. To buy this company I know he'd steal from under me if he got the chance."

"It must be awful to still be so bitter after so long. Did he ever marry?"

Hayden shrugged. "Yeah. He did. I guess it wasn't about love. It was about power."

I got the feeling there was more he wasn't telling me, but he'd confessed so much I didn't want to push. I liked the idea that he hadn't grown up with money—it made his lack of focus on certain things make sense and why he found it so odd that I would offer to unpack for him. I wanted to know more, but I wanted him to enjoy the few hours he had off rather than focus on the reason he was working so hard, so I swallowed my questions.

We walked up and down hills, hand in hand, for hours as if we were just two tourists, enjoying everything Taormina had to offer—dropping into shops, admiring various vistas. It was everything I'd expected and just a little bit more because I was sharing it with Hayden. He was surprisingly interested in the details around us—the people who all seemed to be in such a good mood, the way some of the houses slanted so much it looked as if they were about to collapse.

The road opened up into a small square with trees in the middle and tables from the cafés dotted between them.

"Coffee?" he suggested.

I nodded, and we found a spot in the shade.

"*Due caffè americano per favore,*" he called to the waitress as he held out my chair for me.

"You trying out your Italian to impress me?"

"Is it working?" he asked, leaning back in his chair, regarding me intently as if he were a painter and I was a bowl of fruit.

I narrowed my eyes as the waitress set our drinks down. "Are you fishing for compliments?"

He tipped his head back and laughed from deep in his belly. "I wasn't, but it did sound a little needy, didn't it? I can order a coffee and a glass of wine but that's about where my Italian begins and ends. The UN isn't going to be calling me up to offer me a career as a translator any time soon." He stroked his jaw with his knuckles. "You're feistier on solid ground."

"This is me. My uniform's back on the boat." I took a deep breath, then I held out my hand. "Avery Walker, nice to meet you."

To my surprise, instead of shaking it, he held it in his and didn't let go. "Hayden Wolf. What you see is what you get." Was he jibing me, accusing me of being a fake?

"My job requires me to be professional, to not always say what I think, to suck it up when guests annoy the crap out of you. That's just life."

He didn't respond right away, just stared at me as if he was taking it all in. "I know. I just like Avery Walker better."

I smiled. "Me too. But I do what I need to in order to succeed at my job. You should understand that—you're in the middle of the ocean for two months to be good at yours."

He raised his arm, resting it on the back of the empty chair next to him, and stroked his thumb across the wooden slat. "I hadn't thought about it like that. I guess it's just a different kind of sacrifice."

I couldn't help but laugh. "Yes, being on a luxury superyacht traveling down the Italian Riviera is *such* a sacrifice."

He smiled, and the way he scanned my face showed he was smiling because I was laughing, as though he took pleasure from my happiness rather than because I was teasing him. Joy bloomed in my chest.

"You sound like my brother," he said. "And it's definitely beautiful, but it's always a sacrifice when you'd rather be somewhere else, doing something else."

I blinked and turned away. I didn't want to talk about sacrifice or what I'd rather be doing—the life I'd thought I'd have before my brother's accident. "Is he like you, your brother?"

"No, not at all. He's the brawn. I'm the brain."

My gaze darted down to his muscled arms, strong thighs and tight abs covered by his white linen shirt. "If you're the brain, I'd like to see his brawn."

"Did you just ogle me?" He sat forward in his chair, his eyes narrowing.

I lifted a shoulder. "Bite me. You said it—it's my day off. You're not my guest today."

He chuckled and sat back.

"So your brother didn't end up like you in a corporate job?"

Hayden shook his head. "I guess he wanted a worthier life." He paused and squinted, vulnerability flashing across his face, though I wasn't sure where it came from.

"That's a huge sacrifice," I said.

"Absolutely." He nodded. "I could never do anything like that. Landon's special, built for duty and honor."

Real adoration passed through his voice. In my experience, it was unusual for anyone rich to value anything but wealth, yet Hayden understood there were more important things.

"All I do is make money, but I try to . . ." He winced, and I sat forward, resting my chin on my hand, wanting to hear what he said next. "It sounds ludicrous, but I try to act honorably. Like a gentleman. In the City, business is generally full of snakes. People wanting to make money out of depriving other people, or getting one over on others." He slid his long legs out in front of him. "I don't believe it has to be like that. I think that if you look after people, your employees, you get much better results than if you treat them like shit. If you respect people, generally you get the same back."

I smiled at him. What was he? Some kind of ethical corporate tycoon? Did such a person really exist?

"Don't get me wrong. I'm no angel. I'm shrewd, I'm demanding and ruthless when I need to be. But I don't break my promises. I reward loyalty and I don't lie. And I never work with those who do."

His jaw tightened, and I could tell his mind had shifted to something else. I couldn't help but focus on the man in front of me. The guy I'd judged as being another spoiled millionaire but was anything but. He respected, even idolized, his brother who'd served his country. Hayden was someone who wanted to do the right thing *and* make money.

I'd thought he was just a hot piece of ass, when really, he was so much more.

He swept his thumb across my cheekbone. "For the record, you can objectify me any time you want."

My pulse danced in my wrist. He was acting like this was a date, as if we were lovers. Was it? Would we be? Though today was my day off, Captain Moss wouldn't draw such a clear distinction between on-duty and off-duty behavior, but the more time I spent with Hayden, the more the line between us blurred and faded.

"But what about your brother?" I smiled. "Can I objectify him too?"

He withdrew his hand and chuckled. "That I might object to. I'm not one to share."

I tried to bite back my grin, enjoying the way he'd acknowledged the connection we had. "I noticed. Are you not planning to have any guests on the *Athena* at all?"

He picked up his coffee, his large hand dwarfing the delicate white cup. He took a sip, then shook his head. "I'm here to work—you know that."

I pulled my bottom lip between my teeth, trying to hold myself back from leaning over and tasting the coffee on his lips. "I know. But you're here. I thought maybe things had eased up or you had decided to take in more of the Med."

He pulled his wallet from his pocket and left some notes under the saucer of his coffee cup, then stood and held out his hand for me. "You said you'd always wanted to see Taormina, so here we are."

I stood and he scooped up my hand and we began walking back up the hill.

"Surely we didn't stop here for me?" It had occurred to me it was a huge coincidence that the only time he'd come ashore was in the one place I'd told him I most wanted to come, but I hadn't really thought that was why he'd stopped here.

"Partly. I wanted you to have the chance to see it."

My heart clunked against my ribcage. This stop *had* been about me. This was the real Hayden Wolf, the Hayden Wolf who believed in treating his employees well and never breaking his promises.

"And given you're not one to take a day off, I thought if I came ashore, you'd be forced to . . ."

There was absolutely no point in even pretending I could resist him for a moment longer.

I pulled at his hand, dragging us beneath a stone arch and into a tiny walkway between the houses. "Kiss me," I said, leaning against the brick. I'd never had anyone do something so thoughtful, so selfless, for me, let alone a man who had no reason to think about me at all—I was just the hired help.

He didn't need to be asked twice. He brought his hands to my face, and his gaze dipped to my lips then back to my eyes before he finally placed his lips to mine.

It wasn't enough. I needed more. I slid my hands around his ass, and up and under his shirt to his hot, hard back and pulled him toward me. He groaned, his tongue slipping between my lips as he ground himself against me. One hand trailed down my neck, slipping my top from my shoulder, exposing my skin to the hot air. He pulled back and looked at me.

"You're so beautiful." He dove toward my neck, sucking and biting, sending off buzzes and pops across my skin.

Threading my fingers through his hair, encouraging the press of his skin against mine, I arched into him, wanting more, more, more.

At that moment I didn't care if the rest of the crew filed past us or Captain Moss tried to interrupt. All I wanted was Hayden Wolf's mouth on mine, his hands roaming my body, his erection pressed against my stomach.

Suddenly, he jerked away and took a step back. "I won't be able to stop if I touch you any longer," he said and blew out a breath.

I pulled my bottom lip between my teeth, feeling a little wanton at being able to drive such a self-controlled man to the edge.

He steadied his breathing, shook his head and took my hand, pulling me under the archway again and resuming our walk back up the hill.

His pace was quicker than before, as if we were no longer wandering and now had a purpose or a destination.

"Where are we going?" I asked.

"To my hotel. We're going to have dinner. You're going to need your strength."

"I am?" I asked, jogging a couple of steps to keep up with him.

"You most certainly are, Avery Walker, because I'm going to be keeping you up all night."

A warm shiver ran down my spine. He wanted me just as much as I wanted him. There was no point in pretending. No longer any chance of holding back with this man.

I was off duty, the crew was miles away and I just wanted some time free of worrying about the consequences of anything. A few hours of Hayden before he went back to being forbidden fruit. A few moments that were about me and my wants, needs and desires.

TWENTY-TWO

Hayden

I didn't usually do this—take a woman to dinner, flirt, imagine her naked and clamped around my cock. But I was enjoying this buildup, the talking, the way she looked at me as if I were more fascinating than this beautiful place we were in. Of course, I'd noticed how attractive Avery was as soon as we'd met on the main deck a month ago, but the pull toward her had grown almost without me noticing. She was clever, good at her job, and perceptive. She was funny, feisty and vulnerable, and clearly devoted to her family. She also had an incredible arse, the tiniest waist and a killer smile.

I liked her inside and out. I wasn't sure I'd ever thought that about a woman before.

My non-professional relationships with women were usually a lot simpler. I'd meet them in a bar, on the tube, or coming out of a building—it didn't matter—and then the clock started ticking. How long would it take before we fucked? It was usually less than an hour, it rarely involved dinner and never included handholding. Then there were the two or three women I had established relationships with —they'd call me or I'd call them when I just needed to fuck. In either case, for me, it was all about the physical.

There was no doubt that every part of my body wanted every part of Avery's, but I was enjoying her mind too. Her laugh, the stories of the rich and famous on the yachts she worked on, the look of hope in her eyes when she told me her father was doing well.

"How's your brother doing with your dad being sick?" I asked as we sat opposite each other on the dining terrace of my hotel.

She glanced away from me and out at the darkening sky. "Good, I think. He has a new physical therapist and he's made progress with her."

"You said he had an accident. Was it a sporting injury?"

She blinked slowly. "Not really. We were stupid." She paused, and I didn't fill the silence. "We were swimming in the river. All the neighborhood kids would go every summer. You'd get all ages, from all different friendship groups, the cool kids mixing with the geeks, you know?" Her gaze flitted back to me for a second before resting on the sky.

"We did it every year. Every now and then we'd get chased away by the landowner, but we always went back—it was too much fun." She shrugged. "Anyway, one afternoon we went down to the river; we'd swing on this rope attached to a tree and jump off into the river. I fought to go before Michael. I played the older sister card." She shook her head. "I should have been looking out for him, not competing with him."

Her eyes didn't leave the sky, not because she was transfixed by the darkening view, but because she was remembering, or trying not to.

"Then it was his turn and . . . he let go in the right place, just like all the times before. We all ignored the no-swimming signs. But I was older. I should have followed the rules. Kept him safe." Her words came out fast and desperate and then stopped abruptly.

I reached out across the table and pressed her hand between mine. "It wasn't your fault. You were just being kids."

She shook her head. "He hit a rock. His spine fractured. In the beginning he was paralyzed from the neck down."

"It wasn't your fault," I repeated.

She exhaled and looked down at her lap, as if she'd brought herself back to the here and now, away from the memories.

"It's just easier to live with some days than others. My dad never blamed me. Never seemed angry, just took it all in his stride. We just got unlucky. Even when my mom left I never saw him crack. He must have been heartbroken but he never let it show. He acted like it was all normal."

I wanted to ask about her brother's injuries now and ask her why her mother had left. But I'd reminded her of too much pain tonight and I wanted to heal, not hurt. "He sounds like an incredible man."

Her eyes went glassy and she smiled. "He really is." She tilted her head. "And Michael too."

"And you're here, paying the bills, following the rules, making sure everyone is happy like it's your responsibility to ensure everyone's looked after. Are you atoning for your sins or just incredible? A little of both, I think." She was all about honor and duty—both traits I admired in the people close to me.

"Can I get you anything else?" the waiter asked, interrupting us.

Avery tried to pull her hand from mine, but I tightened my grip.

"Do you want a coffee?" I asked her.

She shook her head, the golden strands of her chestnut-brown hair highlighted by the fairy lights filling the terrace.

"Just the bill please," I said to the waiter.

"We can't see Etna anymore," she said, glancing over at the darkened sky that had swallowed up the volcano.

"I think we can be sure it's still there."

"That's comforting, isn't it?" she asked. "I'll probably never sit in this spot again, won't ever come back here again, but I'll always know what the view looks like. It won't change."

I frowned. "You won't ever come back? Is it not what you'd thought it would be?"

She reached across the table and slid her palm over the top of our joined hands. "It's so beautiful, but I've been doing the Med season for seven years and this is the first time I've been." She shrugged. "I doubt I'll make it again."

My gut churned at her resignation. It was as if she knew that her life wasn't about pleasure or enjoyment—it was about service and duty. She'd accepted her fate without any bitterness. I struggled to accept that future for her. What was it with this girl? I wanted to fix everything for her, rearrange the world to see that smile on her face. "Never say never," I said. "Etna will be here in the morning when the sun rises."

I released her hands, pushed my chair out and stood. It was time for it to be just the two of us. I wanted this selfless woman to myself.

I held my hand out and she paused before accepting it. I led her through the tables. We'd not talked about it, but today we'd morphed into a couple, taking a romantic break together. Going back to my room was the next obvious step, wasn't it?

"Hayden." She slowed as I led us into the hotel lobby.

I glanced back at her.

"If anyone was to find out."

I turned to her. "I promise they're not going to. But if you don't want to do this, then I'll walk you back to—"

"That's the problem, Hayden." She cupped my neck in her hand. "I want you too much. I'm risking everything."

I grasped her wrist. I had no right to ask her to risk anything for me, but the selfish bastard in me couldn't give her up. "I promise everything will be fine. No one will know."

For a fleeting second, I wondered what would happen tomorrow. If she lost her job I could find her something else, something better, couldn't I? But what if I still wanted her? How could one night with her ever be enough? But even if it wasn't, I couldn't give her anything else. It wasn't how I led my life.

She pressed her hand against my chest. "Let's go."

Silently, we made our way to my room. With each step my body wound tighter and tighter and by the time I opened the door my heart was thundering in my chest and my muscles threatened to rip through my clothes.

I slid a hand around her waist and cupped her ass, pulling her toward me as I backed into the suite and shut the door. I exhaled at the click of the lock. Finally, for the first time ever, we were alone.

In private.

We'd spent time together in my office, but we were always only a few feet away from her colleagues. Even watching the fireworks, we'd been aware that Captain Moss wasn't far away. Here, it was just us—Hayden and

Avery. Not guest and stewardess. Right here, at this moment, time was suspended—nothing existed outside of this room.

I pushed her against the wall, resting my forehead to hers. I couldn't rush this. I had to keep my lust from boiling over.

"Hey," I said.

"Hey," she replied, placing her palms on my chest, her fingers sneaking between the buttons of my shirt.

I rolled my hips against hers. "I want you so badly. I've waited so long."

"And now we're here, in this room, the door's locked and it's like we're stepping out of our reality."

Her voice was breathy, and her eyes wide as if she was desperate for me to agree. She didn't want to be wrong about her interpretation of things. She needed my reassurance and there was something about the fact I could do that, anything, for *her* instead of it always being the other way around that shot testosterone through my body and blood to my dick. That was how it should be.

"Yeah. Nothing else exists. Just me and you. Here and now."

She sighed in response.

I pulled her hand from my shirt as she popped open a button. "You first," I said and walked her backward toward the bed. "This needs to come off." I pulled up her shirt, focusing on the skim of my fingers across her ribcage, and tossed it behind me before sinking my teeth into the top of her breasts. I groaned. I'd fantasized about this and now here I was, and the feel of her was even better than I had imagined. I delved my tongue down her cleavage, wanting to go deeper, further, take more. I trailed my tongue up to the dip between her collarbones. She gasped and arched against me as if she wanted me as much as I wanted her, as if that were possible.

I pulled at her skirt. "And this. It needs to come off." I slid it down, pressing my lips to hers, worried if I pulled my mouth from her body, somehow I'd never be allowed back.

I stepped away to take her in. She looked like a fucking goddess in just her pale blue underwear.

I nodded slowly in approval. "I'm going to taste you," I whispered into her ear, sliding my fingers over her lace-covered pussy, my other hand on her ass, keeping her in place. I dropped a kiss on her lips then sank to my knees.

Her wetness was already soaking through the material of her knickers and I gritted my teeth, wondering if I could hold back from fucking her until I made her come for the first time.

I scraped my thumb along the seam of the lace and pushed my fingers underneath, as she threaded her fingers into my hair. Her slick juices coated my fingers and I wondered how long she'd been worked up like this. Since I'd locked the door? Since holding my hand at dinner? Since I'd touched her at the theater?

I grunted at the thought of her wet for me all day, shoved the lace to one side and buried my face in her hot pussy as if I'd find the answer there. She was sweet and wet and her small gasps sent electric currents right to my cock. I tried to ignore everything but the smell of her, and the way her pussy felt like home. I pulled at the lace, dragging it down so I could get more of her. I circled her clitoris and traced my tongue down to her entrance and back up. Her right knee buckled, and I grinned against her wet skin.

"You lose your balance?" I tipped my head back and she grinned sleepily down at me, drugged by my touch.

I slid my fingers up the back of her thighs to the juncture of her perfect arse and around to her hips. "Lie back on the bed."

She frowned. "I want your mouth on me."

I chuckled. "I'm not going to deprive you, but I don't want you to fall."

She stepped back, hit the bed and lay down, spreading her legs, revealing her pussy in the soft glow of the bedside lamp. She was fucking perfect.

I hooked my arms under her thighs, greedy for more, desperate to make sure she couldn't move away from me when she came. I wanted to feel every jolt, every spasm I created.

I worked my tongue through her folds, her hips restlessly shifting under me as she alternated between squirming and thrusting. The pleasure I was able to give her inflated my chest and tightened my balls.

She arched her back and I shuddered when her fingers scraped through my hair as she came, screaming.

"Oh. God. Yes."

The elongated vowels buzzed against my skin, and I was sure I'd never been so hard in my life.

I stood, not taking my eyes from her as she flopped her arms over her head and sighed deeply. "Man, you're good." She slid one knee up and tilted it to the side, covering her pussy, and grinned as if she were in a blissful bubble.

I wanted to be there with her. I wanted to be exactly where she was all the time.

I stripped out of my clothes then grabbed the condoms I had in my wallet. There were four and I made a mental note to buy a condom factory to ensure I had a crate wherever I went. Four wouldn't be close to enough. I'd need to fuck this woman again and again and again. Keep her in my bed for the next four weeks. Fuck Phoenix. Fuck whoever was leaking information from Wolf Enterprises—the only thing I needed was to be inside this woman.

I rolled the latex over my dick and crawled over her, caging her under me. She clamped her hand over my shoulders, her index finger stroking up my neck. I squeezed my eyes shut, trying to block out the feel of her fingers on my skin, her touch enough to drive me to the edge. I nudged her knees apart and settled between them, pressing my cock against her wet, soft pussy.

I stilled and opened my eyes to stare into hers.

Her gaze was soft and encouraging, as if we'd been lovers a lifetime and she already knew my tells, understood how desperate I was for her.

"I want it. So badly," she whispered, her voice lazy and sexy.

"How?" I asked. I needed to fuck her, but I wanted to know how she liked it. "You want it hard? Like you're just here to be fucked? Or do you want it long and deep, like slow torture?"

"I want it all," she said. "I want to get fucked by you every which way."

I groaned because that was exactly what I needed to hear. I had free rein with her body and it was the best gift she could have given me. I sank into her as deep as I could go, her fingers pressing into my skin as if it was almost too much. My mind burst from the perfection of her. She was beautiful, and tight and mine.

I let out a gasp as I nudged the end of her. Fuck she felt good—tight and needy.

She was still wearing her bra, her nipples pointing through the thin lace. Greedy for more of her, I pulled down the cups, revealing the rosy, pink buds. I clamped my mouth around one, slowly, carefully, sinking my teeth into her flesh. She clenched nicely around my cock and her eyes widened, as if she wanted to ask me if I was going to stop, wondered if it was going to hurt. I wouldn't and it would. A little.

She screamed and it turned into a groan, the pleasure slicing through the burst of pain. Fucking perfect.

I released her and tugged at the lace. "Take it off," I growled.

She fumbled behind her, snapped open her bra and shrugged it off. Her freshly bitten breast was red, the white of my teeth marks still visible against her skin. It would sting for a few days and the thought had me pushing farther into her. I rewarded her endurance by pulling out and shoving back in as she clamped her hands around my neck, pushing her thumb against my hammering pulse. If she was trying to calm me, it didn't work, the small, intimate gesture only notched up my desire.

I couldn't hold back any longer. I needed to fuck.

I didn't know where to look—the sleepy desire in her eyes, the bounce of her breasts every time I pushed inside her, the tilt of her hips—everything was perfect.

She moaned and the vibration moved down her body and along my dick, right to my core. I kept fucking her. I wanted to make this last but needed to get to the end at the same time. It was just too good. She was just too much. I doubled down, fucked her harder, my gaze flitting from her face, to her chest, to where we were joined. The clench of her pussy and bite of her nails stole my concentration.

I slipped my hand beneath her arse, tilting her hips toward me and she whimpered at the change in angle, her orgasm seconds away. My heart pounded against my breastbone and I wanted to come before it burst out of my chest. Her breathy moan had me focusing on her face and I watched as a look of disbelief crossed her face and she silently screamed her orgasm.

Her expression and her tightening pussy had me pushing into her once more, then again and then one last time, pouring every ounce of energy into her, all my effort spent. I collapsed on her with a grunt, then pulled her close, needing her to see what she did to me.

Shit.

Fuck.

What was that?

My breathing slowed and I realized I was twice her size and needed to move. I rolled to my back, but she tightened her grip and I took her with me so she was on top. I traced my hands down her back and squeezed her perfect ass.

"What did you just do to me?" she whispered against my chest. She was in my head again. Something shifted. What we'd just done—how she'd made me feel . . . Maybe it was because she'd been the first I'd had in over a month. Perhaps it was because I'd wanted her for longer than I'd wanted any woman without satiating my need. But I didn't think so. It was as if our bodies were designed to be together. As if I could read what she needed, and it was exactly what I *had* to give her.

Before I could work out what that meant or convince myself I'd felt it before and just forgotten, she shifted, pressing her palms against my chest and lifting herself up so she could straddle me.

"I think I might have lost consciousness there for a second," she said, smiling at me. It wasn't her stewardess smile. It was sexy and teasing and warm, and I reached for her hips, wanting as much of my flesh to connect with hers as possible. She slid forward and I slipped out of her. I sat up and pulled off the condom, tied a knot in it and dropped it on the shirt I'd discarded by the bed.

I turned back to Avery as she slid her pussy over my cock, pulling her bottom lip between her teeth.

She wanted more.

And I wanted to give her everything she desired.

Her breasts pushed together as she flicked her hips, teasing my cock, which hadn't had a chance to fully soften. She was slippery wet, her desire coating my dick. She might have just been the sexiest thing I'd ever seen.

She tipped her head back and the ends of her hair skimmed her waist.

Reaching across to the bedside table, I grabbed another condom before things got too far. This woman wanted to be fucked every way, and the temptation to fuck her bareback grew in me but there was no way I'd do that. She slid back, giving me access to put on a fresh condom, her tongue dipping out to wet her lips as she watched. My dick strained, trying to reach her mouth. Before I could roll the latex to the root of my cock, she knelt, nudging at my hands as if she was desperate for me to finish so she could get me inside.

Her impatience gave me a sense of smug satisfaction—I liked greedy Avery. I liked naked Avery. I liked everything about this fucking woman.

She linked her fingers through mine and held herself steady, hovering above me, my crown at her entrance.

She pressed her lips together and blinked, readying herself.

Slowly, she sank onto my cock, stretching to let me in. The pressure was the only thing I could think about, as though I'd lost my vision and the only sense I had left was the way her pussy felt. When I could see again, the sway of her breasts—high and full and perfectly curved—came into focus as she moved. Conflict swam through my veins. I needed the drag of her pussy, but couldn't wait for her mouth. I wanted her sitting on me, wanted to be buried in her. I wanted her on top of me and underneath me, moaning and wearing that sexy smile. I just couldn't get enough.

I swept my hands up her thighs and sank my thumbs just below her hip bones. It was as if they fit perfectly for me. I guided her, slowly, so my cock pulled out, enough to feel it but not enough that I missed her and then pressed her back. I closed my eyes. After the first, frenzied lust, this was just what we both needed—a slow, unhurried fuck. Something we could savor. And though I knew we'd be up all night, exploring each other's bodies, I also knew it wouldn't be enough. I'd want her again. And again. Just as I opened my mouth to talk about tomorrow, she slid forward so only my tip was in her. She pressed a finger to my lips.

Did she know what I was thinking? Did she understand that I wanted to see her again? That I didn't know how we'd make it work but I'd find a way? My attention was caught by the movement of her breasts and I reached out and pressed them together as she slid back on my dick and leaned back, out of reach.

I couldn't take any more. I needed to run this show.

I sat up and flipped us over. "On your front," I growled. The languid fucking was over. I was in charge and I wanted her whimpering for me.

She smiled as if it were part of her plan all along and then rolled to her front, propping herself up on her elbows. Her hair tumbled over bronzed skin, and I pushed it back over one shoulder so I could see all of her perfectly smooth back. I leaned forward and pressed a kiss between her shoulder blades, tracing my thumb down the river of her spine. Christ, she was perfection from every angle.

She glanced back at me over her shoulder and lifted her arse provocatively.

I grunted and shoved into her, crass and raw, and she moaned as though I'd just made all her dreams come true. She collapsed on her front, extending her arms over her head, bracing her hands against the headboard. Good. She knew this was going to be hard and rough and brutal—knew, and wanted it anyway.

I pulled out and thrust back in, the effort and pleasure drawing a guttural roar from the center of me.

I leaned over her, my arms to either side, and dipped to press my lips against her neck.

"Yes," she whispered. "Please." She huffed out a breath as I pulled out. "More."

Arms flexed, I thrust into her, my body heating and the edges of my hair dampening. It was so good, but I wanted it to be *more* for her. I wanted it to be the best. *I* wanted to be the best for her.

"Oh God, oh God, oh God," she mumbled, all her words running into each other, and she scrambled for breath, her fingers curling, her body tensing.

"See how good it is?" I grunted close to her ear. "See how my cock loves to fuck you?"

She whimpered and relief flooded me at the knowledge it was as good for her as it was for me. "See how I make you feel?"

She screamed and her body tensed as she came around my cock, but I couldn't stop, couldn't even slow down.

I was chasing something—my orgasm, her, life. I didn't know but I thrust and thrust and then I was there, and in that moment I had everything I ever wanted.

TWENTY-THREE

Avery

It was as if I were walking in a field of cotton wool and sunlight as I floated along the street. My body should have been heavy from lack of sleep, but it was soft and light, as if gravity had given up on me as I made my way back to the tender. I wanted to feel like that forever. I resisted the urge to spin full circle in the street like an extra in the *Sound of Music*, but it took effort.

The sun was up but the light was dusky, as if the day's eyes weren't fully open yet. The streets were quiet, shutters still closed. I didn't know how long I'd been walking so I glanced at my watch. It was twenty minutes before the tender left for the yacht. I'd be fine. I was only a few minutes away.

I passed a man unloading boxes of vegetables from the back of his Vespa and waved. "*Buongiorno*," he called.

"It's a beautiful morning," I replied, even though I knew he probably wouldn't understand me. But it *was* a beautiful morning and I wanted to shout it out loud. A joyous morning after an incredible night.

Running into Hayden at the theater had seemed like a coincidence, but today it felt bigger than that. As though it had been *inevitable*. I glanced down, embarrassed at the images flashing through my head. The things he'd done with my body? No man had ever made me feel the way Hayden had. He'd unlocked a whole different part of me last night, discovered someone I didn't know existed. Hayden looked at me as though he knew exactly what I was thinking at every moment—the need, the desire, the vulnerability—as though we'd connected body and mind.

I turned left, and the road sloped steeply under me as it led down to the harbor. I didn't feel tired. We must have fallen asleep at some point because when I'd woken, I'd been tucked into Hayden's body, my back to his front, and I'd had to lift his heavy arm from around my waist to escape. I grinned. I couldn't wait to see him later.

The shore came into view and I spotted the tender immediately. Eric was bent over looking at something, but he was the only one there. He wouldn't have been expecting me to stay on the mainland last night. I was the one known for enforcing the rules, not breaking them. Of course, no one could find out what had happened between Hayden and me. We hadn't discussed it, but things had to remain as they'd always been. Nothing had changed. Yesterday was yesterday. Last night was last night. Today Hayden would return to being my client.

Unease settled in my stomach. That wasn't what I wanted. The thought of going the rest of my life without feeling how I did last night, without spending more time with the man who could elicit the sounds, feelings and memories that Hayden had, tasted like vinegar on my tongue.

Lost in thought, my mood slightly soured, I turned right as I reached the seafront. It was deserted other than a man on a bench facing the sea and reading a newspaper. He closed it as I approached and smiled. He didn't take his eyes off me as I continued toward him, which wouldn't have bothered me because Italians tended to be . . . obvious in what they found interesting. But this man wasn't Italian. His hair was ginger and his newspaper was British.

"Avery?" he asked.

I stopped and fixed my mouth with a professional grin. "Do I know you?"

"No," he said as he set his newspaper beside him and stood. "I'm Phil and I know you work on the *Athena*. I was rather hoping I could ask you a couple of questions."

It was usually paparazzi rather than journalists who approached the crew, but this guy knew my name. He didn't seem like a journalist either. I stepped away from him and continued back to the tender, aware of him following me, my heart beginning to clatter in my chest. Without the slope of the hill to give me height, I'd lost sight of Eric, but he must have been less than a two-minute walk away. How had this man known my name and what did he want?

"You're a stewardess on the *Athena*, I understand."

I didn't react, just concentrated on keeping my gait steady, but the stranger caught up. No doubt he'd be able to outrun me if I was to break into a sprint. He wasn't big, but he was stocky and fit looking. The rich liked to use the phrase that wealth attracted wealth but all too often I'd found that wealth attracted trouble.

"It's a beautiful yacht," he said.

He was right, but I wasn't going to engage with him.

"What do you know about Hayden Wolf?" he asked, as if we were talking about the weather.

Did he know Hayden? Who was this guy?

"I'm doing some research. I need some information."

If this guy was a friend of Hayden's, he had no need to approach me. And if he wasn't a friend, did that make him an enemy?

"I just want to know what he's working on. Who does he talk to on the phone? That kind of thing."

I kept walking and kept quiet even though I really wanted to ask him who he was and what he wanted information on Hayden for.

"I can offer you money," he said. "Five thousand US dollars."

Five thousand dollars? That was a big sum of money. I couldn't remember being offered more than a few hundred, even when big Hollywood stars were on board. And how did this Phil guy even know Hayden was on the boat? And how did he know who I was? I shrugged. "I have nothing to say."

"Think about," he said. "There's nothing to lose. I just want a few innocuous details and you'll get a lot of money in return."

It was a lot of money.

"You could shop. Travel. What would you spend it on?"

An extra five thousand dollars worked out to over thirty physical therapy sessions. That was nearly seven weeks of care for my brother. But I couldn't sell Hayden out. I knew how private he was. "I don't know any details. I just serve dinner and change bedding."

"I'm sure a clever girl like you knows more than you think you do. You've already confirmed he's on the boat, so thank you for that."

I snapped my head around. "I did no such thing."

"But you didn't deny it, and that's as good as a confirmation as far as I'm concerned."

Shit, had I given Hayden's location away? He was so careful, so private about everything. It would be horrifying to be the person who fucked that up for him. "I didn't confirm or deny anything. It's none of your business who's on my yacht."

"If the information's good, the money could go up," he said, ignoring my denial. My bliss seeped away, and I wanted to grab him by the collar and force him to confess that I hadn't confirmed who our guest was, but of course, I'd just make things worse. It would cement what he clearly already knew.

"Five thousand dollars? Come on, it's easy money. Just tell me what he's working on, who he's talking to. Think of it as a tip. You're used to tips, right?"

Easy money? Was there any such thing? Five thousand dollars would mean a great deal for my family. Didn't I owe more loyalty to my family than a near-perfect stranger? If I asked my dad I knew what he'd say. He'd tell me my character was priceless. I couldn't take the money for my family when I knew they'd be disappointed if they ever found out how I'd come by it.

As we rounded the corner, the tender came into view.

"Eric," I shouted, and I waved when he looked up. I turned to the man. "I don't have anything to say to you, sorry," I said, then broke into a run. It wasn't worth it. I would just work harder for bigger tips rather than take money to steal secrets and sell them. That wasn't how I was raised, and more than I wanted that extra money, I wanted to be my father's daughter.

I didn't look to see if he was following me. I just focused on Eric, the tender and getting back to the yacht.

"Hey, I thought you'd go back to the yacht last night," Eric said, taking my hand as I stepped into the boat. "You weren't at dinner."

I frowned as I turned to see Phil had disappeared. I hadn't told him anything, yet he'd twisted it and made me feel bad.

"Avery?"

I turned away to look at Eric. "Sorry, yeah." Should I tell Eric about the approach from Phil? Maybe he'd approached other members of the crew while they'd been ashore. What had they told him? Was Hayden under surveillance or something?

"Did the guy I saw you with get lucky?"

It took me a couple of seconds to see which dots he'd connected. Eric had assumed the man I'd been approached by was my lover. I'd not thought about what I was going to say about where I'd been last night. I'd been too wrapped up in the shadows of last night, still drunk on Hayden's touch, to think through my excuses and get my story straight. I shrugged. "You can't ask me that," I said and winked at him.

Eric clearly hadn't recognized the guy, so perhaps Phil had only approached me. I'd mention it to the captain so he could remind everyone to take their duty of confidentiality seriously. I wasn't sure if I'd tell Hayden. I'd not revealed anything to Phil but whoever he was, he'd intimated that I had. I hated the thought Hayden might get the same impression, might believe I wasn't on his side or didn't have his best interests at heart.

I knew the truth. But would he believe me? Or was it better to just keep quiet?

TWENTY-FOUR

Hayden

"Can anyone here play chess?" I asked as I wandered into the galley. I was waiting for a phone call from the U.S. and had forty minutes to kill. As the deal progressed, the bulk of the work I needed to do had tapered off and I became increasingly reliant on the lawyers to move things along.

Three people turned to look at me, and though Avery kept her head down, the blush in her cheeks was all the attention I needed.

"Not me. I'm a card man," Neill said.

"I can set you up with a Jet Ski if you like?" Eric offered.

I shoved my hands in my pockets. "I only have forty minutes."

"Avery, you do that thing on the board. Isn't that chess?" August asked.

Avery looked up. "Backgammon," she said simply.

"That will do," I replied. I enjoyed the thought of some one-on-one time with Avery, even with the rest of the crew milling about. "Come on, Walker." I turned and headed to the smaller salon and dining room, where the games were kept.

"What are you doing?" Avery hissed, bending to pull out the red leather backgammon set from the sideboard.

I frowned. "Killing some time until the next draft of the agreements is circulated. What's the problem?"

"Main deck?"

"Sure, do you want a drink? Skylar," I called, and she popped her head out of the galley. "Can you get me a glass of water please? Avery, what do you want?"

Avery glared at me, so I shrugged. "That's fine, just the water."

Taking the backgammon set, Avery headed out to the main deck.

"You can't offer me a drink like I'm your guest, Hayden. It's weird."

"It's weirder that you're at my beck and call after . . ."

I'd woken up to an empty bed this morning, but I couldn't remember having fallen asleep. We'd fucked until we were both raw and exhausted, but neither of us had talked about what happened next. I hadn't told her that this didn't feel like a one-time deal for me.

I couldn't remember ever *knowing* I'd want to fuck a woman again before I'd fucked her for the first time. These feelings and experiences were new. Different. *Avery* was different.

"It is what it is," she said, sliding the fastening of the case open and laying the board flat on the table. "I have something I need to tell you later," she said as she pulled out the red and cream counters and began arranging them on the board so they were completely aligned.

I knocked her hands out of the way. "Stop. I'm red."

She shrugged. "That's fine." She nudged my hands away, trying to place the red counters on the red and cream triangles in front of me. "Did you hear what I said?" she asked.

I stroked my hands over hers. "I can set out my own counters."

"You don't like me doing things for you?" she asked.

"I like you doing things *to* me," I replied, remembering how her eyes watered when my cock hit the back of her throat.

She sank her teeth into her bottom lip and her blush told me she was remembering the same thing.

"Hayden," she whispered.

Christ, she was so fucking sexy when she blushed. So innocent. So perfect. I took the red counters from her hand and linked my fingers through hers. Our eyes locked and for a few seconds the rest of the world melted away. A horn from another boat sounded and she pulled away, trailing her fingers along mine as if she was losing my touch reluctantly.

"When we're alone, I'm not your guest. I'm Hayden. Understand?"

Her eyes flickered behind me. "But we're not alone. That's the issue. Deck crew are twenty feet away for all you know. Skylar will arrive with your water at any second." She set the cream dots on the triangles. "You *are* my guest while you're on this yacht."

Her gaze flickered up to meet mine and she grinned.

"You gotta give this girl a break and act like a guest or I'm going to get fired, and you of all people know I can't afford for that to happen." She was talking as much to herself as she was to me. The pull between us was undeniable.

I was proud that I understood why keeping her job was so important to her. The fact she'd told me how paying for her brother's medical expenses was the reason she was here made me feel important. Christ, I ran a multi-billion-dollar company and knowing something private about Avery Walker was what made me feel important. How did she have that much power over me? Perhaps it was simply because she was a better person than I could ever be.

"I didn't get to see you this morning," I whispered.

She raised one eyebrow at me as she finished laying out her counters. "I think you saw quite a lot of me last night *and* this morning," she whispered.

I couldn't resist that pouty little mouth and teasing eye roll. I reached across and swept my thumb across her bottom lip.

For a second we were back in that hotel—in a private space, the two of us the only key holders.

The swish of the electric doors interrupted us, and I moved my hand, but it was too late. We'd been caught.

Avery's soft eyes slid into sadness as she looked up to see who had come through. It wasn't until Skylar placed the water in front of Avery that I saw she wouldn't meet my gaze—or Avery's. Skylar's cheeks pinked, and I knew for sure she'd seen everything.

"Thank you, Skylar," I said.

"Can I get you anything else?" she asked, eyeing the closing doors as if she were being timed and if she didn't get through before they shut she'd be stuck in this awkward situation.

"No thank you," I replied, trying to catch her eye to see if I could figure out what she was thinking.

I'd fucked up. I had no idea what the dynamic between

Avery and Skylar was like. Would Skylar report her? Did she want Avery's job?

Skylar scurried away.

"I'm sorry—"

The scrape of Avery's chair, teak against teak, cut me off. "For me, please go down to your office, while I . . ." She shook her head. "I'll come and find you later. I need to tell you something anyway."

"Of course," I said. Never had I been incapable of controlling myself with a woman. What was happening to me? Had I just ruined everything with an uncharacteristic lack of self-discipline?

I was an idiot.

I stood as she began packing away the backgammon. I wanted to help. "I'll do—"

"Jesus, don't you get it?" Her jaw was tight and her words sharp. "This is my job. My livelihood, my way of looking after my brother. This is not your fault—I was weak, it was my decision to be . . . pulled under by . . . but please don't make this worse. Pretend you have a call and *go*."

"Very well." I turned to head back inside, my whole body itching from her words that seemed to press into my skin and burn. Weak? Pulled under? What had passed between us last night had been so much more than sex, certainly more than lust taking over and pulling her under. She'd felt it too, hadn't she?

But I didn't say a word. Skylar catching us in an intimate moment had been my fault. I knew I shouldn't have touched Avery in public. I understood what this job meant to her, how losing it would be catastrophic for her family. I deserved her anger and I couldn't dilute or erase it.

Not yet.

Avery

It was my job to make things right for people, from billionaires to my brother and everyone in between. I was used to solving guests' problems and ensuring my stewardesses, the chef, the captain, my dad and anyone else in my orbit was happy. I just had to do it for myself this time.

I slid the backgammon case back into the sideboard, straightened my skirt, and headed to the galley. I exhaled just before I went in. I hoped to God Skylar hadn't mentioned what she'd seen to anyone. If she'd kept it to herself then there was a chance this situation was salvageable.

Skylar sat at the banquette, flicking through a magazine, while Neill chopped vegetables. If she'd told Neill, surely they'd still be talking about it.

"Can I talk to you in the laundry room?" I asked, trying to keep my voice light and breezy, as if I wanted to catch up about towels and mops rather than discuss the real possibility of me losing my job.

Without looking at me, Skylar closed her magazine and shuffled off the bench.

"Where's August?" I asked.

"Napping. She's on break."

I nodded. I'd been lucky that Skylar had caught us and not August, who I'd chastised several times at the beginning of the charter for even talking about hooking up with a hot guest or mentioning how handsome Hayden was.

I was such a hypocrite.

Skylar shut the door to the laundry room behind us. Despite there being only one guest on the yacht, the washers and dryers were constantly in use and provided the soundproofing we were going to need for this conversation.

"What are you doing?" Skylar asked, her eyes wide as she stepped toward me.

I pressed my fingers against my temples, as if I were trying to stop my brain from exploding. "Did you tell anyone about what you saw?"

She jumped up to sit on one of the washers. "Of course I didn't but, Avery, what the fuck?"

My body sagged and I leaned back against the dryer. Maybe this was still containable. "I'm sorry, I just—"

"Don't be sorry. Tell me what's going on. Is he . . . pressuring you?"

My eyes darted up to meet hers. "No, of course not. I mean, he would never . . ."

"When did it start?" she asked.

Did it sound stupid to say as soon as I laid eyes on him? At least that's where the kernel of desire had been born—for me. "Last night was the first time . . ." The first time I'd let myself acknowledge all the things I was feeling, the first time I'd forgotten to fight the attraction I had to him.

"Got physical? This hasn't been going on the whole charter?"

I reached behind and leveraged myself up to sit on the opposite dryer. "We've never . . . not on the boat."

She drew back. "But you *have* slept with him?"

There was no point in denying it. "Last night."

She let out an exhale. "That's where you were last night. Eric said he'd seen you with some ginger guy."

"It wasn't planned. We ran into each other . . ."

Skylar rolled her eyes.

"I'm serious. I went to the Greek theater to do the whole tourist thing. I had no idea he'd be there. But, I can't say I wasn't attracted to him before that."

Silence sat heavily between us. She had no reason to trust what I was saying. I'd broken the golden rule and crossed the line with a guest, putting my job and *everyone's* tip at risk. "You didn't tell anyone?"

"No, I wanted to speak to you first. But I'm not going to have to tell anyone if he touches you like that again in public—"

"I know. I think he was trying to be nice or something." At least I hoped that was all it had been. I wasn't sure if he'd just been thoughtless or selfish when he'd touched me when I'd just asked him not to. Both, maybe. As much as he might be a moral millionaire, he was still used to getting everything he wanted. He still snapped his fingers and expected people to jump.

"Is it worth risking your career over a one-night stand?"

That was the question. Last night I had felt as though whatever was between us was worth risking everything for, but today? Although we hadn't discussed it, whatever was between us hadn't felt fleeting. "It didn't feel like it was a one-night thing." But what else could it be? We lived in different countries, had different priorities. I couldn't maintain a relationship with a yachtie who had the same lifestyle as me. What hope did I have that things would work out with Hayden Wolf? "I just really like him."

"Well of course. He's gorgeous and rich—"

I scrunched up my nose. "It's not about that."

Skylar sighed and tipped her head back, skeptical. "Seriously. This could get you fired. It's reckless. It's just not you."

"I know." It was out of character. My family's security was everything to me. "It's just he's a really good guy and we've ended up spending time together and—" Physical desire would have been easier to resist but Hayden's kindness, his passion for what he did, the way he talked about his brother. Every time I learned something new about him, I liked him more.

"So what? Are you going to have an affair with this guy?"

I looked away, so the anxiety that churned in my stomach didn't show on my face. An affair seemed so crass. What had happened between us shouldn't have a label that applied to anyone else. It should have its own box, its own atmosphere, it was so different, so special.

"I don't know." I shrugged. "It's only been a few hours since . . . I haven't had time to think."

Skylar slid off the washer. "I don't want to see you fuck up your career so some bored, rich dude can get his rocks off, however hot he might be."

How could I explain that what she was describing wasn't what had happened between Hayden and me? We'd shared things. Connected. Hadn't we?

"Look, I won't say anything to anyone," she said.

I hadn't asked her to keep my secret, but I still felt equal measures of relief and guilt as she spoke.

"I don't want you to get in trouble. I like you and Moss would have a fit. He'd fire you in a nanosecond. But if August or Eric or someone else was to find you . . ." Yachting could be bitchy and there were plenty of second stewardesses who would have taken the opportunity to bury me. I was lucky Skylar was standing in front of me and not one of the countless other, more ambitious girls I'd worked with.

"I know. I'm sorry," I said. "I didn't plan it." I hated breaking the rules, but I especially hated pulling Skylar into this mess.

"I can't imagine you did. You're always so careful about everything. So . . ."

My stomach churned. She was right. Hayden had me making decisions that were against my nature, against my better judgement. What was I thinking? I'd gotten away with it this time. I hoped. But the only way to ensure no one else found out was to put a stop to things. "I should be clear with him that nothing else is going to happen between us." I hated the sound of the words as they left my lips.

"Maybe. I just know that the road you're on at the moment seems to be signposted trouble," she said.

I was so used to having as much in my life nailed down as possible, so used to being focused, to following the rules, that continuing to break them didn't seem realistic. But the alternative of never being with Hayden again seemed unbearable. It was as if someone had opened the curtains in a dark room and shown me I'd been missing daylight this whole time. It was too heartbreaking to shut those curtains right away. But Skylar was right. This sunlight—Hayden and everything he brought with him—could burn, corrode, and ultimately destroy my entire world. And in four weeks he'd be gone anyway. What was I doing?

Skylar opened her arms to give me a hug and I slid off the dryer into her grasp. "Whatever you decide, be careful. We're in close quarters and people are pretty good at sensing chemistry. You only need people to suspect something for things to get difficult for you."

The sensible decision was to put a stop to whatever had started between Hayden and me. Things had gone too far already, and it wasn't as if we were going to ride off into the sunset. It was ridiculous to think it might be the beginning of something. In four weeks, the charter would finish, Hayden would go back to London and I'd continue with the season here. Where did that leave us? And if there was nothing beyond these next four weeks then surely losing my way of supporting my family couldn't be worth it. However painful it would be, I needed to redraw the line in the sand before I lost everything. I had to end whatever there was between us.

TWENTY-FIVE

Hayden

I should be fucking delighted. My phone call with the lawyers had ended. Negotiations were productive and we were ahead of schedule, but all I could think of was the way Avery had looked at me as she'd packed up the game—equal parts devastation, capability and determination. She'd lost all of the softness and vulnerability that I uncovered when we were alone together and her expression when I left her had rusty, sharp edges that pierced my gut.

I needed to keep distracted. I grabbed the satellite phone from my desk and punched in Landon's number.

"Everything okay?" he answered.

"I'm getting impatient about finding this leak. You've been on it weeks now."

"Feel free to hire someone else, you dick. If you want this job done properly, then you're going to have to be patient."

I knew my brother was the best, but I wasn't about to

tell him that. "I just don't understand what's taking so long. Have you been investigating Cannon too?"

"No. We've just been fucking around drinking beer and chewing the fat."

I knew I was being unreasonable, but I was annoyed that I'd been careless with Avery. I prided myself on my self-control. Why the hell hadn't I been able to resist touching her?

"Sounds like you need a shag," Landon said.

I nearly told him I'd gotten plenty last night but held back. It would be my normal exchange with Landon, but for some reason I didn't want to describe what had happened as a shag. Sure, I'd released a lot of pent-up frustration and it had been a phenomenal night but—it wasn't just a shag.

"Whatever. You're the man-whore."

Landon chuckled. "Yeah, that's right. You're a born-again virgin."

Although I liked to fuck regularly, I was a little more discreet than Landon. I was also very clear about my intentions—or lack thereof—before any clothes came off.

But I couldn't remember making any such intentions clear last night. Probably because for the first time since I could remember, I wasn't certain there was a clear boundary or end point to describe.

"Whatever. Stop obsessing over my sex life and tell me where we're at in uncovering the leak."

"We're focusing on Gerald, your financial controller, and Anita. I've called in a favor from a mate in Cayman and I'm due to hear back in a couple of days. Hopefully we can take a look at what's in his account. And we're tapping his phones—home, office and mobiles—he's not spoken to anyone who isn't his wife or his kids."

"And is Anita in the clear?"

"Not until I can find out why she has a spare six figures in a newly opened bank account. I'm warning you that it's not good news that we've not uncovered a rational explanation quickly, but we're working on it."

I'd feel better once she was ruled out. There was no way it could be Anita. She was loyal and had access to everything I did. If Cannon had her, they had everything.

"You've got to get your head around the idea that it might be your assistant. I don't know why you are so convinced it couldn't be her when she's the obvious person Cannon would target if they wanted someone on the inside of your business."

Landon was telling me everything I didn't want to know. Anita potentially being the leak wouldn't just be disastrous because she had access to everything in my office. It was also because I'd never thought to doubt her. I'd never taken any precautions to keep anything sensitive from her. Professionally I'd been an open book as far as Anita was concerned. If I'd been complacent that made me culpable. And I wasn't sure what was worse—having no faith in my own judgement of people or potentially being part of my own downfall.

"Look, you've not found anything yet. You never know. It could be because there is no leak." I'd been racking my brains for another way Cannon could have found out about every deal. "Maybe there's another way that Cannon are stealing every deal from under me."

"*Right*," Landon responded, the word coming out stretched and sarcastic.

"I mean it. Look, they've got nothing since I left my mobile and laptop back in London. Maybe they'd done something with some malware or something."

"I've had your devices thoroughly examined. There's

nothing there, not even on your desktop in your home study."

"How the hell did you get into—never mind. Couldn't it be that kind of malware that disappears after a certain duration?"

"Like the *Mission Impossible* message, you mean?"

If I didn't know my brother far better than I wanted to, in that moment, I would have thought I was on to something. "Fuck you."

He chuckled. "Seriously. We need to drop in a red herring. Something juicy that will tempt anyone who's trying to lie low."

"Like what? I've asked people to get information memorandums. That should have drawn someone out."

"Maybe you need to up the ante. Make an offer."

"Make an offer? On what?"

"I don't know. A company. You need to take it up a step. Whoever is selling you out isn't biting on the crumbs we're feeding them. We need to throw them a nice, fat, juicy steak."

"I can't just make an offer on anything—it would have to make sense. The numbers would have to stack up or it wouldn't be credible. And I don't want to withdraw an offer for no apparent reason. My word is fucking important in this business."

"Jesus. None of this is my problem."

"And who would I let into the loop anyway? To get Gerald in the loop the circle would have to be pretty wide."

"At this point, it will be our quickest option."

I fisted my hand, then spread my fingers wide as I inhaled. It felt as if this would be the final battle, but I hoped there was no losing side. I didn't want to find the leak in my senior team. I wanted there to be another explanation. I didn't want to have been wrong about any of them because it meant my judgement was off—that I had to question every decision I'd ever made.

"Okay. It will take me a week or so." I'd need to find a process to jump into. Maybe I'd go back to the insurer in Mexico that Gerald had run numbers for. I didn't want to be in Mexico, but at least it was a transaction that wasn't being run out of the City, so if I withdrew without explanation my reputation wouldn't suffer. I'd find a way. "I'll keep you posted."

"And make sure next time you call me, you've gotten a shag."

"You going to arrange for me to have company? A security-cleared escort?"

"I always suspected you paid for it." Landon chuckled.

"Fuck you. I'm stuck on a yacht in the middle of the fucking sea. Alone," I said.

"You've always got an excuse for your complete lack of game."

"Go find me the fucking leak. And try to stay out of trouble while you're doing it." I hung up and tossed the phone on the desk. Speaking to Landon more often than normal was nice. I made a mental note to suggest we resume our regular squash game when I got back to London, which led to thoughts of getting home, sweaty, spent and then dragging Avery into the shower with me and fucking her until neither of us could stand.

Except Avery wouldn't be in London with me. She'd be on another charter with other guests who would make ridiculous demands of her and treat her like the help. My jaw clenched. Would she visit me in London? I could fly in, but she rarely got time off. However ready I was to get back to London, I knew that Avery Walker would be difficult to walk away from. Impossible to forget. Women like Avery came along once in a lifetime and I needed to figure something out before my cruise around the Mediterranean was over.

I CHECKED MY WATCH. It was past midnight and it had been hours since Avery had gone to speak to Skylar. I was growing impatient. I wanted to see her.

From what I could make out, most of the crew seemed to finish up around eleven and I'd expected Avery to come down to tell me what had happened with Skylar. I was about to go back up to the main deck when a rap on my office door jolted me upright. I strode across the space and yanked the door open. Avery slid inside, and I closed and locked the door.

Reading people's body language had been invaluable to me during the course of my career. I could tell when people were bluffing, when they were under pressure, when I'd surprised them. It was part of the reason I'd found it so difficult to believe I had a leak in my top team. They were people I knew well, people I thought I could read.

But a blind man would have understood that Avery was unhappy as she leaned against my office door, her arms folded, her eyes downcast.

Shit.

"I'm sorry," I said, stuffing my hands into my pockets. "What did Skylar say?"

She shook her head. "No. I need to tell you something that happened today. This morning after I left the hotel. I've not had a chance—"

"Are you okay? Is this about Skylar?"

"Please just listen to me. This weird guy approached me. He was asking about you."

I didn't understand what this had to do with Skylar and me getting Avery into trouble. "What guy?"

"I don't know. Some British guy. He asked me lots of questions about the boat and you. Offered me money to tell him stuff."

"Tell him what?" I asked.

"I don't know. I mean, sometimes we get paps offering us money to confirm which celebrity's on our boat but this guy wanted to know about your work. And he said I'd confirmed to him you were on the boat and if I did, Hayden, I'm sorry. I got a little freaked out and he was telling me I knew more than I said I did and I was confused and trying to get away from him."

Her words were tumbling out and her voice was getting higher and higher.

"Shhh," I said and moved toward her, but she put her hand out, her palm facing me to stop me. Fuck, I hated that. I wanted to comfort her, to make things better. "Seriously, don't worry. This boat was booked in my name. It wouldn't be difficult for someone to find out where I was. I'm on holiday. That's how it's meant to look if anyone sees me or finds out where I am."

"I didn't ruin it for you? I don't think I told him but maybe I did."

She was so fucking worried about me when she was the one who was potentially going to lose her job. "You didn't ruin anything." I'd mention this encounter to my brother. Maybe it was Cannon sneaking around. But Cannon was the least of my worries right at that moment. "Tell me about Skylar, Avery. What happened? Do I need to go and speak to Captain Moss?"

"She said she hadn't told anyone. That she wouldn't."

I took a half step toward her, but she slid along the wall and out of my reach. "She's covering for me. And I hate that she's had to," she said, shaking her head. "It's not right. Last night was . . ." Her words faded as if she was sinking into the memories of the previous evening. Then she pulled in a breath. "But enough. There's too much at stake for me. This is where it ends."

Shit. I should have prepared better for this, worked up arguments. I needed to convince her that . . . What? We were meant to date? Fuck? What was I offering her?

"We slept together. That's all," she said. "I'm not trying to make more of this—"

I'd had enough of the distance between us. I caged her against the wall, my hands braced on either side of her head.

Her gaze shot up to meet mine and then hit the floor.

"Look at me," I growled.

She lifted her face and focused on my jaw.

"Yes, we slept together but don't dismiss last night as if it's something that happens to you a lot. You know it was . . ." I clenched my teeth, remembering how she'd felt around my cock, how her hair had slithered over her body like water—how we'd connected, mind, body and soul. "It wasn't a one-night stand."

Not only was Avery the only woman I'd known I'd want to fuck more than once before I'd touched her, she was the only woman I'd thought about after I'd come. She was the only one I'd had to *convince* to come to my bed and the only one I wanted there again.

Her gaze darted to my mouth, then up to meet my eyes and back down again. "It can't be anything else. I need this job. You know that."

"You're not going to lose this job." Fuck, I had no right

to make promises I couldn't keep. "Not if Skylar doesn't say anything. We'll be more careful. I'll be more careful." Last night we'd existed in some kind of suspended space and time, and I'd been lazy and selfish thinking that could continue back on the yacht.

"I can't risk my brother's medical bills for some holiday romance with you just because you're bored."

Pushing my hips against hers, I pinned her to the wall and cupped her face in my hands. "I didn't fuck you because I was bored. I fucked you because I couldn't help myself. This isn't a holiday romance." I wasn't romantic and I wasn't on holiday. But more than that, what was between us wasn't fleeting.

"Of course it is." She kicked her leg back in frustration, her heel connecting with the wall.

It took all my self-control not to close the space between us and kiss her, but I held back, determined to prove this wasn't all about lust. "It's more than that for me." I didn't know what was happening between us. I wanted her to understand that what I felt wasn't casual.

"Last night we weren't on the yacht and it was easier for me to pretend the rules didn't apply. Today, it's different. You're my guest. I'm a stewardess. That's how it should stay."

"I won't believe you if say you don't feel this pull between us," I whispered.

"Of course I feel it, but that doesn't mean it's right. It doesn't mean I can give in to it again."

I stepped back from her, wanting her to understand how serious I was. I didn't want her to do something that would cause her pain, but she should know she wasn't just a convenient fuck for me. I leaned against the desk. "I know I look like I'm being a selfish bastard. I know I have nothing to lose whereas you have put your career on the line. But I can't let you walk out of here without telling you how I feel." She deserved my honesty. "I need you to know that I've never had a night like last night. I've never been on the phone to lawyers about any deal, let alone the deal of my career, and found my mind so full of a woman I have no room for anything else." I was usually laser focused and especially at times when I was under pressure, but Avery had everything upside down. "You make me want to blow off work and spend all night talking about everything you ever did before I met you. I want to understand what makes you happy, what makes you sad, what makes you angry." I had an ego to match any man's, but I'd never before believed that a woman existed just for me. That was how I felt about Avery Walker—she was here for me, made for me, created *for me*. "I've never felt so proud to know someone. And I've never felt so fucking lucky that that woman wanted me. I want to scoop you up and bolt off this yacht and go get lost somewhere where it's just you and me until the end of time." It was as if my heart was exploding and I was finally able to find words for what I was feeling. "The thought that we might be over just doesn't make sense to me. What's between us feels like it will last forever, like it's timeless."

Avery sank her teeth into her bottom lip but remained silent.

"I haven't thought about what happens when I leave this boat," I said. "But I know that I can't ever imagine not wanting you in my life. I'm a resourceful guy and you're a born problem solver. We'll figure this out."

She bowed her head. Had I lost her?

I stepped forward so I was just inches away from her "You want to walk away from this?" I asked. "I'll hate it, but I'll never touch you again if you ask me not to."

I glanced up to see unshed tears in her eyes. "I don't want to but I'm afraid. Hearing you . . . I feel all that. And more. But you can't screw up my redemption."

Her words spread hot and sharp through me. Yachting was more than a career for her. This job was more than just a way of paying for her brother's medical bills. This was about sacrifice and atonement—her assumed guilt for Michael's accident. I should walk away, push her away. But I was rooted to the spot, as if gravity had misfired and I'd be pulled to wherever she was. "I won't screw it up," I whispered and placed a kiss on her collarbone. She didn't need redeeming. She was the only one who thought she did. "Believe in me. Believe in us."

Her knees buckled a little and her hands slid over my shoulders. Jesus, just this woman's hands on my shirt-covered skin was enough to bring me to the edge.

"This room is Taormina, right?" I whispered. "In here, we're Hayden and Avery. Just like yesterday. Through that door . . ." I tipped my head in the direction of the exit. "Out there, I'll be the guest and you can be the stewardess. I promise I'll not put you in danger of discovery again."

She pulled her bottom lip between her teeth. She was almost at the point of saying yes, I just had to sweep my hand up the back of her thigh or press my hardening cock against her hip and she'd relent. But I needed more than that. She had to want this.

"I feel it," she whispered. "And I don't know if I'm more afraid of walking away or of the consequences of staying. I think either will hurt me."

I blinked. I wanted to swallow up any hurt she'd ever felt. Any pain she'd ever have.

"My dad wanted me to do something just for me. To focus more on myself. The problem is the only thing I want for me is you. I want this for me." She reached up, searching my face, tracing her fingers over my cheek. "Taormina," she whispered.

"Taormina," I whispered back before I pressed my lips to hers, lazily pushing my tongue through her lips to meet hers and I was home, where I belonged. Her hands curled around the back of my neck and I sighed in relief.

Reaching down, I bunched up her skirt, pulling up the cotton until my fingertips reached her skin. I yanked the skirt up to her waist, leaning back to see the black lace covering her, then pushing the material to the side to examine her pussy. It was pink and perfect and needed to come. She needed to stop thinking and overthinking. Analyzing and overanalyzing. She needed to be reminded of how her body responded to me, how good we were together. I slid two fingers through her folds, gauging her wetness, and I got a sense of smug satisfaction that despite the obvious conflict she had about us, she was still wet for me. As much as her mind tried to resist, her body told me everything I needed to know. I spread my fingers, wanting to feel as much of her as I could as I pushed my tongue back in her mouth to dull her little moans.

I pressed my fingers into her and circled my thumb over her clit. She gasped and pulled back, her hand tightening around my neck, her thumb tracing the pulse hammering under my skin. The sticky, sweet feel of her goaded my cock until it was begging for more.

I pressed my hand against the base of her chest and pinned her against the wall as I circled her clit. I pulled my fingers out, circled, then pushed them back in. I wanted to watch as she came, wanted to see on her face what I could do—how no man had ever made her come as quickly or as hard. She squirmed under my touch and her hand snapped to my wrist but didn't seek to remove it. Instead she spread her fingers as if she was trying to communicate with me.

"Hayden," she whispered. "I want you to fuck me."

I nodded, not letting my fingers still for a second. I was still pushing and pulling, circling and pressing. "I know. And I will. But you need to come. Just to take the edge off. Just as a warm up. I need you relaxed when I shove my cock inside you."

She slumped an inch down the wall as her legs began to shake. She wouldn't last long. My fingers hadn't been inside her pussy two minutes and she was on the cusp of coming all over my hand. Her hips flicked, and I pushed deeper into her wetness as our mouths stilled, connected but quiet, our breaths mingling as I concentrated on the press and quiver of her pussy as she fucked my hand and my hand fucked her. She stiffened, then her hands fell from my wrist. As her orgasm shivered across her body, she looked at me.

I released her as her body sagged.

"You see? You needed that. You needed to let go." I lifted her and spun her around and sat her on my desk.

"And what do you need?" She traced her index finger along my eyebrow. The softness in her expression was back. The determination and practicality had left her, and I took pride in knowing I'd done that. I'd helped her forget, just for a few minutes.

"I need you," I replied.

Avery

I slid my legs wide open on the desk, still boneless from my orgasm but ready for more. Ready for everything he could give me . . . and for any consequences that would follow.

I opened his shorts, but he was so hard against the buttons that my fingers faltered with impatience.

He gasped as the fastening released and his cock burst out, hard and hot and ready to fuck me. My pussy twitched, and I licked my lips.

He groaned, and my eyes shot up in warning.

"We have to be quiet," I whispered.

It was as much a warning to me as to him. Last night the hotel had provided freedom in more ways than one. But now we had to be more careful.

He grinned as he fingered the edge of my polo shirt, then pulled it up. I lifted my arms and he tossed it over his shoulder. He reached into his pocket and pulled out a condom before letting his shorts drop.

I swallowed and reached for the condom, but he pulled it from my reach.

"Patience. You'll feel me soon enough," he said as he tore the wrapper and rolled the latex over his tip.

Soon wasn't soon enough. I clenched at the thought of his cock and how it felt as it pushed inside me—hard and soft, brutal and gentle.

I grunted and arched my back at the memory. Hayden chuckled. "If that's what just the sight of my cock does to you, what about this?" he asked, pushing into me in one deep, unexpected movement.

He glanced down at me, his eyes soft. "Breathe."

I exhaled, my chest lowering as I tried to relax so he didn't feel as if he were going to split me in two. I looked down to where we were joined, and he was deep inside me. Just a fingertip's width of his cock was on display. I reached down and smoothed my finger over his hard, silky skin. He tipped his head back and gasped. I didn't know which I liked more, the feel of him so deep or the sounds I could elicit from him.

I slid my palms up his strong stomach to his chest and he watched me. He didn't need to say anything. We were just there, in that moment, joined.

Eventually, he started to move, slowly and deliberately. "Feels good," he said, part question, part statement. The vibration of his voice skirted over my skin and I wondered if anything would ever feel quite as good again.

I nodded, inhaling sharply as he thrust into me again with such force it was almost painful.

His hands pressed into my ass, keeping me in place and pinning me to the desk. He bent his head, his end-of-day shadow scratching against my cheek, setting sparks of lust desperate to burst into flame.

I wanted more, harder, faster, longer. I reached for him —his face, his chest, his arms, his stomach—every part of me trying to convey what I needed. "Please," I whispered through clenched teeth.

"Avery," he whispered back as he thrust in again. "Avery. Avery. Avery." He set out in a rhythm of pleasure and skin and sweat as he pistoned in and out of me. It felt as if my body was made for this. For him. For what we were doing.

I reached around his neck and braced my other palm on the desk, steadying myself so he could get deep, so deep. I caught my breath as he dipped lower, changing the angle so it felt as if his cock was even bigger than before.

Something landed on the floor and even though it felt like it happened two rooms away, I knew one of us had knocked something off the desk. We were making more noise than we should—the creak of furniture, the slap of skin against skin, the buried sounds of ecstasy. It was all louder than it should have been, but I couldn't stop, didn't want to. Whatever the consequence, it was all worth it for how he looked at me, touched me, what he did to my body.

I curled my fingers, my nails biting into his skin as my orgasm murmured out of my belly and up my spine. As if he knew how close I was, our eyes met, and I panicked because I didn't want it to be over so soon . . . but I didn't think I could stop it.

He nodded as if he could see what I was thinking. I frowned but he dropped a kiss on the top lip of my open mouth. "Come," he said.

I had no choice but to do as he said. My body convulsed as my climax ran through me like lightning through water—hot and bright and everywhere.

My grip gave way and Hayden's hands left my hips and guided me down so I was lying on the desk. My fear about it being over was unwarranted, and I smiled as Hayden continued to fuck me on the desk, his fingers skirting my body. Absentmindedly, he flicked my hard nipples as his hands traveled over my skin. As if there was a connection right to my groin, I moaned. He leaned over me and covered my mouth with his palm as his pace increased. He knew I'd lost all control. I would do anything he asked right at that moment—fuck him on the main deck, in the galley. Whatever he wanted, wherever it pleased him.

His thrusts became sharper, harder, and with his free hand he reached between us and his thumb found my clit. I arched my back and mumbled into his palm, tightening around him.

His eyes didn't leave my face, and because I wanted to watch him as he came, I tried to keep my lids from falling closed, overwhelmed from the sheer perfection of it all. This time, my orgasm came quickly and the force of it was unexpected, leaving my legs shaking and my body shuddering. My climax was the final straw for Hayden. His jaw tightened and his fingers left my clit and clamped over my upper arm, holding me in place as he thrust into me, once, twice.

"Avery," he spluttered in a choked whisper as he came, our eyes locked together, our bodies pressing and joined. In answer, I threaded my fingers through his hair and smiled at him. How could I have thought I might give him up? Even if I only got to have him for a few more weeks, I had to take as much as I could get.

He curled over me, pressing his skin against mine as our heartbeats crashed against each other, the rest of our bodies still, anchored to each other. I'd give anything if we could just press pause and exist only in this room and let the rest of the world melt away.

TWENTY-SIX

Avery

I woke the next morning, grinning. Who did that? Not me, certainly not in the middle of a season. Like most yachties, mid-season slump normally kicked my ass. By then tips had become the norm rather than a treat. The lack of sleep took its toll and there had been enough difficult charters and spoiled guests for time to drag and tempers to fray. It was the point in the season where we woke up sobbing, not grinning. But there was nothing normal about this season. Not the length of charter, not the lack of guests and certainly not the sex. If Hayden was even a tiny percentage as good at his job as he was at fucking me, it was no wonder he was a gazillionaire. I shivered at the thought of his mouth, his cock, his dirty words. I pulled the covers off and headed to the bathroom. A cold shower was the first item on the agenda.

After fucking me as though it was his job, Hayden had promised we'd be discreet. I should have given him up, redrawn the line in the sand, but there was so little about my life that was for me that I wanted to cling to Hayden and how I felt about him for as long as I could.

I wasn't on duty until ten this morning, but I tended to keep my hours to whatever Hayden was doing. I showered and changed. Put on some tinted moisturizer and a coat of mascara and then, wet-haired, I picked up Hayden's satellite phone from beside my bed. He'd insisted I take it last night when I told him I'd not spoken to my father for a couple of days.

"Daddy?" I asked as my father answered the phone.

"Avery. How are you?"

I took a seat on my bed, running my free hand through my wet hair, separating the sodden strands. "I'm sorry I didn't call last night, there was some stuff here I had to sort out. Did you hear anything from the insurers?"

Since my father's diagnosis, I'd persuaded him to have some additional help, just to assist with getting Michael up in the mornings. We just had to get the insurer to pay for it, and given the premium increase I was paying this year, they'd better.

"Oh, you know what they're like. I'll manage just fine."

"No, Daddy. Lifting isn't good for you."

"I said I'll manage. The insurance company isn't going to pay."

"You heard from them?" I asked.

"I got through yesterday. They're reassessing our benefits or something."

"Well that sounds good. Like they're trying to help."

My dad snorted. "I don't think that's what they meant."

My father always tried to keep bad news from us. He was always the one marching forward at the front telling us it wasn't as bad as we thought it was. But I'd learned to read the signs. He wasn't telling me something. "What did they say?"

"We don't know anything for certain, not yet."

"What does 'yet' mean? Please don't keep this from me. I need to know."

There was a long, deep sigh at the other end of the phone. "I don't know, Avery. Apparently, unless he's making significant improvement with the physical therapy, the insurance company said it could be cut."

"What?" I leapt out of my bed. "They can't do that. He is making progress. He's working really hard."

"I don't know, honey. They said something about it being chronic or preventative or—I can't remember. They're saying they'll drop his sessions down to once a month."

I was already paying for three sessions a week and that was only because I had a forty percent pay rise this season. I couldn't pay for an extra three. "But we didn't call about the physical therapy. We wanted additional home care. I don't understand why they would decide to stop what they've been doing since the accident."

"I guess our request for additional help led to a review of the entire file. I don't know, sweetheart. But we'll manage. We always do. I don't want you to worry about it."

I wanted to scream. I'd paid a fortune in premiums over the years and now they were cutting treatment? It wasn't fair.

I had little in savings as I'd just finished paying for adjustments to the house so Michael's wheelchair would fit and we could adapt the garage to a downstairs bedroom.

I pulled out my notebook from the shelf above my bed where I noted down my budgets. I'd always gotten into trouble as a teenager for being reckless with my allowance, but since Michael's accident I'd coveted every penny—allocating every dollar and cent I had carefully. Maybe I could pay for the additional home help, but there was no way I was going to be able to pay for additional physical therapy too.

"He's been making so much progress, Dad. The physical therapist said so. And you know how much he wants to walk again." I might not be able to turn back time and stop us from going down to the river, but I would do everything I could so Michael lived the best life available to him. Maybe I could get a promotion to a bigger boat or go work on one of those Russian oligarch's yachts and dodge bullets and the sexual harassment for more money.

"I know, honey. They've told us they're putting it in writing, so let's just wait for the letter and see exactly what's going on."

This was the last thing I wanted my father to be coping with. Another setback, another hurdle to climb. With his recent health scare he should be thinking about reducing his hours at work and taking things easy, but there was no way he'd do that now.

"Okay. Will you send me a copy—" Shit. I still wasn't used to not having email on board. "Email me a copy of the letter when you get it. I'll go ashore to an internet café and pick it up. In the meantime, I'll see what ideas I have for bringing in some more cash. Maybe I'll hold up a bank or something."

My father chuckled. "Yeah, I don't see you as an armed robber."

I smiled. No matter what, my dad always found the funny side. "It won't be long until I'm home."

"It will be good to see you."

My heart tugged at his words. He wasn't a sentimental man and he'd never admitted he wanted me home or that he missed me. He always insisted that there was nothing in Sacramento for me, and that I was much better off travelling the world. His words, and the dull way they sounded across the phone, made me think that maybe things were changing. Maybe his positivity was floundering. I wasn't sure what I would do if he lost his bright smile and easy charm—it was who my dad was. No, I had to find a solution to this and things would go back to how they'd been for the last seven years. I had to find a way to restore hope to our family.

TWENTY-SEVEN

Avery

I needed tequila. Or a whiskey. What was it that people drank when they got bad news?

I stared at the letter in my hands, wanting the words on the page to be different to what I'd read on screen before I'd pressed print. I'd hoped my dad had gotten mixed up when I'd spoken to him a few days ago, but it was true, the insurance company was cutting Michael's physical therapy. I slumped back into the chair in the internet café. They must have made a mistake. Surely.

My instinct was to go to the nearest travel agency, book a flight home and try to fix things. But it would only make everything worse, because now, more than ever, I needed my job. I'd spent the last few days with a pen and paper and calculator trying to figure out whether I could bridge the gap between what the insurance would cover and what Michael needed.

Whichever way I cut it, I was twenty thousand dollars a year short.

Guilt rose in my throat. It was heavy, suffocating. If I'd been a better sister, he wouldn't have had the accident in the first place and if I was a better sister now I would be able to find a way to pay for his care. I should have gone to college, done pre-law or medicine—at least then my income would be going up every year instead of plateauing. I could have trained as a physical therapist or learned coding and come up with a great idea like Facebook or something.

I'd wasted my life. I'd walked away from college and the future I wanted for the money and it *still* wasn't enough. What else was left? I didn't know where to go from here.

I had nothing of any value that I could sell, and even if I got a job on one of those Russian yachts, I couldn't make another twenty thousand a year.

Folding up the letter, I placed it into my bag, determined not to cry. I just had to find a way. I'd felt hopelessness like this when Michael was in the hospital, before we'd known if he was going to make it. And again when my mother left. Each time it had eventually lifted, or I'd become used to it—I wasn't sure which—but for some reason, this time felt worse. Like before I'd had obstacles to get over but this time we were staring at a black hole that was threatening to consume the three of us.

For once, I wanted this to be someone else's responsibility. I knew my dad was the parent here but there was nothing he could do. This was down to me. And that burden bore into me until all I wanted was just a moment without it. Maybe that was what I'd found in the time alone that Hayden and I had shared—a few minutes or hours where I felt lighter. It wasn't as if the responsibility disappeared, more that being with him made me stronger somehow, as if he were lifting me up, reinforcing my strength. He'd be gone soon, and I didn't know if this news about my brother's insurance would have been easier to bear if I hadn't escaped for a little while, if I hadn't glimpsed a different life for a few hours.

I stood up, a little dizzy, and headed outside. I'd told Eric I wouldn't be longer than thirty minutes. Hayden didn't like me away from the yacht and anyway, I hadn't touched his room this morning and I needed to clean the bathroom and change the sheets and do the hundred other things that needed doing even though we only had one guest on the yacht.

I squinted as I opened the door of the internet café and slipped my sunglasses on. Usually I enjoyed the heat, the sunshine and the blue skies, but today I wanted it to rain, hail, snow—anything that didn't say vacations or money or happiness because that felt like someone else's world. Not mine.

I started down the hilly, cobbled streets back to the boat. The last time I'd taken this route, I'd been in an entirely different frame of mind. I'd been so happy I couldn't stop myself from smiling, talking to strangers—I'd wanted to sing out loud. Today everything was different.

"Avery." A man called my name and a figure appeared beside me, as he tucked a newspaper under his arm. "How's Mr. Wolf?"

I kept my pace the same, heading toward the sea as I realized that this was the same redhead, Phil, who'd approached me the morning after I'd slept with Hayden.

"What do you want? I've told you I have nothing to say to you." There were more people around than there had been the previous time I'd met him—tourists wandering around and locals going about their business—but there was something in his overfamiliarity that made me feel exposed and vulnerable. As pleasant and polite as he was, there was something sinister buried below his pale skin and hard eyes. I stared right ahead.

"I like you, Avery," he said, his tone cheery as if he were selling fruit or ice cream. "So I'm going to cut to the chase. I want to know what Hayden Wolf is working on."

"I don't know what you're talking about. I don't discuss my guests and who may or may not be on board." I didn't glance at him and just kept walking.

"Maybe not, but we both know Hayden Wolf is on the *Athena*. And we both know you could use some extra cash."

My stomach flipped over. How did he know anything about me? Who the hell was this guy? "You need to leave me alone."

"You don't want to hear me out, even for your brother's sake?"

I stopped in my tracks and turned to him. "What did you say?"

"I know you take care of your family, Avery. All I'm suggesting is a way you can do that."

"You don't know anything about me or my family—"

"It's my job to find out these things. I know about your brother's condition and how you pay for his insurance. Not to mention all the things you pay for that aren't covered by your policy."

How had this guy found out all this stuff? I turned back to face the water. "How do you know this?"

"I just had a friend ask a few of your neighbors. People will do anything for a little cash."

Our neighbors had talked to strangers about us? For what? A few dollars?

"And that's not a bad thing. I'm not judging. Everyone has their own circumstances to consider," he continued. "It helped me a great deal. What I'm asking from you is nothing. We just need eyes and ears on the ground. That's all. You're not hurting anyone. In fact, you'll be helping your brother."

"How would sneaking around and spying on people help my brother?"

I glanced across at him and he was smiling and relaxed as if he were offering me suggestions on the best beaches in the area. "We're prepared to pay you a lot of money to tell us what we need to know."

"I'm not interested in your money."

"Even to help your family? That sounds pretty selfish to me." He tilted his head, looking at me as if I'd just said something ridiculous.

"My family wouldn't want money that I've had to lie for."

"Oh gosh, no. I don't expect you to lie. In fact, all I want is the truth. You might even have what I need to know already. Tell me what Mr. Wolf is working on and I'll give you—"

"I'm not interested," I said and started walking toward the tender again.

"You haven't heard what I have to offer you yet. For your brother's sake, you should hear me out."

"I'm not interested," I said. All I wanted in that moment was to get back to the tender and put some distance between me and this red-headed creep.

"Would a hundred and fifty thousand dollars change your mind?"

I stopped walking.

He couldn't be serious. He was going to give me a hundred and fifty thousand dollars? What kind of shit was Hayden mixed up in? This couldn't just be one company buying another. Or a long-held grudge. For that kind of money, there had to be more to it.

"I thought that might get your attention."

"A hundred and fifty grand?"

He smiled. "Right? Easy money. How many seasons would you have to work to make that money? Think of all the amazing things you could do. You could have a holiday, you could take some time off, maybe even go to university."

My head was spinning. A hundred and fifty grand was *so* much money.

He pulled out a business card and held it between his index and middle finger. "When you've thought about how you'd spend the money, which college course you'd like to take, how happy your dad and brother would be with that extra cash in the bank, call me and we'll arrange a time to meet." He pulled out a satellite phone from his pocket and held it out.

I stared at his hands as though I was seeing a hundred thousand dollars right there, baking in the Italian sun. All I had to do was reach out and take it.

"You've resisted, Avery. You've said no. You've proved to yourself you're a good person. Now your brother needs you to say yes."

My head snapped up and his eyes were warm and calm, and if an outsider saw us, they might think we were friends or that he was making a pass at me.

I didn't like him, not one bit, but he wasn't wrong. My brother *did* need me, and a hundred and fifty thousand dollars was a lot of money.

I glanced back to the tender and then swallowed. Would my dad expect me to give up so much money? So much cash would be life changing for my entire family.

Including me. I needed more time to work out what would be the best thing to do.

I snatched the card and phone from his hands and ran toward the tender where Eric would be waiting. I'd never seen a yacht as a place to escape to rather than from, but I'd never been more ready to leave solid ground. I didn't know which way was up and being back on board was at least a familiar place. There I could decide whether I should betray Hayden or my family.

TWENTY-EIGHT

Hayden

I barely recognized myself and these feelings of longing I had for Avery Walker. It had only been a few hours since she'd been naked on my desk and already I missed her sweet taste and her fingers through my hair. We'd managed time alone each day since Taormina and instead of quenching my desire, it set it on fire. How would I feel back in London without her? It didn't make sense. After all, I hadn't known the woman long and I wasn't one for emotional entanglements, but I couldn't imagine my world without her in it. I needed a plan.

I wasn't sure if it was because I didn't have any other distractions, but she'd become the thing I looked forward to most in my day. Usually the buzz I got from the process of buying companies was better than any drug, better than sex. It made everything else slide away and took my focus. There was something freeing in that. Nothing was more important. I was clear what my responsibilities and objectives were when I was trying to close a deal. Avery complicated that tunnel vision. She seemed to exist outside it, splitting my focus. I basked in the way she cared for me, made sure I had everything I needed, but more, she challenged me, told me what I didn't need.

I smiled at the knock at the door, which I knew would be Avery. "Come in." I kept my gaze on the shiny walnut door. The first thing I was normally faced with when that door opened was Avery's beautiful smile and wide eyes, but when she opened the door only as much as it took for her to slip inside, her face was a little dull, her smile more forced than usual.

"You're a sight for sore eyes," I said, reaching for her as she pressed the door closed.

"I am?" she asked, walking into my outstretched arms. "Can I get you something?"

I sighed. However close we'd gotten over these past weeks, I couldn't get away from the fact that she saw herself as the help.

"I wish it wasn't like this," I said.

She froze, her knees touching mine as I wrapped my arm around her waist and pulled her to my lap. "Like what?" she asked.

"You having to wait on me. Pick up after me. You're worth more than that."

She huffed out a breath and relaxed in my arms. "I'm worth exactly that. Anyway, I like doing it for you." She ran her palms over my arms.

"I don't like the thought of you doing it for other people when I'm gone."

She tipped her head back and kissed my jaw. "You want me as your own personal chief stewardess?"

"You make me sound like a pervert."

"That's because you are a pervert." She poked me in the ribs and I grabbed her hand, kissing the inside of her wrist as I ground my hips against her.

"You never thought of what you might want to do other than this?"

Her mouth fixed in place, a glaze of professional coating her expression. "This is my job. You ever thought of what you might want to do other than buy and sell companies? At least I get to see daylight in my job."

She had a point. I worked long hours in personality-less rooms for weeks on end. She was the one on a yacht off the coast of Italy. "Yeah, I accept that my job is ridiculous. You can't make me feel bad about that—my brother was in the SAS, remember? I've learned to live with how shallow what I do can be. But it pays really well."

"Well then, I don't see your point."

I traced the dip between her collarbones and trailed my fingers between her breasts. "I was thinking through logistics."

She pressed her lips together, trying not to smile. "You were thinking through *logistics*? Did anyone ever tell you how romantic you are?" Her fingers rippled through my hair and I closed my eyes, savoring her delicate touch.

"Is that what you want? I'm not sure I'm very good at romance, but I can work on that." I was going to have to shift a lot of things. I'd never done relationships, never loved anyone, but I would do whatever it took for Avery.

"But even if I moved the head office, you're not in one place all the time. We need to figure something out that's going to work for both of us."

I bit at her neck and she moved toward me, asking for more. "I'm not sure romance is what you want," I growled.

She tucked her hand to the back of my neck where it fit so perfectly and stroked her thumb along my jaw. This. I could stay like this forever. It wasn't fucking. It wasn't talking. It was intimacy and something I wasn't sure I'd ever had before.

"I don't have any answers. You and me beyond the *Athena* seems impossible. My life is split between three places—Sacramento, the Med and the Caribbean. You're in London. I have my family to provide for and you have a business to run." She squeezed her eyes shut and I pressed my mouth to her forehead. "I don't see how it can work."

"We'll make it work," I said. "I can fly down to the Med between charters if I have to."

She sighed. "You can't do that. And what happens when I'm three thousand miles away?"

"I *can* do that. We'll figure it out."

"You seem so sure, but I just don't see a way," she said, looking at me as though she wanted a solution right then and there.

"Maybe I'll buy an insurer based in Florida, so I can work out of the States. Perhaps you'll get a job in London. We'll make it work."

"I don't know." She sighed.

Surely she couldn't doubt how I felt? I'd laid myself bare to her more than I'd ever done in my life. "You don't realize how special you are to me. I'll find a way," I whispered. "I promise. Trust me." I didn't want to agree with her, but our situation wasn't an easy fix. I could give her the money she needed to care for her family or offer to employ her at Wolf Enterprises, but I knew her pride wouldn't let her take either of those options. And short of becoming a deckhand, how was I supposed to spend time with her if she continued working on yachts? Would I have to accept I only saw her for days here and there during the season? I couldn't imagine that would work in the long term. Along with closing the Phoenix deal and finding out who the leak was, I now had to figure out how I made sure I didn't lose Avery. And the clock was ticking. I didn't have long left.

TWENTY-NINE

Hayden

I was so close to the finish line with Phoenix, I could almost taste it. At the last minute they'd asked for an increase in price. I couldn't get hold of the CEO and no one could explain why the change at the eleventh hour. I had a gun to my head—pay more or have wasted the last two months on an aborted deal. I couldn't agree to the increase without my investors being on board and they were determined to torture me by going through some of the financials with a fine-toothed comb. When I'd arrived on the *Athena*, buying Phoenix had seemed like an almost-impossible task, and now I was within touching distance. It was torture. All I could do was wait and while I did, hopefully I could find out who was the leak at Wolf Enterprises. When Phoenix closed I couldn't continue to do all my business from a superyacht. I dialed Landon's number.

"Looks like Cannon are spending a lot of time and effort on you," Landon said before I'd even said hello. "They've got to one of the crew members."

"On the *Athena*?" My pulse began to throb in my neck.

"As opposed to which other crew members?"

"But nothing's leaked. I'm just waiting for my investors. We're nearly done." Shit. I couldn't lose things this late on, could I? Was this the reason Phoenix had asked for money? Had they had a better offer from Cannon?

Mentally I scanned through which crew member it could be. The only one I'd anything to do with other than Avery was Skylar. Was it possible someone was sneaking about among my things when they thought I was sleeping or on the main deck?

"Do you have the name of the crew member you think is compromised?" I asked.

Taps on keyboards echoed down the phone. "Avery Walker. She's the chief stewardess, right?"

I tried to swallow but my throat constricted and I coughed. "No, it won't be Avery. You've got it confused. Do you have a photo? Is it a woman? Does she have white-blonde hair?"

"No, brown hair. It's in a ponytail in one shot. Down in another."

My heart stammered in my chest, as if it were knocking at my ribcage, trying to get out. "No, there must have been a mistake."

"Have I ever steered you wrong?"

"Yeah, but Avery wouldn't betray me. And like I said, Cannon haven't managed to disrupt this and steal this company from under me." Not yet anyway.

"Look, my man over there has spotted her three times with the same guy in different locations. We looked into him and he's some kind of ex-MI5 guy. Works for a firm we know Cannon pay for intelligence. A Phil Dyer, but he uses various aliases. James Cree is a favorite. Alfie Molloy is another."

It couldn't be true. There must be some mistake . . . but Landon didn't get shit like this wrong. "You have photos of her and this guy? And even if you do, that doesn't mean anything though, right? Perhaps he approached her, but that doesn't mean she told him anything. He might have been coming on to her, trying to compromise her and failing."

Landon's silence on the other end of the phone told me he thought I was being an idiot and was trying to piece together why.

I ended his torture. "I've been sleeping with her."

"Jesus, you're an idiot. I told you I'd arrange company if—"

"Landon," I growled. I didn't want to hear how he thought I was a teenager who couldn't do with my fist for a couple of months in exchange for a successful deal that would feature in my fucking obituary. It hadn't been like that. Not that lust hadn't played a part, but it was more than that. I couldn't have stayed away from her if I'd tried. And I had tried.

And she'd tried to keep away from me. As much as she wore a mask, the way she fought against crossing the line between guest and crew couldn't have been faked. Could it? If I'd not bumped into her at the theater, we may never have ended up spending the day and night together.

Had she engineered that?

Had she deliberately played coy to throw me off guard?

Fuck. I didn't know anything anymore.

"You're sure it's Avery?"

"Can you get to shore? I can have someone meet you with the evidence in thirty minutes."

"But it's just photographs of her talking to some guy?"

"In one of the photographs, she was given a satellite phone."

She'd told me the yacht only had one satellite phone and that she wasn't allowed to use it much. That was why she'd had to use mine. Had that been another lie?

"She has an established line of contact. This wasn't a one-off."

My only hope was this wasn't Avery. That Landon was confused. At a push, August's hair could be described as brown, although it was so dark, wouldn't most people call it black or at least *dark* brown?

I stood up. I had to see more evidence. I trusted my brother, but it was hard for me to believe I'd been so wrong about someone. I had to find that phone, see those pictures with my own eyes and confront her. "I need to see the evidence."

THIRTY

Hayden

Did she suspect I knew what she'd done? As much as I didn't want to look, I couldn't help but be drawn to Avery standing on the main deck as the tender got closer to the boat. As usual, her hair was scraped back into an efficient ponytail.

Unfortunately, Landon hadn't mistaken August for Avery. The photographs his contact had shown me had been conclusive. Avery had met with an ex-MI5 agent on three separate occasions. Once might be explainable. Twice even. But three times she'd spoken to this guy, once just after our night together in Taormina.

Avery knew I was buying Phoenix. She'd seen the bloody documents. She could have worked out the price and the main terms . . . but the deal hadn't been stolen from me. Not yet.

Why hadn't Cannon stepped in? Was Avery part of a longer-term approach? Perhaps there were plans in place I didn't know about.

I'd spoken to my investors onshore, and they'd agreed to the price increase. I was an inch away from completing the deal of the decade, the most significant transaction of my career, and yet I wasn't elated. Adrenaline ran through my veins, but it wasn't victory that had put it there. It was anger.

Betrayal.

I'd thought it cut like a knife when I found out I had a leak at Wolf Enterprises, but it was a flesh wound compared to the way my heart felt as if it had been yanked out of my chest and displayed on a stake right at that moment.

The boat was booked until the end of the week, but I had no reason to stay after we completed the sale. Not anymore. But before I left, I wanted an explanation. To look Avery Walker in the eye and ask her how much they'd paid her to fuck me and whether that made her feel like the prostitute it made her.

Avery

Something was wrong.

As much as Hayden and I were super careful, even when we were surrounded by others, I always knew he was aware of me. A look or the tilt of his head gave it away. But as he came aboard all I got was his averted eyes and the back of his head as he swept past me and into the main salon.

Asking Eric to take him ashore with no notice and without telling me was weird enough, but now he was avoiding looking at me? Had his deal gone south? Last time I'd spoken to him they'd been about to finish things. Something must have gone wrong.

Hayden was never anything but cool. Charming. In control. But he looked as if he wanted to circle his hands around someone's neck and squeeze until he'd choked the life out of them.

"Everything okay?" I asked Eric as he appeared at the top of the stairs, squinting into the sun.

He shrugged and slipped his sunglasses over his eyes. "This is the weirdest fucking charter I've ever been on, that's for sure."

"Did he collect something or meet someone or what?"

"No idea. He disappeared as soon as we docked and came back forty minutes later. Didn't say a word to me on the way there or back. He's a weird son of a—"

I put my hand up to him. "I'll go check on him."

"I hope the tip is worth it."

The tip was the least of my worries. I hated seeing Hayden anything other than the man I knew him to be. Something must have gone seriously wrong and I was concerned about him.

I knocked on the door to Hayden's office as I'd done so many times this charter. Next week the office would be back to a bedroom and I'd be blushing thinking about all that had happened between us in this room.

I'd miss him.

I'd wish things were different.

But as my dad always said, no one promised life would be fair. He also loved to tell me I had to play the hand I was dealt and then he'd fall back on a perennial favorite: suck it up, buttercup.

"Come in," Hayden barked. He usually met me at the door, dragged me inside, pushed me against the wall and kissed me raw. Something was definitely wrong.

I turned the handle and stepped through. He was behind his desk, his gaze down. When I followed his eyes, I could see he was looking at photographs spread out on the white, glossy surface.

I stepped forward and the upside-down images sharpened, their familiarity pulling me toward them.

As I moved closer, he steepled his fingers over the images and spun them around so they were facing me.

All were of me and the redheaded man who'd approached me and offered me money to spy on Hayden.

"You care to explain?" he asked, raising his eyes to look at me. His anger rolled off him, but he was also in complete control. This was a man no one would want to go up against. This was a man ready to battle.

I stepped forward and peered at the first image. It had been taken weeks ago in Saint Tropez. I hadn't made the connection before, but the photographer who'd asked me who was on my boat had been the same redheaded guy who'd offered me a hundred and fifty grand to tell him which company Hayden was buying. "It's the same guy," I said almost to myself.

"You two seem cozy."

I glanced up. Hayden towered over me, his eyes dark and heavy.

"Why are you taking pictures of me?" Didn't he trust me? Was he spying on me as well as this red-headed Phil guy who wouldn't leave me alone? What the hell had happened and how was I the girl caught in the middle of it?

He didn't answer. He just stared at me as if he were about to unleash his wrath.

"Have you been keeping tabs on me?" I asked.

"Answer the question," he said, his jaw tight and his words clipped.

"He was offering me money," I said, squinting at the first photograph, still confused as to why I hadn't recognized that it had been the same guy who'd approached me in Taormina. I'd clearly just not thought anything of it. Perhaps the camera had thrown me off. I'd been excited to get off the boat and was looking forward to speaking to my dad. "This was the guy."

"Are you working for Cannon?"

His question was like a jolt of electricity and I snapped upright and stepped back.

"What?" He thought I was a spy? I must have misheard him. He knew every inch of me. We'd spent hours together, working, kissing, tracing the contours of each other's bodies. He couldn't think that I'd been faking all of that. Surely.

"It's a simple question. Yes or no."

"Who is Cannon? Who the hell do you think I am?"

"Then explain the pictures. Why are you meeting this guy—who works for Cannon, but I imagine you already know that."

"I don't know who this Cannon is, and this guy approached me. I never *met* with him. I told you about this time." I tapped my finger on the middle photo.

"You didn't tell me you'd spoken to him on at least three occasions." His hand swept up, indicating the photos. "I guess telling me about once gave you cover in case you'd been spotted. Very clever."

Gave me cover from what exactly? "Did it occur to you that he kept coming back because I *wouldn't* give him what he wanted?"

My emotions ricocheted between panic and anger at being accused of something I hadn't done, but mostly, I was so disappointed that Hayden would think I was capable of spying on anyone, let alone him.

"I'm showing you the photographs and asking you to explain them. I think I'm being more than reasonable." His tone was flat and lifeless, as though he was the boss of an organization and I was some faceless employee he'd never met before who he was about to fire. He'd already made up his mind about what those photographs meant. It pierced me to my core that we'd spent so much time together and yet he still thought I was capable of betraying him.

I'd just have to explain. Surely when he heard what had happened, he'd chastise himself for being such an asshole.

"This one?" I said, turning the glossy print around so it faced him. "This was the first time I left the yacht. You can see he's wearing a camera around his neck. He looks like he's paparazzi. He asked me who was on the *Athena*."

Hayden's silence contained an unspoken question.

"No, I didn't tell him anything. It's not unusual to get approached, especially in Saint Tropez. All of us do, but we don't say anything." I wasn't sure that was true of some of my colleagues, but I certainly hadn't. "Unless the guest wants us to."

"The guests want you to tell the press they're on board?" Hayden asked, narrowing his eyes suspiciously.

I shrugged, taking a seat opposite him. "Sometimes. I mean, this lifestyle is expensive. People like to show off."

"So explain why you didn't tell me you'd been approached?"

"This happens all the time. I'd forgotten it had even happened until I saw the photograph."

"So what about this then?" he asked, tapping his finger on the middle image of the redhead. "That was the night after we stayed at the hotel. You can't tell me that's a coincidence."

"What's a coincidence?" I asked. I didn't understand why he was being so cold and sharp with me.

"That was the night we first slept together. Had he been waiting for you to report back to him or—"

I held up my hand to stop him. He made me sound as if I'd slept with him for information or something. He wasn't about to tell me what happened. I'd been there, and I'd told him about it. "He was on a bench. I was walking back to the tender in the morning and he was there. I told you all about it later that day after Skylar caught us. I was a little freaked out. He offered me money—five thousand dollars—to tell him what you were working on." I winced as I remembered how he'd told me I'd confirmed that Hayden was on the boat.

"You made it sound like it was no big deal," he said.

"Me? I couldn't get you to focus on it. You said that you being on the *Athena* wasn't a secret and then you kept asking about Skylar. Do you not remember this?"

"You never mentioned it again. And you conveniently forgot that he'd approached you before. Very convincing."

I sighed. Jesus, why was he so ready to assume the worst of me? I couldn't believe I was having this conversation with Hayden. Hadn't he told me he'd never felt the way he did about me before? Didn't that count for anything? Didn't he trust me? "I even told you he convinced me that I'd given him some information that I shouldn't have because he kept peppering me with questions and I was trying to dodge them. I told you he said I'd confirmed that you were on the yacht."

"So you admit you told him? What other information did you give him?"

"No." Had I? "I don't think so, but it all happened so fast and my head was everywhere. If you remember, we hadn't had much sleep the night before and the guy caught me off guard. Maybe I didn't refute it or maybe by refuting it I confirmed it for him. I don't know."

Hayden shook his head. He clearly didn't believe a word that came out of my mouth. "So this guy approached you a third time, even though he knew by then that it was futile? What happened the third time you met him?"

My heart sank and guilt crawled across my skin. I tipped my head back and stared at the ceiling. "That's when he offered me a hundred and fifty grand to feed him information about the deal you were working on."

"Wow," Hayden said. "A hundred and fifty grand. Five thousand just wasn't enough. I guess we know your price now."

Anger pushed through my guilt and erupted. Why did he just assume I'd taken it? I hadn't done anything. I'd been tempted for a second. I'd thought about it. That money would have meant as much physical therapy as my brother needed and it might have meant a different life for me. At the very least it would have meant breathing space, room to pause.

I pushed out of my chair and leaned over the desk. He was being so harsh and unfair. This wasn't the man I'd given my body to. He wasn't the man I thought he was. "You're an asshole," I replied. "I didn't take his money. You're still working on your deal, aren't you?"

"Yeah, despite you." His words were nasty but his tone was flippant, as if I were an irritation.

"Surely if I'd told him, then someone else would have bought the precious company, that guy who hated your dad."

He folded his arms. "I have no idea how your mind works or what your plans are. I hope it was worth it. You sold your character, your soul, for that money."

"You think if I had a hundred and fifty thousand dollars I'd stick around here to get caught? I'd have taken the next flight out."

"There's no point in denying it, Avery. I found the phone and the guy's business card under your bed. The same phone you're being given here." He tapped the photo with his finger.

"What the hell?" How had he gotten that phone? I'd stashed the phone and the business card, unsure of what to do with them. "You've been in my room?"

"You should try harder to hide stuff if you don't want people finding them."

"You've been through my things? Who are you?" Jesus, how long had Hayden had suspicions about me? Had he fucked me despite them or because of them? I shivered, uncomfortable in my skin. I needed to get out of there.

"Fuck you. I didn't take the money. If I had, my life would be a lot better right now. My *brother's* life would be a lot better. I'm not that girl. I wouldn't have done it to anyone, but *especially* not to you. Not the way I feel—felt—about you." I straightened and took him in. Still so handsome, but this wasn't the man I'd shared so much with. That man would know I couldn't ever take money for selling someone out. "You think you're isolated on this yacht in the middle of the sea? It's your suspicions, your mistrustful heart, that isolate you. I'd rather lose every dollar I have than live like that—trusting no one, loving no one, having no one love me. You might end up with an empire and more money than God, but take a look around and you'll see all the backs of the people who loved you who you turned away."

Had all these weeks been a lie? Was he pretending to be someone he wasn't? I shook my head. "I didn't take that money. I know that, and the man I kissed under the fireworks all those weeks ago knows it too. I don't recognize the man standing in front of me. And I don't want to know you." He'd believe what he wanted. Resignation took hold. I wasn't going to win this battle. I'd known as soon as I got back to the yacht that I could never betray Hayden like that. I'd paid a high price for my character because either way I was guilty, either of betraying Hayden or my brother. Even now, with Hayden accusing me of taking the money, I didn't regret my decision, but I did regret having put so much on the line for him. I'd been a fool. I pulled open the door and left, and Hayden didn't try to stop me. As I slammed the door behind me, I let out a breath, trying to stop myself from screaming out loud at the injustice of it all. For a second I thought I'd found someone, the one. For a moment I'd imagined a life full of fun and love and happiness rather than duty and burden and sacrifice. My heartbeat scattered in my chest and all of a sudden disappeared as if my heart had simply given up the fight.

THIRTY-ONE

Avery

"All crew. All crew, this is the captain. Meeting in the galley immediately." The anticipated announcement echoed out from my waistband as August and I folded towels in the laundry room. It was Captain Moss's call to the post-charter meeting where the captain brought up any concerns he had about our performance as a team and then distributed the tips.

Hayden had left the charter yesterday, the day after our argument in his office over the photos. I hadn't seen him again. I couldn't bring myself to leave my room while he was still on board. I didn't want to be reminded of the anger in his voice or the mistrust in his glance. Skylar had found me crying and told me to stay in bed. She didn't ask any questions and I hadn't argued with her. Even I wasn't able to paint a professional smile over my broken heart. I needed to piece myself back together and now Hayden was gone, it might be possible.

"I really hope this tip is decent. Ten percent at least. I

know we didn't have a whole lot to do, but eight weeks is a long time to have a shitty tip." August's words came in and out of focus for me. I was exhausted. Emotionally, physically—every kind of tired.

We made our way through the narrow corridor to the galley, and I slid into the banquette, the last to sit for the all-crew meeting. Now that Hayden's charter had finished, the energy on board had ratcheted up and everyone's voice was a little louder, their smiles a little wider. On the other hand, I felt as if I was coming out of a fog. I knew the people around me, but still felt as if there was a wall between us, that we were in different worlds.

"Beers?" Neill asked, opening the fridge. Charter was officially over if we were drinking.

"Yeah, I'll take one," I said. Alcohol couldn't make me feel worse.

"Are you sure you should?" Skylar asked. "Is your stomach better?"

I hadn't been there to see Hayden off the boat. It was the first time I'd ever not said goodbye to a departing guest, but I just couldn't bear it. My professional mask had crumbled, and I wasn't sure I would have been able to hold it together. I was angry that he thought I'd betrayed him, but ashamed by the fact I'd taken the phone and card, that I hadn't told him and possibly avoided everything that had come after. My heart ached at the thought of never seeing him again, but my head told me things ending this way would probably be easier—there were no what-ifs or what-could-have-beens.

Since our first kiss, I'd tried hard not to think about what would happen when Hayden left the yacht. Although he'd told me he wanted things to continue between us after he left, I knew the *logistics*, as he'd put it, were difficult. He was based in London with commitments and a business to run, and my job made a long-distance relationship almost impossible. Any time I had off I spent in Sacramento. As much as I might wish it were otherwise, the likelihood of Hayden and I existing outside this yacht was almost none, even before he'd accused me of being a corporate spy.

But now none of that was even a fantasy. He thought I'd betrayed him and through his assumptions and accusations, I *knew* he'd betrayed me.

I'd risked my career for him. I'd put my brother's care at risk for him. And yet he'd turned on me in an instant. He'd made up his mind about those photographs before he'd even asked me about them, and then assumed I was lying.

Captain Moss entered the kitchen and all eyes gravitated toward the ten brown envelopes he held in his hands. I should care more than I did. The tips I earned this season were all allocated to my brother's health insurance premiums. I knew that whatever was in that envelope, it wouldn't be enough to cover the additional expenses.

"No real issues on this trip," Captain Moss said as he sat down. "But we've not been tested. This was a very easy charter for everyone apart from Avery. You feeling better?" he asked me.

I nodded. "Yeah. It must have been something I ate," I said, flashing my best fake grin at Neill. "I threw up, but feel fine now."

"Cheeky," Neill said.

"You worked hard," Captain Moss said, lifting his chin in my direction.

Guilt unfurled in my stomach. If he only knew what had been going on between Hayden and me. I'd betrayed too many people for someone who wasn't worth it.

"You're a good girl, Avery." From anyone else, a statement like that might have been condescending, but at that moment it was exactly what I needed to hear. I wanted to be a good person. I needed to be a *good girl*, because if I wasn't, why hadn't I just taken the money and helped my family?

"You should have plenty of energy for our next guests who arrive next week." He dealt out the envelopes to each of the nine crew members. "We want to keep the bar high. We got a fifteen percent tip. Anything less for this next one will be a disappointment."

The crew gasped as they peered into their bulging envelopes. It was at the top end of what tips normally were, and because charters were usually shorter, none of us were used to having so much money handed to us at once.

"No room for complacency," Moss continued. "Go have fun tonight, but tomorrow I want every one of you up on deck at ten sharp. We've got to get this boat looking like it's brand new. No excuses." Captain Moss stood and headed back to the wheelhouse, leaving the rest of the crew to make plans for the evening. Why plans were necessary, I wasn't sure. We always did the same thing—drink as much as possible, dance and find someone to make out with.

But making out with anyone wasn't in the cards for me, and a new charter was the last thing I needed. The idea of seeing other people where Hayden and I had shared so much seemed wrong. Even though things had ended badly, I didn't want to erase it. I just wanted the pain of not having him to drift away. I wasn't sure that would ever happen, but I knew new guests wouldn't help. Neither would vodka.

"Wanna come and help me pick out an outfit for tonight?" Skylar asked.

I shrugged and followed her out of the kitchen. "That pink dress you showed me the other day would be nice," I said, trying to act as if my world hadn't turned upside down and inside out.

I followed her into her small cabin that she shared with August and she shut the door behind us. "Are you okay?" she asked. "You don't look okay."

"I'm fine," I said, taking a seat on August's bed, dipping my head so I didn't knock my head on Skylar's bunk.

"So, what happened with you and Hayden? Are you going to see each other again?"

I hadn't expected her question. We'd not discussed me and Hayden since our conversation in the laundry room. "No, of course not."

"Of course not?" She squinted at me as she hitched up her leg and sat on August's bed. "You must have been in love with him. Why wouldn't you want to see him again?"

Her statement hit me like a punch to the gut. "In love with him?" I clutched at my stomach, trying to find my breath, disorientated and dizzy. "Why would you think I was in love with him?" It couldn't be true, could it? I couldn't have fallen in love with a man who thought I was capable of betraying him for money, someone who clearly didn't know me at all.

My limp body and my aching heart suggested otherwise.

"Avery, you're not that kind of girl. You wouldn't have risked everything you've worked so hard for just to get laid by a pretty face." She sighed, and a grin curled at the edges of her mouth. "Although he did have a mighty pretty face. And a gorgeous ass. And I swear, one time the breeze lifted his shirt and I got a look at—"

She stopped as I fixed her with a glare.

"I'm just saying that to have put all that on the line, he must have meant a great deal to you."

I swallowed. I couldn't love him, could I? I couldn't love a person who'd treated me so cruelly. I wanted to scream at the top of my lungs. Why was everything so fucking unfair? I didn't want to be in love with a man who'd left me so easily. But of course she was right. Of course I loved him. Or a version of him at least. I loved the way he seemed to want to peel back my layers and know my deepest, darkest thoughts, the way he was so driven and determined that sometimes he'd forget the time of day and the day of the week but still kept the perspective that his brother had a job far more worthy. I loved the man who was the best man I'd ever known. I would never have risked everything for anything less. But it didn't matter what he'd meant to me. He'd hurt me. Despite what he thought, he was the one who'd betrayed me. I squeezed my eyes shut, willing myself not to cry. "He's gone now. It doesn't matter."

"You should totally call him. You swapped numbers, right?"

I shook my head. "We had a huge fight. It's done."

"Tell me what happened." Skylar pulled me into a hug and I let her. I needed someone to show me they cared in that moment.

I explained Hayden's accusations to Skylar, and explained what really happened. Talking about it was like putting a period at the end of the relationship. I could no longer pretend to myself that things were different, that what he'd accused me of had just been some big mistake and that he'd be back soon, begging my forgiveness. It was done.

I'd never felt that irresistible pull that I had toward Hayden for anyone else. I couldn't imagine I ever would again. No one would be able to pin me to the spot with just a look, rile me up to the point of almost coming with just a kiss. No man would ever make me feel as if it was an honor for me to share the weight of my responsibility with him. Even just talking to Hayden about my family had helped lift the burden slightly.

People like Hayden Wolf came around once in a lifetime. Things might have been different if I'd never taken that phone and business card. Maybe then, we might have found a miraculous way through the distance and contradictory lives and lifestyles, but the chance for miracles was over.

Now I had to focus on what I should have always put first—my family.

THIRTY-TWO

Hayden

The driver opened the passenger door. I dipped my head to get in, then groaned at the sight of my brother. "I hope you're here to tell me good news."

"Welcome home, brother. I thought I'd meet you at Heathrow as I knew you'd be so pleased to see me."

"I've had quite enough of you at the moment. Especially after a commercial flight." I was exhausted.

"Christ, you poor bastard. You had to fly commercial from your superyacht? Did the world run out of private jets?"

I pressed my lips together, trying not to let him see the grin threatening at the corners of my mouth. "And? I presume you came with news."

"I've found your leak," he said as he pressed his thumb against the side of his tablet, his fingerprint bringing it to life.

"About time. I thought I wasn't going to be able to go back to my office."

"It was Gerald," he said simply.

I recoiled. "I thought that having an offshore account wasn't conclusive? How can you be sure?" As financial controller for Wolf Enterprises and right-hand man to my finance director, he would have a lot of access to a lot of information.

"Because I'm that good."

"It's taken you nearly eight weeks—you're not that good."

"What can I say? He covered his tracks well. We had to wait for him to make a mistake."

"Prove it to me." When he'd told me about Avery, I'd refused to believe it until I'd seen the evidence for myself. And even after I'd found the phone and the business card, I still went ashore to see the photographs for myself. When I'd confronted her, her explanations were a little too polished. She'd had an answer for everything. I'd wanted to hear more—when had she started with Cannon? Had she been in their pocket all along? But she'd stormed out of my office, indignant. There was only one piece of the puzzle missing with Avery. Landon hadn't been able to track the payoff to her account.

Landon swiped through various documents and photographs, showing me records of Gerald receiving large payments into an offshore account on dates just after Cannon closed the four deals they'd stolen from under me. Landon had also had people search Gerald's home and recovered various electronic files stored in a safe, which were full of confidential details about the transactions Wolf Enterprises had been working on.

"Jesus. He's worked with us for years. He was so competent and professional; he'd be the last person I would have thought capable of something like that."

That wasn't true. *Avery* was the last person I'd ever have thought would betray me. I might have known her for a fraction of the time I'd known Gerald, but I'd been certain I'd looked into her eyes and seen nothing but honesty and truth. Her selflessness was one of the things I'd liked most about her. The way she had such strong values—the way she'd sacrificed so much for those she cared about. I'd just thought I was one of those people. Apparently it had all been an act, a means to an end.

"Does that mean Anita is in the clear?" I asked.

"Yes. That was an inheritance from her grandparents. They paid some before the sale of some real estate and some after."

I hadn't even known her grandparents had died. I liked to keep things professional but my assistant should be able to tell me about things like that. But I'd have the chance to put that right. At least she hadn't been the leak.

"I'll have Gerald's pass cancelled and his desk cleared." I tipped my head back on the headrest. "At least that's done." I'd expected it to feel more like a victory. Perhaps all my adrenaline had been used up completing the deal, but I wasn't elated or triumphant at catching the guy who'd threatened everything I'd worked for. Instead I was hollow and gray inside. Avery's warmth had left me. I had only known her a few weeks, but she'd carved a place in me that was so deep and profound that I didn't feel like myself now I knew I'd never see her again.

Was I so easily manipulated?

I hadn't seen Gerald betraying me over the course of months and I'd known that man years, sat across a board table from him a thousand times, met his wife and kids.

Why did Avery's betrayal feel bigger?

The image of her smiling face—an expression I knew

her other guests never saw—her long hair wrapped around my wrist, her panting little moans that went straight to my cock. I couldn't get any of it out of my head.

"You heard anything about Avery?" I asked Landon.

He shook his head. "I told you that it would be a few weeks. I'm tracking her finances and her father's. The payment will show up."

"But if she was the leak, how did I manage to get Phoenix done? It still doesn't make sense."

"What do you care?"

I had no idea why I still cared. I'd completed the Phoenix deal and now owned the company I'd always dreamed of. I should feel ten feet tall, but it felt as if I'd got to the summit of Everest and found the vista was nice and everything, but it wasn't that different to the view a couple of thousand feet down. I don't know what I was expecting—a coronation, a key to the city? Yes, I'd outwitted Cannon, but the victory echoed it was so hollow.

"We uncovered it and now you'll never see her again."

I'd never understood women who stuck around while their husbands and boyfriends abused them physically and mentally—why couldn't they just walk away? But I wasn't sure that if Avery was here right now I wouldn't want to take her back to my flat, strip her naked and fuck her into next week. Despite watching the guilt on her face, hearing her excuses as she sat across from me, I'd never stopped wanting her. Had the last year of Cannon's attack on my business undermined more than my net worth? Had it chipped away at my judgment and instincts about people? I still wanted to believe Avery couldn't have betrayed me. I needed that final puzzle piece to slot into place before I gave up hope and accepted I'd opened up to someone who was just using me.

"I want to know, Landon. I want to see the money move. She just didn't strike me as a woman who would . . ." Would what? Do anything to care for her brother? It was one of the things I'd liked most about her. She'd sacrificed her own life ambitions for her family. Taking money for their future wouldn't be so difficult.

"Like you said, everyone has their price," Landon said.

"Maybe," I said. "But I want to see it for myself. And can you track that ginger guy down? I'd like to talk to him."

"Jesus, that pussy must have been good."

"Don't be a dick. I want to know we were right about her. At the moment, she had an explanation for everything. As soon as that money hits, there are no more excuses that make sense. As you know, I'm all about the details. I'm ruthless but I'm fair. And for the record, I'm going to kick your arse at squash."

As soon as I saw the money in Avery's account I would be able to close that chapter in my life and move on. Until then, I'd still wake in the middle of the night with the sensation of her hair between my fingers, still see her every time I closed my eyes. I needed to see the price she'd been bought for and then I could forget she ever existed.

THIRTY-THREE

Three months later

Avery

I plastered on my best fake smile as I stepped through the sliding doors of the salon and out onto the main deck carrying two platters of appetizers—oysters on one, caviar on the other. It was the last service of the season and I couldn't wait for it to be over and to wave goodbye to these guests tomorrow morning.

"You have a really fantastic body," the oldest male guest, Gus, said, looking me up and down as I leaned over the table to set down the platters. August followed with two additional bottles of champagne.

I ignored him, my smile never faltering. The grin wasn't real and so wasn't affected by rude, sexist comments. Usually, I brushed them off and didn't give them a second thought, but there was something about this guy that made me want to knock him over the head with an empty bottle and toss him overboard. Maybe it was just because it had been a long season. The Mediterranean was one of the most beautiful places in the world, but five months was a long time at sea, whatever the surroundings.

"She really does," another man said, and he patted me on the ass.

Were we in 1977? I wasn't an object to be leered at or an item for sale. Why did people with money think they could grab all the pussy they wanted?

I moved away from the grabby hands and lecherous stares and guided August back through the doors to the galley.

"Urgh, why is it always the ugly ones that want a slice? If he was good looking I wouldn't mind. If Hayden Wolf had ever grabbed my ass, I'd have enjoyed it, but this lot?" She pretended to barf. I should have discouraged her, but I didn't care if the guests heard. Hayden Wolf wouldn't have grabbed August's ass—he'd have been clear about what he wanted. I'd certainly found him impossibly persuasive and seductive, but he'd never taken anything from me that I hadn't given him willingly.

The echo of his arms circled my waist and my professional smile disappeared. I should have forgotten how it felt to be held by him. Three months was long enough. But the ache for him was still there, it had settled under my skin and I wasn't sure if it would ever leave.

"Avery, Avery, this is the captain. On the bridge, please."

Grateful for the interruption, I snatched the radio from my waist.

"On my way," I replied, then turned to August. "Keep an eye on the table, but I don't want you going out there on your own, okay?"

"If you're with the captain for long, I'll go out with her," Neill said, knowing full well why I didn't want her to go alone. We really shouldn't need a buddy system, but that was yachting.

I trailed upstairs, my feet heavy with fatigue, and knocked on the wheelhouse door.

"Come in," Captain Moss said. "Those handsy guests behaving?"

I shrugged. We both knew they weren't, but it wasn't so bad we were going to endanger our tip . . . which probably meant they had bought us. Maybe Hayden had been right and I did have a price. I did things I hated every day only for the money. It couldn't have been such a stretch for him to think I would have taken a hundred and fifty thousand dollars. The line had been clear to me, but maybe to him I was on the wrong side of the line every day I woke up on a yacht. "They're manageable."

Captain Moss rolled his eyes and indicated for me to take a seat. "You've had a good season. I know you didn't get a break in between charters, so it must have been tough on you."

"I'm looking forward to getting back to California, that's for sure." My flight was already booked. I wasn't even staying the night after the charter finished. I wanted to get the hell off the continent Hayden Wolf was still on. Maybe then I'd be free of him.

It had been months, but I still thought about him constantly. At times I hated him for what he'd accused me of, for how he'd so easily thought me a liar. But other times I just missed him—missed the way he held me, pressed his lips to my forehead. It was worse at night when I dreamed about him—about *us*—in London, having dinner, watching television, in a real relationship. It had only ever been a fantasy, but it was one that had felt so very real.

"You've held this ship together with your professionalism and commitment this season, Avery. I'm proud to work with you. I'll start the Caribbean season in three weeks and I'd like you back with me."

It took some effort, but I pulled my mouth into a smile. "That's really flattering, Captain Moss. I just . . . I don't know if I can think about next season yet." All I wanted to do was get away from this boat where I'd fallen in love and my life had morphed into more than being a yachtie for a few weeks. The promise of a different life meant facing my daily reality was harder than usual. Loving Hayden had meant anything was bearable. But now? Every time I opened my eyes, the daylight stung as if it were reminding me of how ridiculous I'd been to think there might be more for me. That I might build a life and a future with someone. I'd dared to love someone, and my heart was now permanently scarred.

He frowned. "I've always seen you as a lifer when it comes to yachting. You thinking of switching things up?"

Yachting had never been my passion, certainly not in the same way the sea was Captain Moss's. It had always been a means to an end. "I'll be back. I think I just need a break." I had no choice but to return. I might not have chosen the life of a yachtie, but it had chosen me. "I'd be delighted to join you for the Caribbean season." I forced my smile a little wider. "But I need a month off."

He nodded. "You earned it. I was going to suggest we bring August and Skylar along with us, if you think they're up to it."

I'd spent the first part of the season distracted and wrapped up in my feelings for Hayden, but despite my lack of attention and the rude awakening we'd all gotten when Hayden left and twelve guests arrived for our second charter of the season, we'd gotten along famously. August had learned quickly, and Skylar had been loyal and hard-working, even if she hadn't found the rich man she was looking for.

"I'll ask them. The three of us make a good team."

"Show me a good team, and I'll show you a good leader. Nice job, Avery."

I sucked in a deep breath. "Thank you, sir."

Tomorrow I'd be on the way home to my family. I was ready to shut the chapter on the promise of love and happiness and to accept my future.

THIRTY-FOUR

Hayden

Landon had tracked down the guy in the photographs. Why the bloody hell he wouldn't meet us in London, I had no idea. I was paying him enough. It had been a nearly two-hour drive out to Essex. I hoped it would be worth it. I bowed my head as I entered the dark, old-fashioned pub. An inglenook fireplace that had horse brasses pinned to its breast stood at one end and a bar at the other. This place hadn't seen a paintbrush in a thousand years.

I scanned the room and caught sight of my brother. I paused and slid my eyes to his companion sitting opposite him. The familiar stranger's hair didn't look so ginger in the dim light of the small-windowed room.

"Hello," I said as I pulled out a chair.

"Good, you're here," my brother said, stating the obvious. "I've got you a beer." I glanced at the three pint glasses on the table filled with different shades of brown liquid. I hadn't had a beer since I'd left university. I preferred a good whiskey, but alcohol wasn't the thing I was focused on.

"You'll recognize Phil from the photographs. As I said to you on the phone, he was a hired hand for Cannon, not an employee."

"I work for the highest bidder, simple as that," Phil said. His accent was non-distinct, and he matched the tone, looked as if he would blend into a crowd.

Phil seemed ready to launch into an explanation of his life story, but my brother interrupted him. "It seems he doesn't know a hell of a lot, so I'm not sure what use he's going to be."

When we'd uncovered Gerald's treachery, I'd ordered a full security check on all senior members of my staff. I was satisfied there would be no more leaks, but for me, it wasn't over. Not yet. And not because Cannon wasn't going to be held to account. I'd been clear I didn't want to press charges against them or Gerald. I wanted the rot cut out and the focus back on being the best at what I did. I'd claimed my power back, kept my investors happy and bought Phoenix. I wasn't out for revenge. The best way I could get my own back was by being successful despite Cannon's best efforts to ruin me as they had my father.

But it wasn't over. Not quite. We'd not managed to trace the payments into Avery's—or any of her family's—bank account. And if that money never showed up, I would always have a doubt in the back of my mind. I was sure I would replay our conversation where I confronted her about the phone and the photographs again and again and again. It had been three months, but the memory was fresh as if it were yesterday. I was fighting an internal war, where I changed sides every time I thought back to that conversation. Should I have believed her? I needed certainty to shut down any memory I ever had of Avery Walker.

As the money hadn't shown up, unless I confronted

Cannon's board, who would simply deny the entire mess, then the only person who could confirm Avery's guilt was Phil. I needed closure, because thoughts of Avery Walker were haunting me. I'd tried everything I could to bleach my mind of her, but despite the long hours, the booze and training as if I was trying to make the Olympic team, I still yearned for her. I'd assumed being with other women would help, but for some reason I couldn't do it. Since leaving the yacht, I'd made do with my fist and some bad porn.

I nodded. "Let's see," I told Landon. I wanted to hear exactly what had happened from the horse's mouth. I had nothing to lose at this point. "Phil, I'm going to pay you a lot of money and in return, I want to hear about all your dealings with Cannon, directly or indirectly, and from the beginning. If I find out you've lied to me or spared me the truth or misled me in any way . . . Well," I said, glancing at my brother. "I know some very dangerous men. Let's leave it at that, shall we?" I'd never resorted to physical violence or even threats of physical violence before. Even at school, I always left that to my brother, but I'd never been so serious. Up until now the evidence had been compelling but circumstantial. I wanted certainty when it came to Avery Walker.

Phil shrugged. "Like I said, I'm a gun for hire. And like you said, you're paying me a lot of money."

"Okay, go on," I said.

"I've been working for the firm that put me on the Cannon job on and off since I left MI5. I'd done a few jobs for Cannon. They were good clients. It was easy work. Just surveillance and information gathering mainly."

"And they learned to trust you?" Landon asked.

"I guess. Then this job came along and they were offering good money to spend some time in the sun. What's not to like? They said it was surveillance and questioning. Nothing big." He paused as if he were trying to recall the details.

"Did they give you a list of people to surveil?"

He shook his head. "No. They told me to find your boat and report back to them. That was it at first. That took a few days because you weren't in the marina. And then I called in a few favors, got details of the crew on board. Avery Walker was the easiest target."

I winced as his thin lips curled around her name. I hated the sound of it coming from his mouth.

"She wasn't working for Cannon?" I asked.

He took a sip of his drink and the few seconds delay in his answer felt as if it lasted hours. "No, it was my job to get her to talk. I thought it would be easy. I knew her family needed the money and that she sent most of her salary and tips home. I thought five thousand dollars would be enough. But not a chance."

Five thousand dollars hadn't bought her. At least she'd tried to resist. "So you didn't approach any other crew members at all? No deck crew? It was just Avery?"

"No, I was convinced she'd break. Especially for so much money." He picked up his pint and took a sip as if we were discussing the latest Six Nations match. "I can't believe she turned down that money. I've never offered so much to a source for so little. I mean, it was just the name of the company you were buying and how much you were going to pay."

"You were surprised she didn't take the five thousand?"

"No, the hundred and fifty thousand. That's what I got told to offer her." He shook his head. "It was a lot of money she walked away from just for a few bits of information. I wasn't asking her to plant listening devices or really do anything that would put her in danger."

She'd turned it down? I knew how much her family needed the money, how much it would have meant for her to have that amount of cash for her brother. She probably could have skipped a season or at least got a job back in Sacramento. Guilt churned in my stomach. What had I done?

"They were stunned when she didn't bite," he said, interrupting my thoughts. "I was surprised. Especially as it kept getting better for us. Cannon pulled a few strings and had her brother's insurance coverage reassessed. Her brother's entitlements were cut. We thought she would have been desperate for the cash. I thought it was a perfect moment to make that final, big offer. But she said no."

I leaned back and tried to take in what I'd just heard. Avery's brother—the person she worked so hard for, had given up her own dreams and aspirations to provide for—had had his health insurance cut? Because of me. Her brother, her guilt about the accident and her need for redemption were Avery's Achilles' heel and she'd still not sold me out?

"But she still didn't take the money?" My heart began to thunder through my chest. I'd been right about her the first time. She'd not betrayed me. She'd protected me. I'd always known Cannon were lowlifes, and I'd been content to walk away from the immoral, illegal things they'd done in order to try to bury me. I'd been determined to take the high road, clear in my mind that my revenge would come with my success despite them. What this guy was saying changed things. Now I wanted to bury them. I might not like it, but I understood that her telling some guy Phoenix's name in return for her brother's wellbeing would be a small price to pay. It had been an impossible situation for her.

"Nope. Not a penny. When she called me from the satellite phone, I thought I had her. I really did." He shook his head in disbelief. "But she wanted to know who else I'd approached on the crew. Didn't even ask for more money. Just a flat-out no."

Could she really be that good? Would she sacrifice her brother . . . for me? Everything he was saying rang true to me. The Avery he was describing was *exactly* the woman I knew. The woman I'd kissed on the upper deck while watching the fireworks, the woman who'd worked tirelessly to keep me happy, even when it wasn't her job, because that was her nature. She was kind and sweet and loyal just as I'd always thought. She really was that good.

And I'd thrown her away, assumed the worst, accused her of betraying me when really, I'd been the one who betrayed her. I'd not believed in her. I'd not trusted myself.

I was an idiot.

"And that's it? There's nothing else?"

Phil shrugged. "A couple of days later Cannon cancelled the job."

That must have been when my acquisition of Phoenix had been announced.

"I want to hear from you if you ever get another job offer from Cannon. I'll make it worth your while."

Phil tipped back the last of his pint and pushed out his chair, leaving me heavy with guilt and unsure of my next move.

"What was all that about?" Landon asked when Phil left.

"All what?" I asked. He'd known why we were here.

"This whole conversation was about Avery. Are you still

hung up on her or something? Surely she was just a convenient fuck."

I leaned back, staring out the window into the black, and let the dark wave of guilt wash over me. What had I done? "We weren't just fucking."

"What does that mean?"

I wasn't sure what it meant. I just knew that between us, it had been different. The connection we had was inexorable. We'd proven that. I'd been drawn to her despite it being the most demanding time in my life, when all I'd worked for, all I'd become was on the line. And she . . . she'd risked her job, her *redemption* for me.

And it had all worked out for me. I'd bought Phoenix, defeated Cannon. But our relationship had brought her only misery. I'd believed her guilty of a betrayal she wasn't capable of. Her being with me had ruined everything for her, yet I'd walked away with a bruised ego and an aching heart and I'd thought I was the one badly off. "It means I fucked up."

"There was plenty of evidence," Landon said. "You were well within your rights to think she was selling secrets."

He was wrong. Avery had never shown herself to be the kind of person who would betray me. "I had no right whatsoever. She'd put her career on the line for me. If people had found out about us, she wouldn't have been able to get another job. Why would I think that after that, she'd betray me? I must have lost my mind." I thrust my hands through my hair, my body hot with panic. What had I done?

"Jesus, you sound like this woman was really important to you."

I sighed, sliding down in my chair. "She was."

"Then go apologize."

I scoffed. "Oh yeah, because it's that easy. Integrity and loyalty are at her very core and I accused her of having neither."

Landon winced. "We all make mistakes. Even you, Hayden Wolf."

"You saying you do too?"

He rolled his eyes. "Of course not. But if I did and I had a way of setting things right, I'd like to think that I would try."

I groaned, remembering our last conversation. "She'll never forgive me. I was nasty. Spiteful. I just felt so . . ." Betrayed wasn't a strong enough word. *Vulnerable* was how I'd felt, but I wasn't about to say that out loud. Landon wouldn't understand. "I'd just thought things were different with her. I mean, we talked. Shared stuff. I thought I knew her and I wanted her to know me."

Landon nodded, and spared me the shit I'd assumed he'd give me. "Sounds a little out of character for a guy who divided women into two categories: those he worked with and those he shagged."

I cringed at his accurate reflection of my relationships with women before Avery. Avery had felt like a friend, a partner, a soulmate. She wasn't anyone to put in a category. "Yeah, Avery was different."

I had to do something, make it up to her. She'd turned down that money from Cannon only to have me turn on her. And now, because of me, her brother's insurance was fucked. "I'm going to need you to help me with some stuff. I don't know how Cannon managed to get to the insurance company, but I need to find a way of setting it straight."

"I have her address in Sacramento," he said. "It's just a private jet away."

"Why would you want me to chase after this girl? I thought you didn't understand monogamy?"

"I don't, but it sounds to me like you *have* to have this girl."

He was right. My pull toward Avery was as strong as ever. It had never wavered, even when I suspected the worst of her. But I couldn't just turn up on her doorstep. I didn't even know if she'd be there, let alone if she'd agree to see me.

"No, this is about paperwork. She suffered, her brother suffered, and all because Avery was part of the crew on the yacht I chartered. I can't let that stand. She's done nothing wrong, and yet her family is bearing the brunt of being associated with me. This isn't about me getting what I want—even if I do want *her*. This is about me making things right for her and her family."

Landon grinned around his pint glass and after taking a sip, set it down. "If you tell anyone I said this, I'll deny it, but you're a decent guy, Hayden. I'm kinda proud you're my brother."

Landon was a war hero. He'd fought and sacrificed for his country. For him to be proud of me was beyond anything I could hope for. "I won't tell a soul," I replied and clinked my glass against his. I might be terrible at relationships with women and I might have become a paranoid control freak, but my brother and I had something in common: we were men of action and we didn't stop until we'd got what we wanted. I'd make things right with Avery. It was the least I could do.

THIRTY-FIVE

Avery

The bruises on my heart still ached as if I'd last seen Hayden yesterday. I'd expected Sacramento to revive me, to make me forget the weeks that had come before. But a month at home had passed too quickly and I was dreading leaving for Miami later that day.

"Come over here and have breakfast with me and your brother before you go," my dad said.

I glanced over at them both. "Sure. Has the mail come yet?"

My dad cocked his head to the counter top where a stack of mail lay unopened.

"Dad!"

Since I'd gotten back from France, I'd spent all of my free time on the internet, finding charities that supported people in our situation and talking to them about what had happened, writing to apply for grants from foundations and trusts, investigating what I could do to appeal the health insurance company's decision regarding my brother's care.

I'd been busy and it had started to pay off. Some donations were just a few hundred dollars, but yesterday we'd received a check for five thousand from a sports injury charity. It wasn't going to go far, but it had given me hope and more than anything, that was what I needed.

My father had seemed content to accept what had happened, as if he knew the odds had never been in our family's favor, knew that the house always won. He'd shrugged and done the best he could with what he had.

That was his coping mechanism.

Michael and I hadn't talked about it at all.

The way I dealt with it was to try to fix it. It was who I was—I fixed things for people and the five thousand dollar check yesterday was evidence I could fix this too.

I grabbed the mail from the counter and dropped into a seat at the table, sorting through the envelopes. Most of them were junk.

"You want juice, honey?" my dad asked as he held the jug over my glass.

"Sure, thanks," I said, sawing my finger across the sealed top of a brown envelope. "You're going to have to check these when I'm gone. You know that, right? You can't leave it for me to come home to in five months. Some of them you need to respond to right away. Those you should just scan to me and I'll deal with them." I unfolded the letter. I didn't need to read the line and a half of writing—anything that didn't require at least two paragraphs was a no.

"I can email you on this boat you're going on, right?"

"Yes, and call me. I'll have my phone with me. It will be much better than last time." I wasn't sure it was the relief at being able to contact my father that made my shoulders sag or if it was the thought that if I had my cell my guest wasn't Hayden Wolf.

I'd tried not to think about him, but he was still there, haunting me at the edges of my smile as I settled back into Sacramento, and in that time just before I fell asleep when I couldn't press down the memories of him anymore. I hoped that if I could block him out for long enough, eventually I wouldn't have to try, and he'd dissolve into a pot of bad decisions and might-have-beens.

My rage had faded, at least.

I couldn't be angry at him for his accusations. They'd hurt. They still hurt but I understood it. And I deserved it. For a second I'd been tempted. And it hadn't been how I felt about Hayden Wolf that had stopped me. I just couldn't do that to my father or brother. Neither one of them would have forgiven me if they'd thought any money they'd received had been from a source like Cannon. It was hard enough for my dad to accept the checks that had been coming from charities and foundations since I'd started applying. He was a man of honor and principle and I wouldn't sully his legacy by taking money for stolen secrets. I wanted to be worthy of calling him my father.

My feelings for Hayden remained almost overwhelming whenever my heart and mind grew weak and let memories of him escape. There was no sign of them diminishing, but I kept telling myself it would happen. Surely, thoughts of him would fade and weaken and I wouldn't have to try so hard to keep them at bay.

"That's weird. This one's to Michael," I said, pulling out a thick cream envelope from the pile. Most of the letters and applications I'd made had been in my father's name as next of kin. One or two had been in mine, but I hadn't made any in my brother's name.

"Can I open it, Michael?" I asked.

He shrugged, focused on his food rather than his mail,

and I grinned and blew him a kiss. I flipped the envelope over and worked my thumb under the flap.

No check, but it was two pages long. I flipped to the second page to see an application with boxes and dotted lines sprinkled down the page. They were asking for bank account details and addresses. That was weird.

I turned back to the first page, glancing to the headed notepaper. Lycan Foundation. I couldn't remember writing to them, but I must have sent off four hundred applications, so it was perfectly possible that I had just forgotten.

I read it once all the way through and then paused. I must have read it incorrectly. They were offering to pay Michael's physical therapy, for a full-time caregiver and for any health insurance premiums.

That couldn't be right. My pulse began to throb in my ears and I started again from the top.

"I want you to eat something," my dad said. His voice sounded tinny and far away.

"Hang on, Dad," I said, pressing the letter flat against the table and tracing the lines of typed text with my finger. I needed to read more carefully. I had to subdue the fluttering in my gut that was squealing that this letter was a winning lottery ticket.

I'd been wrong. It wasn't what I thought. It wasn't just Michael's physical therapy, a full-time caregiver and insurance premiums they wanted to pay. It was *"all and any costs associated with Michael's medical or occupational needs for the rest of Michael's life."*

Surely I had this wrong? This would mean that if Michael needed other things as he got older or as my father got older, this charity was going to cover it. I flipped over the page. This couldn't be happening.

I stood, vaguely aware of my chair falling back

behind me.

"Avery, sit and eat something. Please," my dad said.

"Hang on a minute. I just need to check something." When had I contacted these people?

I grabbed the laptop, brought up my spreadsheet of applications I'd made, but I couldn't find anything.

I typed it into Google. Nothing came up.

Was this a scam? Would anyone be so cruel?

"Daddy, did you apply to any charities? Or did anyone we know do that?" For a flash I wondered if my mother had had something to do with it but of course she wouldn't have. We didn't exist to her anymore.

"No, Avery, you know how I feel about that. It's hard enough seeing you do it but I tell myself it's for Michael. But I don't like to . . ."

I turned back to the computer and searched Google again. "You ever heard of the Lycan Foundation?"

My dad chuckled, and my heart thudded against my ribcage. Was this a joke? "Lycan? Is this Dungeons and Dragons or something?"

"What are you talking about?" I held up the letter. "This charity is saying they'll pay Michael's medical bills. All of them. Forever. But I don't remember applying to a Lycan Foundation."

My dad froze. "*All* of his medical bills?"

"Yes! Do you know who they are?"

He shrugged, his brows drawn together as he strode over, took the paper from my hands and read the letter himself. "Lycan is . . . I don't know. It was the name for a werewolf, I thought, but I guess it's just a surname."

Werewolf? Memories of Hayden burst through my mental barriers. It couldn't be him, right? He had no idea where we lived or that I'd applied for anything. I'd never told him that Michael's medical insurance had been changed and that his physical therapy had been cut. And he hated me. He thought I was a liar and a thief. Of course it wasn't him. I shook my head.

"Call them." My dad handed me back the letter. "There's a number on the letterhead."

I scrambled to pick up the phone. I had to confirm what they were offering was real. I punched in the numbers, chewing on the inside of my mouth.

"Lycan Foundation, Alyson speaking."

I took a deep breath and explained why I was calling.

"Yes, that's right," Alyson said as I relayed the contents of the letter. "You just need to fill in all the details. It might take thirty days for us to organize all the payments, but we'll back pay from the date of the letter."

I pressed my lips together, trying to take in what she was saying. I swallowed. "And this has no end date?"

"That's right. It's for the rest of Michael's life."

It was as if she'd unlocked a brace from around my chest and suddenly there was more room to breathe.

"Thank you," I said. "I just don't remember ever making the application, so it's a lot to take in."

"I understand," she replied. "Other charities and third parties refer cases to us from time to time. That must be it."

I nodded. "I guess. I don't know what to say. Thank you so much."

"You're welcome. Just let us have the forms and we'll make all the necessary arrangements."

I put the phone back down. My father's eyes were wide. "It wasn't a hoax?"

"I don't think so," I replied. "I guess we fill out the forms."

"That means you don't have to go to Miami," he said.

I'd never told my dad the only reason I did the yachting season was to take care of Michael, just like he never told me he didn't want to retire because it meant the cost of health insurance premiums would skyrocket.

This donation gave us both hope for a different kind of future.

I stood and pulled him into a hug. "I still have to go to Miami. I've made a commitment and anyway, I'd like to see this Lycan thing actually happen before I think about making any big changes." My whole life had been about working to care for my brother. If Michael was really going to be looked after, where did that leave me? My entire focus had been on making enough money to look after my family.

If I didn't have that focus, I wasn't sure I knew who I was. I'd never allowed myself to think about what I was missing or how life might have been. I wasn't sure if I knew how to do that.

"If this is really happening, Avery, then promise me you won't stay doing a job you don't like. Promise me you'll do what you want to do, wherever in the world, whatever that is."

I had no idea what I wanted. Hayden had been the only thing in my life I'd had just for me in seven years and to him I was nothing, just some woman who'd betrayed him.

My heart swelled at my father's desire to have me happy and at the thought of finally being able to do something for me. Although I was excited, I wouldn't let myself believe something so wonderful could be happening. I'd been there before. I'd thought Hayden and I would carve out a future together. Believing things could be different had caused me misery and disappointment. This time I'd hold myself back, protect my heart until I'd seen the change it promised.

THIRTY-SIX

Avery

Another day, another blue sky, another superyacht, but it might be my last first day of the yachting season. I glanced across the marina from the upper deck of the *Venus*. The view always looked prettier just before the guests arrived.

At the start of my last season, I'd been standing on a deck waiting to meet the man who would break my heart. I couldn't help but wonder what Hayden was doing right now. At the beginning of the last season I hadn't even met him, which seemed ridiculous since my feelings for him were so strong, as if we'd been joined together in a previous lifetime then found each other again. Yet he'd discarded me so easily. He couldn't have felt as strongly as I had—still did. I hated myself for being in love with him. He'd betrayed me, yes, but I couldn't hate him for it. Couldn't switch off my love for him just like that.

My radio crackled. "Avery, Eric and Josh. This is the captain. Preferences meeting in the crew mess."

I pulled the radio from my belt. "Roger that." I turned

and headed inside to the main salon. The guests were due to arrive within the hour so this was late for a preferences meeting, but we received it whenever the guests filled it in.

"This is pretty standard stuff, but we don't have much time," Captain Moss said, starting the meeting before we'd all sat down. "Six guests. They have three more for lunch today who will be leaving tonight. They're combining business with pleasure, so they may have guests on and off the boat during the course of the charter."

Charters that combined business entertaining tended to be a little easier. They'd want to spend a lot of time eating and drinking and all the bedrooms wouldn't be occupied.

"One of them is a vegetarian," the captain continued. "And one of them doesn't eat meat, but eats fish. Another doesn't eat carbs."

Josh rolled his eyes but we all knew the dietary requirements could be far worse.

"They like mojitos and champagne and only organic sparkling water."

It was my turn to roll my eyes. The guests were perfectly happy to drink cocktails but of course their water had to be organic. Captain Moss scanned down the page and we followed his lead. "No expensive whiskeys or cigars . . . They want the *Wall Street Journal*, *New York Times* and *Washington Post* every day." We got through the rest of the sheet in record time.

"Right, that's it. I'll see you out on the main deck." He checked his watch. "Eric, make sure you've got crew down there to deal with luggage. They'll be here any minute."

I stood and pulled out eleven champagne glasses. Two for orange juice—in Miami there was always someone who abstained from alcohol. The remaining nine I began to fill with champagne.

"Can I help?" Skylar came in behind me.

"Sure, grab the orange juice and fill two glasses."

Our radios crackled. "All crew, all crew. Guests are on the jetty."

"Shit," Skylar said.

"Early. Just our luck," I said.

We got the champagne out and practically ran to the main deck, lining up just in time to see the first guest emerge from the stairs.

I held my tray and plastered on my best superyacht smile. This might be the last time I would open a season and I was excited about what that meant for my future.

We greeted the primary and his wife, Brad and Jennifer, and their guests began to fill the deck. I tried to pick out the ones we'd had photographs of who were staying over.

"We're missing someone," Brad said. "Oh, here he is." He turned to the stairs as their final guest appeared. "Hayden, we thought we'd lost you. This is Hayden Wolf, a business associate of ours."

It was as if the whole world dropped away, leaving just him and me. For what seemed like a thousand years I was totally paralyzed—unable even to blink.

Our eyes locked, and he smiled. I couldn't respond. What was he doing here?

The world whooshed back, and I heard the captain chuckling as he and Hayden shook hands and Skylar gasped beside me.

"Avery, Skylar, August, Eric. Good to see you." He took a glass of champagne from my tray and lifted it slightly as if he were toasting something.

Was this a coincidence? He didn't seem shocked to see me, so had he known I would be here? Did he want to question me again? I had nothing left to tell him. I hadn't had any more approaches from anyone.

Was he here to cause trouble for me? Make me feel worse about something I didn't do? Maybe he was here to get me fired?

"Avery, do you want to leave the tour until later? That way you can all enjoy your meal and we can do the tour after when those who aren't staying have left?"

Trapped in a fog, I took the guests to their table, asked them about wine and made sure everyone was happy. I avoided looking at Hayden and tried to remember the preferences sheet we'd only just been through. I would have seen his name and photograph if he was staying over, right? I might be able to get through a lunch, but I couldn't handle a week with him. Not here. Not after all those things he'd accused me of. Not when I still loved him despite it all.

He seemed engaged in talking to Brad, so as soon as I could, I headed back to the galley, trying to fight back the nausea building in my stomach. Why was he here?

"Are you okay?" Skylar asked as I walked into the galley, my legs heavy, my brain fuzzy with trying to process what was going on. "Did you know he was going to be here?"

I shook my head as I slid the tray onto the counter. "Not a clue." I looked up at Skylar, who shrugged.

"I think you should take a moment. He's only here for lunch and August and I can cover that."

"What's going on?" Chef Josh asked as he pulled open the refrigerator.

"Nothing," Skylar and I chorused.

"Yeah, if you and August can do lunch service that would be good." Hopefully Skylar was right and Hayden would leave soon. Avoiding him would be the best for both of us. I had to be the last person he wanted to see.

"Sure, you stay here and . . . You think he's here to say sorry?" she asked.

I frowned. "No. He made up his mind. This is just a coincidence. Right?"

She shrugged and took out a fresh bottle of champagne from the cooler. "It's just . . . I don't know. You look good together."

My stomach somersaulted. He looked good. He *always* looked good, but I knew his heart wasn't mine. I just had to hide in here for a couple of hours and then I could get on with my last charter season.

THIRTY-SEVEN

Hayden

This could have been the very worst idea I'd ever had. There was no doubt Avery had been shocked to see me on the main deck. I should have expected it, I supposed. I'd just thought I might see something other than shock. I thought that her professional exterior might melt a little and I'd see that she loved me—as I loved her.

"Can I get you a top up, Mr. Wolf?" Skylar asked as she tipped the bottle of champagne toward my glass.

"Thank you," I replied. "Where's Avery?" I kept my voice low and quiet so only she and I could hear. Avery had disappeared as soon as she'd shown us to our table. Skylar and August had served lunch. Was she avoiding me?

"She's in the galley," she replied.

Brad had regularly invited me to join him on his yacht. I'd always declined, but this time I'd preempted his request and told him I'd been very happy with Captain Moss and that he should consider chartering the boat he was captaining. Brad had taken my suggestion and I'd accepted his subsequent invitation, although I'd declined a stay over.

Once I'd started to make things right, attempted to neutralize some of the poisonous things Cannon had done in order to bring me down, I'd been desperate to see Avery, and getting on a yacht was the quickest way I knew how. As soon as I'd laid eyes on her all my feelings magnified and multiplied and more than ever I realized what an idiot I'd been. Avery Walker wasn't capable of betraying anyone. I knew that, had always known it deep down, so why had I accused her? I'd let the dirty tricks of a business rival color everything around me and in the mindset where everyone was either a suspect or guilty, I'd lashed out. Avery had borne the brunt of my frustration with Cannon and my desire to defeat them.

I'd tried to rehearse an apology on the plane ride over, but I hadn't been able to get the words to fit together properly. I couldn't think of a single reason why she'd forgive me. But I had to try. I couldn't just walk away.

As lunch finished up, I said my goodbyes to Brad and his wife and the other guests and excused myself. Instead of heading straight off the yacht, I made my way inside, making some excuse about using the loo. I spotted the entrance to the galley and my heart began to clatter in my chest. I didn't want to get her in trouble, but I wasn't about to leave this boat without having a conversation with her.

I exhaled when I saw her sitting at the table, writing notes in her neat handwriting, the profile of her perfect ponytail exposing that long, soft neck. "Avery," I said.

She closed her eyes in a long blink, and then she turned and looked up at me as if it were the last thing she wanted to do. Her resistance plowed an ache deep within me. I wanted her, needed her. Did she hate me? Was I irredeemable?

She glanced across the room and my eyes followed hers. There was a guy in the kitchen I didn't recognize, though his eyes were fixed on me and Avery. He grinned and turned his back on us as he continued with his work.

"Can I have a word?" I asked, focusing my attention on Avery. "Perhaps you'll see me off the yacht?"

"Of course." Her professional smile overrode her sadness as she slid out from the table, then led the way off the *Venus*. I wasn't sure which I preferred—her sorrow or a smile that wasn't real.

She led the way as we walked off the deck and down the stairs. She stopped when we got to the bottom, folding her arms and inspecting the wooden slats of the jetty.

"Let's walk," I said. I'd forgotten what it was like to be this close to her, how much I liked having her by my side, walking, working, fucking. I liked doing everything with her.

When we were out of sight of the yacht, I stopped.

"I have an apology to make that's so big it had to be made in person."

She glanced up at me, her eyes narrowing.

"I know you didn't accept the money from Cannon," I said.

She stayed perfectly still. She didn't even blink.

"I know you're not capable of such a thing. I should never have questioned it in the first place. I knew you better than that."

She closed her eyes and shook her head. I wasn't sure if she was blocking me out or telling me she wouldn't forgive me.

"I don't know what to say." I wasn't used to apologizing.

I was rarely wrong, but I'd never been so sorry and I'd never been so wrong. And I needed her to believe me. I needed not to have messed up so badly that I'd lost her forever. "I'm so sorry. I'm an arsehole and I fucked everything up." The words spluttered from my mouth in a desperate attempt to say everything all at once. "I trusted you. I loved—love— you. I knew you were on my side. I don't know what happened." Looking back, I didn't know why I'd doubted her. Everything she'd said made sense. "I think there was so much going on, my focus was all off and I couldn't see the truth when it was right in front of me."

Her brow crumpled, and she uncrossed her arms as she gazed up at me, blinking as if she'd just seen the sun. "You believe me? You love me?"

I nodded. "I do, of course I do. I'm an idiot. A very sorry idiot. I should never have ever doubted you."

She sighed. "Finally," she said, her voice quiet with relief. "I couldn't betray you. Not for any amount of money."

Of course she wouldn't. She was too good. Too decent. Too self-sacrificing. I wanted to reach for her, pull her into my arms and protect her for the rest of time. From the likes of Cannon, from idiots like me who didn't appreciate her.

"Cannon pulled strings to get your brother's health insurance reassessed. They were trying to make you take the money," I said, wanting to fill the silence, wanting to earn her trust back.

"Jesus," she said, stamping her delicate foot on the worn wood of the jetty. "That was them? Fuckers."

"That we can agree upon." I wanted to take every drop of her pain away.

"They were trying to ruin my life so I'd be forced to take the money." She crossed her arms and gazed out at the sea. I wanted her to look at me. I wanted to see forgiveness in her eyes.

"It would seem so. Again, it was my fault. If I hadn't been on this yacht, your brother's health insurance would never have been affected."

"Wow," she replied. "These people have so much power."

"Too much power." She shouldn't have to live with the sword of Damocles hovering over her family. She'd done nothing but do right by everyone in her life.

"For a second, I imagined what my life would be if I'd taken that money," she said, squinting at the sun. "I took the phone. I thought about it."

"Don't feel bad about that. They made it as tempting as they could for you, and you know, if it had been my brother, I probably would have taken the cash."

She laughed, and I couldn't help but smile as I saw that open, genuine joy on her face, but she stopped herself abruptly and turned to me. "But your deal went through, right? They didn't win?"

I couldn't believe that with everything she'd been through, the way I'd treated her, she was still worried about me. "Everything is fine with Phoenix, but I don't care about that. I'm here. I want to make things right with you."

A breeze interrupted the still, hot air and blew a stray strand of brown hair across Avery's face. Instinctively, I brushed it away.

"I missed you," I said, cupping her face and sweeping my thumb over her cheek.

She closed her eyes as if it were too painful to hear the words.

"I missed you," she replied.

"I know I don't deserve it, but forgive me."

She leaned into my palm. "It's done already. I couldn't be angry at you, even before you came here. Well, I was at first, but I saw the pressure you were under, the betrayal you were having to deal with."

My heart soared. I knew I didn't deserve her forgiveness but to have it? To hear her say it? This was the summit of Everest. Looking at her was the best view in the world.

"Forgive but don't forget, that's what my dad always says."

My stomach flipped over. Of course she couldn't forget. What I'd done was question who she was. But did that mean there was no chance of a future together?

"Did you find your leak?" She placed a hand on my chest and I stepped forward so there was just an inch separating us.

I nodded. "I did. They'd been paid very well by Cannon over this last year or so."

"What people will do for money, huh?" she said.

"I'd do anything for you," I whispered. "Rob a bank, bury a body, whatever you want me to do."

Her silence expanded as her palm seared into my chest and my thumb stroked her cheek.

"I should get back," she said eventually. "I can't leave Skylar and August on their own any longer."

Were we done? Had whatever she'd felt for me fizzled and died as my accusations took over? I needed a way back. I couldn't give up. "Come back? Later? Tonight?"

"I can't leave the yacht. You know that."

By forgiving me she'd given me more than I could have possibly hoped for. But I still hoped for more. I wanted her heart, her body, her soul. "Then I'll wait. When can I see you again?"

She tilted her head. "Go back to London, Hayden. I'm

here all season." She pulled her bottom lip between her teeth. "You have a life there."

"I want *you* in my life. I just—"

"This . . . We're . . . I don't know what you want or what you're expecting, but I have responsibilities. I have five months here and then . . . We're not compatible."

I hated hearing her say that. I'd never met anyone I was so compatible with. "That's not true and I don't think you believe it, either. If you can forgive me, then we can go back to—"

"To what? We had a fling on a yacht for a few weeks. You said yourself that the 'logistics were challenging'."

"If you're telling yourself it was just a fling then you *are* a liar."

She didn't respond. She didn't have to. We both knew what we had wasn't some kind of fleeting, throwaway connection.

"I'm not saying it won't have challenges," I said. "But I like to face my battles—and win them. I'm not going to slink away because it might be too difficult. You're worth more than that."

She glanced back to the boat. "It's not just that." She paused and as her eyes flickered over my face, I could see she was trying to decide whether or not to tell me what she was thinking. "I just don't think I can. I saw the promise of something when you and I were together, Hayden. I need you to be the man I thought you were. The one who was in my corner, who respected me, believed me to be on his side. I deserve that man."

"You do," I replied, trying to keep my voice from breaking. She was right. I wasn't good enough for her. "And I want to be that man for you. Perhaps I wasn't then but meeting you has changed so much for me. More than that, losing you turned my world upside down and made me reassess everything. I can't lose you. I want to spend the rest of my life working to be the man who deserves you."

Silence surrounded us. I didn't want to even breathe in case I missed the next thing she said.

"I need to go," she said.

Had I lost her? I couldn't just walk away. I pulled out a business card. "My mobile number is on this card. Promise you'll meet me when this charter is over. That's just five days away."

"You're going to fly back in five days?"

"No." I shook my head and I was certain I saw a trace of disappointment flicker over her face. "I'm not leaving Miami. Not until I've convinced you that I love you."

Her teeth caught her bottom lip, but she reached out and took the card. I wanted to grab her, kiss her, hold her, but I held back. I shouldn't push her, no matter how hard I wanted to. Not yet, not now.

"I have to go," she said.

"Promise me. Five days."

"I won't make promises I don't know if I can keep. But I promise I'll call to let you know."

It was a small victory, but I'd take it. I was impatient to get to the bit where I could kiss her, hold her. When she'd be mine.

She looked back down the jetty. "I really have to go."

I couldn't bring myself to respond. I didn't want to say goodbye.

"I've missed you," I said. She nodded and turned, then made her way back to the yacht.

She glanced over her shoulder as she walked away and gave me a small smile. I'd do anything it took for that not to be the last smile of hers I saw.

THIRTY-EIGHT

Avery

I had a mammoth decision to make and for the first time in a long time I didn't know what to do. My heart had been thudding through my chest all morning. We were just off the coast of Bermuda and Captain Moss had pulled up the anchor to take our guests back to shore. This was it. The charter was almost over, and that meant I owed Hayden Wolf a phone call.

His dog-eared, ragged business card was under my pillow, which was where I'd kept it since he'd given it to me. Each night, I'd take it out, turn it over in my hand and ask myself whether I should call.

Because I wanted to. I really wanted to.

He believed me, and I'd long forgiven him for questioning my loyalty and character.

And I loved him. I truly loved him. And he said he loved me.

So it was simple, right? I should just call him.

The problem was, I'd hurt so much during these months

since he'd left the yacht. The pain had been raw and visceral but I was beginning to heal. Sort of. At least, I had accepted a future without him. Then he showed up five days ago, while I was trying to plan a future that didn't include him. Things had been made easier because I knew he hated me. And because he clearly hadn't shared the deep, fundamental feelings I had for him. I wouldn't have assumed the worst of him and called him a liar. The imbalance in our feelings made it easier to see the future without him.

"Can we get you anything else?" I asked the six guests still seated at lunch.

"I think we're good," Brad said, glancing at his watch. "We need to pack."

There were only a few minutes of this charter left, and the ticking of the clock was booming in my ears.

"I think August has done that for you, while you've been at lunch," I replied.

His wife patted his hand. "It's all handled."

That's what they'd paid for, and that's what we'd done. It had been a good charter. The guests had been friendly and fun without being too much of either. As the kickoff to what may well be my last season, I couldn't complain.

Skylar and I cleared the table and tidied away the kitchen while the deck crew docked the yacht and then hauled all the luggage up from the bedrooms. The last half an hour was always busy, but it was also when the crew wore their biggest smiles.

"I can't wait to get wasted tonight," August said as she shut the dishwasher with her hip. "It's still so hard to get used to pouring champagne for other people when you can't drink it yourself. Where are we going?"

I shrugged and looked at the other crewmembers gathering in the galley, ready to say goodbye to the guests.

"Can we start drinking right away? Like before tonight? As soon as they're gone?" August asked.

"It's going to be a very long season if you need to drink that bad already," I replied. "But as long as Captain Moss says we're on free time until tomorrow, then you're good."

"I just want to make a martini and get to drink it myself, you know what I mean?" August asked.

I knew exactly what she meant. My dad was right. We spent so much time looking after others that along the way, I'd forgotten what I wanted. What I liked. What I loved. The only interruption on my horizon of other people's needs and wants had been Hayden. He'd been mine. Just for me.

I'd told him I'd call him whatever my decision was and although I had all these fears, all these reasons why Hayden and I couldn't be together, I wanted him to change my mind. I wanted him to be mine again.

The next hour passed in a blur. We said goodbye to the guests, we had the tips meeting and we were dismissed for a full twenty-four hours. That was a lot of time to drink.

"Whoop," August called as Captain Moss left the galley. "Freedom and a stack of dollar bills." She waved a white envelope with her tip in it. "It's good to be alive. Can we crack open the beers?"

Crew began to crowd around the fridge and I took the opportunity to slide out of the banquette. "I have to go make a call," I whispered to Skylar.

She slid an arm around my waist. "Be careful. Remember you are an incredible woman who sees only the best in others." I'd told Skylar about my conversation with Hayden. She was skeptical about him flying to Miami, about his protestations of love. And I understood that. I'd forgiven him but that didn't mean I could accept him back in my heart.

"I don't know where we'll end up, but I figure I'll listen to what he has to say." The fact was, even if we could put everything about Cannon in our past, which I believed was possible, the practicalities of dating someone like Hayden were *impossible*. But I wanted to hear him out in a way that he'd never really listened to me when I told him I wasn't Cannon's spy.

"You deserve to be happy," she said.

I kissed her on the cheek and then, without anyone noticing, I dipped out of the galley.

I didn't even change. I just grabbed my bag and Hayden's number and headed off the yacht. All I could think about was the way he held me so tightly and protectively. The way he looked at me when I was talking as if I were saying the most interesting thing he'd ever heard, the whisper of his lips against my skin, his reluctant smile. I just wished it had meant as much to him as it had to me.

I gathered speed, wanting to find a quiet place to call as soon as I could. As I got to the end of the jetty, I scanned the marina, trying to think about where I might go.

"Looking for someone?"

I spun around and came face-to-face with Hayden Wolf.

THIRTY-NINE

Hayden

Patience had never been my strong point, but sometimes that wasn't a bad thing. After all, it meant I was standing here in front of Avery. I couldn't just sit in a hotel room and wait for her to call. I'd come down to the marina to watch her yacht dock.

"What are you doing here?" she asked, her smile pulling up the corners of my mouth as I stepped toward her.

"Waiting for you," I replied, sliding my hand over her hip.

She tried to step out of my arms but there was no way I was going to let that happen. "I said I'd call."

"And I said I'd wait."

"I was just . . . We'd just . . . I was about to call you," she said, her hand sliding over my chest. I shuddered at the perfect feel of her.

"What were you going to say?"

Her smile faltered. "I was going to say I'll hear you out."

"Like I should have done to you," I mumbled. She was a

better human being than me. I'd questioned her, accused her and here she was, still offering me a chance to set things straight. "I understand I betrayed you. You have every reason to hate me."

"I don't hate you. But I also know that you can't possibly feel for me what I feel for you. Because if you did, we wouldn't be standing here heading in different directions. And I can't be with someone I love more than they love me. My heart is fragile enough. It can't cope with the inevitable disappointment that comes from that."

I groaned, desperate to take on all the pain I'd caused her, all the pain she felt inside. "I was an idiot. I accept that, but let me prove to you that I have learned my lesson. I should never have questioned you. But don't ever think it was because I didn't love you enough. I stand here, not just believing but knowing that I will love you until my last breath. That's true whether you walk away from me or you let me keep proving my love to you for the rest of our lives."

She covered her face with her hands in the same way I'd seen her do through binoculars all those weeks before. "I'm here for the next five months, Hayden. We don't work together."

"Look at me," I said, circling my hands around her wrists and uncovering her face. I swiped my thumbs below her eyes, hating that I'd caused her grief. "Five months is nothing." I pulled out her hair tie, letting her chestnut-brown locks fall free, the ends caught by the falling sun. There she was. My Avery. "It's all details. We'll figure it out."

She swept her fingers over my cheekbone, shaking her head. "They're important details and I can't open myself up again. Not to you. Not when I don't know how it's going to end."

"I'll tell you how it's going to end. You're going to marry me, we're going to have twenty kids and we're going to grow old together." Fuck, I'd never thought a wife would be in my future, let alone kids, but being with Avery, that was all I could see. Her. Forever.

She rolled her eyes. "I need you to be serious. If we can't make dating work then what hope do we have?"

"We're way beyond dating, my love. Don't you get it? You need to understand that when we met there was no going back. I belong to you now. You belong to me. Tell me it's not true."

"I can't. I love you."

My heart swooped. She was mine. "I love you more than you will ever know."

I took her hand and strode down the dock. "But if you want to nail down the details, plan it all out? Let's go."

"Where are we going? Not to your hotel because—"

"What? You won't be able to keep your greedy little hands off me?"

She laughed and part of me died that I'd had to wait so long to hear that again.

"No, we're going to my car. I have my laptop. We're going to make a plan."

"A plan?"

"Yeah, I'm going to figure out how much time I can spend over here. Maybe I'll get an office or something."

"In Miami? You're just going to move to the States, just like that?"

I stopped suddenly and faced her. "You don't get it, do you? I want you. And I'm going to do whatever it takes, and that means doing whatever you need."

"I think this might be my last season anyway," she said. "My brother's insurers were a pain in my ass but we have a charity that's pledged to step in—" She stopped talking and looked at me, her eyes narrowing. "You found out the insurers had reassessed my brother's benefits," she said. "It *was* you! Lycan. Wolf. Shit, Hayden." She stamped her foot on the ground but didn't try to drop my hand.

It was time for my final confession. I'd hoped to tell her once she'd agreed to be mine. I didn't want money or any weird sense of obligation to color her decision. "The Lycan Foundation is my charity. They've agreed to fund your brother's care. It really was the least I could do. I was the reason it was cut in the first place."

"You can't do that. I can't be dependent on you. What if we split, then what?"

"Didn't you just hear me?" I cupped her face in my hands. "We're not going to split up. Not ever. And anyway, the money is ring-fenced for your brother. There's no going back on that."

She sighed, her head resting against my palm. "It's too much. I can never repay you."

"I don't want you to. This was the right thing to do, whether or not I'm in love with you. I caused your brother's health insurer to stop funding his care."

"No, Cannon did."

"Exactly. I brought them to your door. You can't say no to this. It's for your brother. And it's excellent for my tax planning." I released her and took her hand as she swatted at my arm.

"Thank you," she said as we began to walk toward the car again. "That's an amazing thing you did."

"It's nothing compared to what you've done for other people your whole life. This was just money. It's nothing."

"You think we can figure out these logistics?" she asked, looking up at me.

"I know we can. As long as we're together, we can do anything."

"I'VE NEVER BEEN erect over a spreadsheet," I announced as Avery pressed save.

"Are you hard because of the spreadsheet, or because it's finished?"

We'd agreed I'd fly to the Caribbean as much as I could to catch Avery between charters, and in the meantime she'd figure out what she wanted to do now she could pursue her own dreams.

"Because I'm looking at you," I said as I reached for her, threading my fingers into her hair.

Her gaze slid to my crotch as my dick pressed against my zip, trying to escape.

She rose from where she sat and straddled me so we were face-to-face. "I think I want to go back to school. College," she said. "I'd like to teach." She shrugged as if she was almost embarrassed.

"You're amazing." Even now, able to do anything she liked, she wanted to do something that would help people. "I love you more every second I know you."

She grinned and pressed her mouth against my jaw. "I like hearing that."

"That I love you?"

She pulled back. "Yeah. I don't feel so stupid for falling for you as hard as I did, for loving you as much as I do."

I groaned and pressed my hand against her ass, pushing her against my straining cock, and she ground against me. Fuck, she felt good.

"You think college would work? I mean that's four

years. And my dad and brother—they're in California. You're in London."

"They can move, or we can move, or we'll just split our time. Whatever you want."

"Are you sure you're not just saying this so I'll get naked?" She fumbled with my fly.

"I'm definitely saying it so you'll get naked, but I'll still mean it after we're dressed again."

"I only have twenty-four hours," she whispered into my ear. "It's not long enough. I know how good you make me feel."

I groaned and stood, carrying her to the bed. "Then I'd better get started. I don't want you to miss out on anything." I undressed her, then dumped my clothes on the floor until we were both naked. I stood over her, staring down at her perfect body, trying to take it all in. Jesus, I was a lucky fucker. I knew that whatever happened, however many more times Cannon tried to bring me down, they'd never succeed. I had Avery Walker and that made me a winner every day of the week.

I didn't know where to start with her. I was always so sure of everything in my world . . . except when it came to the woman in front of me. She constantly had me off-balance. Maybe that was why I loved her. I leaned over her, trailing my fingers over her thigh and dipping over her pussy. Her skin was hot and tight and as I pushed between her folds, *so* wet. Twenty-four hours? Jesus, I wasn't sure I was going to be able to let her leave this room after a *week*. I had too much I wanted to do to her, too much I wanted to share with her.

"We'll have more time soon," she whispered, as if she understood what I was thinking. She usually did. She circled her hand around my cock and my hips bucked toward her; I needed more, wanted to feel every part of her on me, over me, surrounding me.

"There are so many things I want to do to you." I crawled over her and rolled to my side, pulling her toward me, her back to my front.

"As long as it involves me having an orgasm, I'm good with any of them."

I chuckled and hooked her leg back over mine and buried my face in her neck, savoring the feel of her skin sliding against mine. I pressed my palm to her stomach, shifting her toward me so my cock rubbed over her sex from behind. Her heat and wetness and the promise of what came next chased the breath from my chest. I dipped my fingers into her pussy and she sighed.

"Fuck—condom," I spat. I'd been so focused on getting her naked and touching her, I'd forgotten.

I pulled away, but she stopped me. "Do we have to?" she asked, her voice small and quiet.

She didn't have to say anymore. I knew what she was asking.

"There's been no one since you," I whispered, circling her clit. "No one except the memory of you."

"Me neither," she said, shifting a little so she could look at me.

Relief shot out of my chest as it became clear that although our feelings for each other had been stretched, they'd never reached a breaking point. On some level, we'd always remained committed to each other, even through the darkest of times. It was what I needed to hear from her.

"I never wanted anyone but you." She smoothed a palm over my jaw and I pressed at her entrance, so deliciously smooth and wet. I wanted this to be slow, wanted to savor it, but I knew it would be impossible. A low buzz hummed just beneath my skin, trying to get out, and I knew I needed to fuck this woman. I'd known we were connected from the first moment I'd laid eyes on Avery, but I still had a primal desire to make her mine. To fuck her so hard she'd feel me in every move she made for the next week.

"Make it good, Hayden. Fuck me."

My control snapped at her request. I groaned and pushed her to her stomach, lifted her hips and rammed into her, right to the hilt.

She cried out, her sounds muffled by the mattress, as she braced her hands against the headboard.

"Let me hear you," I grunted. So much of our time together had been dominated by caution and an inability to let go, but now I wanted to hear all her sounds, to own them, categorize them, then create new ones.

I fucked her harder, faster, plowing her into the bed as her moans grew louder. "You see how good I fuck you? No one else will ever have you again. You're all mine. This pussy is all *mine*."

She chanted beneath me, "Yes, Hayden, yes, please. More. Hayden. Fuck me. Please." Her breathy voice moaning my name, begging me to fuck her as my cock drove into her, was more than I could ever have hoped. She was mine. I heard it in her desperation. The only reason I lasted longer than ten seconds was because of the blood pounding in my ears, taking the edge off the sounds of her pleasure.

Her hands clenched into fists against the wooden headboard and she tightened around me. I wasn't going to be able to stop myself from coming. It was too much, too good, too perfect.

Her cries grew louder, less controlled, sharper and she convulsed around me. I couldn't stop the staccato growls of desire resonating from my chest every time I pushed into her, as her pussy tightened and tightened. My orgasm circled at the base of my spine then shot up and across my body as I stabbed my hips forward, fucking her orgasm out of her, claiming it for myself.

Knowing how much she loved to make other people feel good, the ability to make *her* feel good was power I'd never experienced before. It was far more thrilling than any business deal or acquisition.

Still gulping for air, I lay over her and rolled to my side, pulling her with me.

"Every time I come with you, it's always the orgasm to end all orgasms," I said.

She shuffled around in my arms. "And then, all too soon, you're chasing the next one," she said, finishing my sentence. I pulled her closer, wanting the press of her hot skin covering me. There should be no space between us. She was mine and I was hers.

She slid her legs over mine and tipped me to my back so she straddled me. Although my limbs were heavy and weak, there was nothing that would stop me from fucking Avery. I sat up and we came face-to-face and I pulled her bottom lip between my teeth, released it and stole a kiss from her already reddened lips. I cupped her hips and brought her closer to me, my cock rubbing against her pussy. She hummed a note of contented pleasure as she circled her hips, coaxing my dick back to life. It didn't take long. Just being in the same room with this beautiful woman got me hard. Having her naked and in my arms was almost too good to comprehend. She stroked her hands up my arms, watching them as if she were inspecting my body, then pressed her fingers along my collarbone and up my throat.

"I'm all yours," I said.

"I want to know every part of you," she said, circling her

hips a little faster, the slickness between us growing.

I groaned, and my dick twitched beneath her.

She trailed one hand down my chest and grasped my straining cock, lifting up on her knees as she placed me at her entrance. She gasped, and I knew that was my cue. I tightened my fingers around her and pulled her down onto me.

She threw her head back and screamed. Christ, I loved her sounds and how they vibrated around my cock. I pushed her back, the drag of my flesh against hers sending shockwaves across my body, and then slammed her against me again. She liked to be on top but she also liked me in control.

"Yes, Hayden," she said on an exhale and I began to plot out a rhythm, pushing and pulling, grinding and slamming. Fucking and fucking.

Part of me wanted to close my eyes and savor the feel of her soft flesh beneath my fingers, her pussy around my cock, but I couldn't stop gazing at her, the jut of her breasts, the rosy pink nipples, temptingly pointing at me, the white expanse of her throat that I promised myself I would lick later, her hair tumbled across her shoulders.

I flipped her over and her legs went around my waist as I set to work to drive us both toward our climax. I thrust and thrust, wanting to solidify our connection, make her mine, stop her from ever leaving me.

She arched her back, digging her fingernails into my shoulder as she began to come. The pulse of her pussy and the bite of her nails set the touch paper on my own orgasm as my balls tightened and I pushed into her as far as I could get, not wanting this perfect connection to end. No matter what came next, fucking Avery, loving her, being with her would be the most satisfying thing I'd ever do in my life.

EPILOGUE

Nine months later

Hayden

As I pulled into the driveway, Avery stood in the doorway in jeans and what looked like one of my old shirts. It drowned her petite frame, but still managed to be impossibly sexy. Would I still get that rush of heat in my gut when I saw her waiting for me twenty years from now? Christ, I hoped so.

She raced toward the car, the gold edges of her hair flashing in the noon sun as I pulled to a halt.

"Hey, beautiful," I said as she swung open the car door before I'd even unclicked my seatbelt.

"Can you believe we're doing this? Like, really doing this?"

Her wide smile always coaxed mine from wherever it was hiding. I slid out of the car and she linked her hands around my neck. I pressed my lips to hers.

"We're really doing this." I glanced up at our new house. We'd bought it the day after we landed in London. We'd had twenty viewings lined up over three days, but we'd walked into this one and hadn't bothered looking at another. It was a modern house, about an hour outside of London, in a leafy village and set on five acres of land. It had taken two months to get the owners out and another two to get the renovations done but it was finally ready.

"I'm going to get to welcome you home from work every day—"

"Naked?" I asked.

"Maybe *some* days." She scrunched up her nose. "A lot of days, probably. But not today. Not yet. I've had a thousand deliveries."

"Well, I'm about to make another," I said, opening the door to the back seats. I pulled out a cardboard tube and handed it to her.

"Are they good? Did you look?" she asked, popping out the plastic end of the tube and peering into it.

"I thought we should look together." She gazed up at me and I placed another kiss on her lips before grabbing a small black gift bag and slamming the door.

"This is our home, Hayden. I like live in the UK and everything now," she said as we approached the threshold.

"I couldn't be happier about that," I replied as we went inside and I shrugged off my jacket. I glanced around. We'd only moved in the day before, but the place still looked pretty empty apart from the basics. Avery didn't have much to ship from the U.S. and we'd kept the flat in London, so we were starting from scratch here. As long as we had a bed and a sofa, I didn't care about anything other than what made Avery happy. "I'm sorry I had to go into the office today, I just needed to—"

"It's totally fine. It was fun straightening things out. I ordered some more stuff online and I started my reading. There's a lot. They're going to work me hard."

"No doubt. Kings College is one of the best universities in the country." I pressed my lips to her forehead. I couldn't be more proud that she was finally doing what she wanted to do.

"Which is why I can't believe they took me."

"I never had any doubt," I said and got a now-familiar eye roll.

She slid the cardboard tube onto the dining table, turned and pressed her hands against my chest. I exhaled and gripped her waist, knowing I was the luckiest guy in Europe.

"Welcome home," she said, smiling up at me. I pressed my lips against hers and we kissed and kissed and kissed. Pressing my lips to Avery's never got old. I ached to kiss her whenever I was away from her.

"Let's look at this." I lifted my chin, indicating the plans I'd collected from the architects. "Then let's crawl into bed and make sure the mattress works."

She inhaled. "Okay. I'm nervous, though. That mattress is going to see some action. It needs to be robust."

I growled and buried my head in her neck before releasing her and turning to the table. I slid the thin sheets of paper out of the tube and without me saying anything, she held one end while I unrolled the other.

"Wow," we said in unison at the front elevation.

"Hang on, I'm going to get something to hold down the corners." I disappeared into the kitchen and grabbed a handful of cutlery. That should do it.

"I knew spoons would be useful," she said, weighing

down the corners so the pages didn't curl. "It looks amazing. What do you think?"

"It's great—let's look at the floor plans."

I pulled off the first sheet of paper to reveal the floor plan of the one-story building that would be twenty feet from our house. "The rooms are all big, with wide walkways." We poured over the details as if we were looking at a treasure map.

"Great, though we might not need wheelchair access forever. I mean, Michael's standing now. Still, my dad will love it. Michael will love it." She shook her head. "Are you sure you're okay having them so close?"

She couldn't think I had a single doubt, could she? "Of course I'm sure. I like your dad and Michael and I want them to be happy, and I'm grateful they said yes."

When Avery had finished up the season and her yachting career I'd met her in Miami and we'd flown back to Sacramento for two weeks before coming to London. While we were in California, I'd floated the idea of Avery's family moving to England. Her father had said he'd be open to it down the line, but in the meantime he'd insisted that Avery apply to universities in London. Avery had resisted at first, until her dad had made her see that if she went back to Sacramento every holiday, she'd still end up seeing them more than she would have if she'd continued to work on yachts. It was the sort of thing my father would have done, and I admired how Mr. Walker put his daughter first.

"And if there's a house right there, next to us, they can stay for as long as they like, right?"

"Exactly. That's why we bought this place, after all," I said as I slid my hands around her waist, looking over her shoulder at the life we were building.

"I don't think my dad realized. Not at first."

"Realized?"

Her hands slipped over mine. "You know, understood how this was it. That we were forever."

Happiness tugged at my chest as the certainty in her voice took hold. Avery had such an open heart—it hadn't taken long for me to convince her that I'd never let her down again. I'd never again question her integrity or wonder about her loyalty. She was more than I deserved, and I'd do everything in my power to be worthy of the trust that she had in me, in us, for the rest of our lives.

"I love you, Avery Walker."

She turned around in my arms and cupped my face in her hands. "I know. I love you, too."

I released her for a second and picked up the black gift bag I'd brought in from the car.

"You and I have been to some beautiful places. We've taken in breathtaking scenery, gazed out onto the ocean together, watched the sunrise over the water. But I thought being here, in our home, looking over these plans would be the most suitable place to propose." I pulled out a velvet box from the bag.

"Propose?" she asked.

"Are you surprised?" We'd been clear about how we felt about each other, wasn't this the next step?

"I don't know. I guess it already feels like we're married. I never expected a formal proposal." Her eyes flicked from me to the box.

I chuckled. "Are you saying no?"

"You haven't asked." She traced her finger over the edge of a blue-velvet corner. "And I haven't seen the ring." She winked.

I got fun, relaxed Avery all the time now. Since she'd finished her last season, the only time I'd seen the chief stewardess was when she'd been applying for college courses or talking to the therapists about her brother's progress.

"So if the ring's ugly, you might say no?" I asked.

She pulled in a breath as if she was thinking about her response. "I don't know. I guess it depends on how ugly."

I snapped open the box to reveal the princess-cut diamond solitaire.

She pressed her lips together and nodded. "I would say that's a pass."

"A pass?" I asked, chuckling. The ring was four carats and the highest quality diamond I could find. "I thought this size was wearable, but if it takes something bigger for you to say yes, just say the word." I sighed in mock exasperation.

She shrugged. "I guess you won't know until you ask."

I pulled her toward me and dipped to press a kiss to her lips. "Avery Walker, will you marry me?"

"Hayden Wolf, I'll marry you anytime and every time you ever ask me."

She was right. We didn't need a ring or a ceremony to know we would be together forever. Our feelings—our love and respect for each other—were what bound us together. I'd gone looking for a way to save my business and found a woman who brought me to life. I'd never need anything other than Avery Walker. She was my sunset and my sunrise. My choppy waters and my calm seas.

My everything.

Another year later

Avery

I kept a careful eye on my speed as I made my way back from college on the last day of the school year. I was just so eager to get home. Three months of no studying lay ahead of me as I pulled into the driveway. Hayden waved and strode toward the car as I parked.

"School's out for summer," he said as he opened the door.

"Sure is, and I got a first for that paper I handed in last week."

"The Piaget one?" he asked.

How he kept track with all the course-related stuff I talked about, I had no idea. He always seemed so interested in every little detail I ever told him about it.

"That's the one." I squeezed his hand before he released me to grab my books from the backseat.

"I have some pretty interesting news myself, actually," he said as we wandered into the dining room. "I got a call today—Cannon is being sold."

"Wow, are you going to buy it?" Although I'd admired the way Hayden hadn't wanted to go after Cannon in revenge, I'd always wanted them to get their comeuppance, not just for what they'd done to my family, but also what they'd done to Hayden's father.

He shook his head. "There's no way he'd ever sell to me. But it was good to get the call. Apparently, they aren't expecting any cash for it. They just want someone to take on their debt."

I stopped walking and turned to face Hayden. "What, so it will be free as long as whoever buys it takes on their loans?"

"Exactly. I was right. They overpaid for the companies

they stole from me. The man who sent my father into bankruptcy and tried to destroy us is paying the ultimate price."

"Wow, how do you feel?" I asked as I headed inside.

"Pleased that I wasn't the cause of their failure. I never wanted one man's bitterness to affect the way I lived my life."

"God, you know how hot it gets me when you're all principled and ethical and shit."

Hayden chuckled. "Hold that thought. My brother's inside, talking with your dad and Michael."

I huffed as if I'd been deprived of Hayden's body for weeks, when in reality he'd fucked me this morning before classes.

"Hey, guys," I called as we wandered into the kitchen.

"You really should get a games console set up in here," Michael said. "I want to kick Landon's ass at Sniper Elite."

"Yeah, as if," Landon said. "You know I was in the SAS, right?"

"As far as I can tell, you just sit behind a desk now," Michael shot back.

I'd gotten used to Landon and Michael. They'd become firm friends and were always poking fun at each other.

"Aren't you going back to America anytime soon?" Landon said, though he knew they lived here now.

"Landon," Hayden called over in warning as he opened the fridge to take out some wine.

"Don't worry, son," my dad said, bringing up a plate and opening the dishwasher. "You'll never get rid of us now. Can't get enough of this beautiful weather," he said, nodding to the windows where it had just started to pour with rain.

I laughed. "Thank God you're handsome or I might

have had to call this engagement off rather than live with the rain all year. It's June, for Pete's sake."

"I thought you'd have had enough sun to last you a lifetime," Hayden replied. "But perhaps we should charter a yacht this summer? Are you missing life on the ocean waves?"

I slipped my hands up his chest. "I don't miss anything when I'm with you."

"I'll tell you what I'm missing," my dad interrupted.

"Maybe a charter for two is a good idea," I said, laughing.

"I'm missing a wedding and grandchildren," my dad said. "When are you kids going to get on with it?"

"Ask your daughter, sir. I'm ready whenever she is," Hayden replied.

"I wanna finish college, Dad. Life's so good right now. I just want to enjoy it for a while, just as it is."

My dad huffed and turned back to the dining area where Michael and Landon were arguing about something.

"You know, we could get married this summer," Hayden said. "We don't have to think about the babies thing until you graduate, but I'd like to marry you before you finish school."

"You would?" I said, stroking his chin with my finger, and he dipped to kiss me.

"I really would."

How was it possible I'd gotten this lucky? As much as life had turned on a dime that afternoon down by the river, it had shifted again the day I'd met Hayden Wolf. And for nothing but the better. I had him in my life forever and that gave me a certainty that no matter what was ahead of us, the future was only full of happiness.

"I'll marry you this summer—hell, I'd marry you tomorrow. But let's not do the babies quite yet. I want you to myself for a while longer."

"Want to do it in Taormina? I know how much you love Italy," he asked.

"I don't care where we go. I just don't want my honeymoon to be on a yacht." It might rain a lot in England, but I'd never missed the constant sun of the Mediterranean and the Caribbean.

He pulled me closer and kissed the top of my head as we stood watching our families laugh and joke together. "No yachts, I promise. Just you and me and whoever else we want to invite, wherever you want it to be."

"As long as I get to walk down the aisle to you, then the rest will just fall into place." As long as I had every sunrise and sunset with him by my side, nothing else mattered.

OTHER BOOKS BY LOUISE BAY

Sign up to the Louise Bay mailing list to see more on all my books.
www.louisebay.com/newsletter

Duke of Manhattan

I was born into British aristocracy, but I've made my fortune in Manhattan. New York is now my kingdom.

Back in Britain my family are fighting over who's the next Duke of Fairfax. The rules say it's me--if I'm married. It's not a trade-off worth making. I could never limit myself to just one woman.

Or so I thought until my world is turned upside down. Now, the only way I can save the empire I built is to inherit the title I've never wanted-- so I need a wife.

To take my mind off business I need a night that's all pleasure. I need to bury myself in a stranger.

The skim of Scarlett King's hair over my body as she bends over . . .

The scrape of her nails across my chest as she screams my name . . .

The bite of her teeth on my shoulder just as we both reach the edge . . .

It all helps me forget.

I just didn't bargain on finding my one night stand across the boardroom table the next day.

She might be my latest conquest but I have a feeling Scarlett King might just conquer me.

A stand-alone novel.

Park Avenue Prince

THE PRINCE OF PARK AVENUE FINALLY MEETS HIS MATCH IN A FEISTY MANHATTAN PRINCESS.

I've made every one of my billions of dollars myself—I'm calculating, astute and the best at what I do. It takes drive and dedication to build what I have. And it leaves no time for love or girlfriends or relationships.

But don't get me wrong, I'm not a monk.

I understand the attention and focus it takes to seduce a beautiful woman. They're the same skills I use to close business deals. But one night is where it begins and ends. I'm not the guy who sends flowers. I'm not the guy who calls the next day.

Or so I thought before an impatient, smart-talking, beyond beautiful heiress bursts into my world.

When Grace Astor rolls her eyes at me—I want to hold her against me and show her what she's been missing.

When she makes a joke at my expense—I want to silence her sassy mouth with my tongue.

And when she leaves straight after we f*ck with barely a

goodbye—it makes me want to pin her down and remind her of the three orgasms she just had.

She might be a princess but I'm going to show her who rules in this Park Avenue bedroom.

A stand-alone novel.

King of Wall Street

THE KING OF WALL STREET IS BROUGHT TO HIS KNEES BY AN AMBITIOUS BOMBSHELL.

I keep my two worlds separate.

At work, I'm King of Wall Street. The heaviest hitters in Manhattan come to me to make money. They do whatever I say because I'm always right. I'm shrewd. Exacting. Some say ruthless.

At home, I'm a single dad trying to keep his fourteen year old daughter a kid for as long as possible. If my daughter does what I say, somewhere there's a snowball surviving in hell. And nothing I say is ever right.

When Harper Jayne starts as a junior researcher at my firm, the barriers between my worlds begin to dissolve. She's the most infuriating woman I've ever worked with.

I don't like the way she bends over the photocopier—it makes my mouth water.

I hate the way she's so eager to do a good job—it makes my dick twitch.

And I can't stand the way she wears her hair up exposing her long neck. It makes me want to strip her naked, bend her over my desk and trail my tongue all over her body.

If my two worlds are going to collide, Harper Jayne will have to learn that I don't just rule the boardroom. I'm in charge of the bedroom, too.

A stand-alone novel.

Hollywood Scandal

HE'S A HOLLYWOOD SUPERSTAR. SHE'S LITERALLY THE GIRL NEXT DOOR.

One of Hollywood's A-listers, I have the movie industry in the palm of my hand. But if I'm going to stay at the top, my playboy image needs an overhaul. No more tabloid headlines. No more parties. And absolutely no more one night stands.

Filming for my latest blockbuster takes place on the coast of Maine and I'm determined to stay out of trouble. But trouble finds me when I run into Lana Kelly.

She doesn't recognize me, she's never heard of Matt Easton and my million dollar smile doesn't work on her.

Ego shredded, I know I should keep my distance, but when I realize she's my neighbor I know I'm toast. There's no way I can resist temptation when it's ten yards away.

She has a mouth designed for pleasure and legs that will wrap perfectly around my waist.

She's movie star beautiful and her body is made to be mine.

Getting Lana Kelly into my bed is harder than I'm used to. She's not interested in the glitz and glamour of Hollywood, but I'm determined to convince her the best place in the world is on the red carpet, holding my hand.

I could have any woman in the world, but all I want is the girl next door.

A standalone romance.

Parisian Nights

The moment I laid eyes on the new photographer at work, I had his number. Cocky, arrogant and super wealthy—women were eating out of his hand as soon as his tight ass crossed the threshold of our office.

When we were forced to go to Paris together for an assignment, I wasn't interested in his seductive smile, his sexy accent or his dirty laugh. I wasn't falling for his charms.

Until I did.

Until Paris.

Until he was kissing me and I was wondering how it happened. Until he was dragging his lips across my skin and I was hoping for more. Paris does funny things to a girl and he might have gotten me naked.

But Paris couldn't last forever.

Previously called What the Lightning Sees

A stand-alone novel.

Promised Nights

I've been in love with Luke Daniels since, well, forever. As his sister's best friend, I've spent over a decade living in the friend zone, watching from the sidelines hoping he would notice me, pick me, love me.

I want the fairy tale and Luke is my Prince Charming. He's tall, with shoulders so broad he blocks out the sun. He's kind with a smile so dazzling he makes me forget everything that's wrong in the world. And he's the only man that can make me laugh until my cheeks hurt and my stomach cramps.

But he'll never be mine.

So I've decided to get on with my life and find the next best thing.

Until a Wonder Woman costume, a bottle of tequila and a game of truth or dare happened.

Then Luke's licking salt from my wrist and telling me I'm beautiful.

Then he's peeling off my clothes and pressing his lips against mine.

Then what? Is this the start of my happily ever after or the beginning of a tragedy?

Previously called Calling Me

A stand-alone novel.

Indigo Nights

I don't do romance. I don't do love. I certainly don't do relationships. Women are attracted to my power and money and I like a nice ass and a pretty smile. It's a fair exchange—a business deal for pleasure.

Meeting Beth Harrison in the first class cabin of my flight from Chicago to London throws me for a loop and everything I know about myself and women goes out the window.

I'm usually good at reading people, situations, the markets. I know instantly if I can trust someone or if they're lying. But Beth is so contradictory and confounding I don't know which way is up.

She's sweet but so sexy she makes my knees weak and mouth dry.

She's confident but so vulnerable I want to wrap her up and protect her from the world.

And then she fucks me like a train and just disappears, leaving me with my pants around my ankles, wondering which day of the week it is.

If I ever see her again I don't know if I'll scream at her, strip her naked or fall in love. Thank goodness I live in Chicago and she lives in London and we'll never see each other again, right?A stand-alone novel.

The Empire State Series

Anna Kirby is sick of dating. She's tired of heartbreak. Despite being smart, sexy, and funny, she's a magnet for men who don't deserve her.

A week's vacation in New York is the ultimate distraction from her most recent break-up, as well as a great place to meet a stranger and have some summer fun. But to protect her still-bruised heart, fun comes with rules. There will be no sharing stories, no swapping numbers, and no real names. Just one night of uncomplicated fun.

Super-successful serial seducer Ethan Scott has some rules of his own. He doesn't date, he doesn't stay the night, and he doesn't make any promises.

It should be a match made in heaven. But rules are made to be broken.

The Empire State Series is a series of three novellas.

Love Unexpected

When the fierce redhead with the beautiful ass walks into the local bar, I can tell she's passing through. And I'm looking for distraction while I'm in town—a hot hook-up and nothing more before I head back to the city.

If she has secrets, I don't want to know them.

If she feels good underneath me, I don't want to think about it too hard.

If she's my future, I don't want to see it.

I'm Blake McKenna and I'm about to teach this Boston socialite how to forget every man who came before me.

When the future I had always imagined crumbles before my very eyes. I grab my two best friends and take a much needed vacation to the country.

My plan of swearing off men gets railroaded when on my first night of my vacation, I meet the hottest guy on the planet.

I'm not going to consider that he could be a gorgeous distraction.

I'm certainly not going to reveal my deepest secrets to him as we steal away each night hoping no one will notice.

And the last thing I'm going to do is fall in love for the first time in my life.

My name is Mackenzie Locke and I haven't got a handle on men. Not even a little bit.

Not until Blake.

A stand-alone novel.

Hopeful

How long does it take to get over your first love?

Eight years should be long enough. My mind knows that, but there's no convincing my heart.

Guys like Joel weren't supposed to fall for girls like me. He had his pick of women at University, but somehow the laws of nature were defied and we fell crazy in love.

After graduation, Joel left to pursue his career in New York. He wanted me to go with him but my life was in London.

We broke up and my heart split in two.

I haven't seen or spoken to him since he left.

If only I'd known that I'd love him this long, this painfully, this desperately. I might have said yes all those years ago. He might have been mine all this time in between.

Now, he's moving back to London and I need to get over him before he gets over here.

But how do I forget someone who gave me so much to remember?

A long time ago, Joel Wentworth told me he'd love me for infinity . . . and I can't give up hope that it might have been true.

A stand-alone novel.

Faithful

Leah Thompson's life in London is everything she's supposed to want: a successful career, the best girlfriends a bottle of sauvignon blanc can buy, and a wealthy boyfriend who has just proposed. But something doesn't feel right. Is it simply a case of 'be careful what you wish for'?

Uncertain about her future, Leah looks to her past, where she finds her high school crush, Daniel Armitage, online. Daniel is one of London's most eligible bachelors. He knows what and who he wants, and he wants Leah. Leah resists Daniel's advances as she concentrates on being the perfect fiancé.

She soon finds that she should have trusted her instincts when she realises she's been betrayed by the men and women in her life.

Leah's heart has been crushed. Will ever be able to trust again? And will Daniel be there when she is?

A stand-alone novel.

ACKNOWLEDGMENTS

Thank you so much for reading. I hope you enjoyed Hayden and Avery's story. It took me a little longer to get to know these two and these two took a little longer to get to know each other. They think a HEA was worth the wait. I hope you did too.

Elizabeth—And exhale. The next one will be easier, won't it? Thank you for your commitment to this book and me and my writing. I really couldn't do it without you.

Najla—We did a LOT this time!! Holy moly. You're so talented, sweet, hard working. You're the best and I love working with you!

Stevie thank you for all your love and support. I miss you! Come back!

Sophie! You're a breath of fresh air. Thank you for all your help and support. I couldn't have done this without knowing you were there, picking up when I dropped things and coming up with great ideas.

To Kimberly, it's so great to be on the same wavelength about publishing *and* Lisa Vanderpump. Thank you for kicking ass on my behalf.

To Kate – thank you. To Charity, Davina, Sallyanne and Ruth—thank you for your help! There was a lot this time.

To all the amazing bloggers and reviewers who connect me with readers: you are amazing! Thank you for all your help.

I am so grateful to the amazingly talented romance writers who live in abundance, lifting each other up, cheering each other on—I'm so proud to be a part of such a great community of women. Thank you.

KEEP IN TOUCH!

Sign up for my mailing list to get the latest news and gossip
www.louisebay.com/newsletter

Or find me on

www.twitter.com/louiseSbay
www.facebook.com/authorlouisebay
www.instagram.com/louiseSbay
www.pinterest.com/louisebay
www.goodreads.com/author/show/8056592.Louise_Bay